BIONICLE®

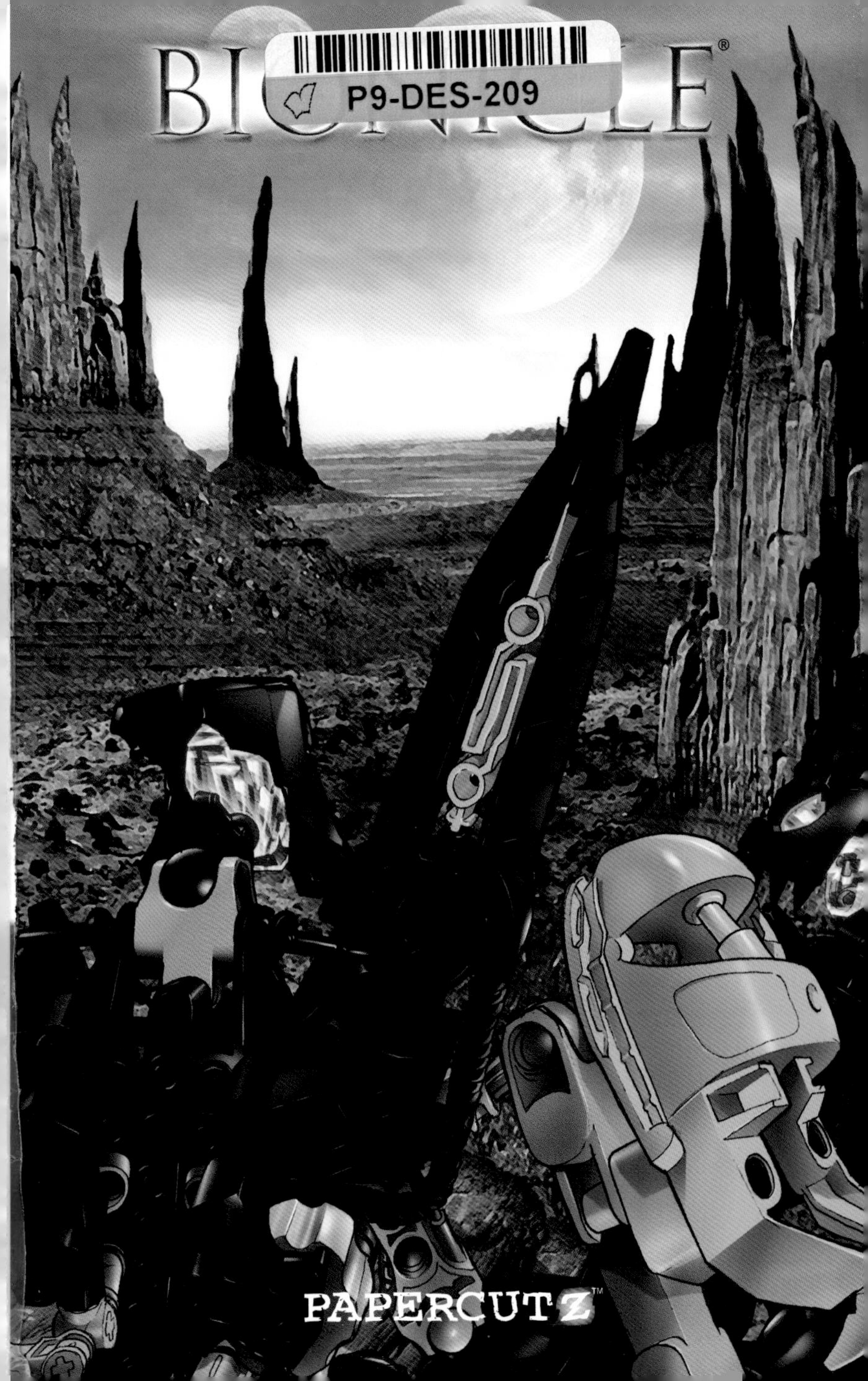

PAPERCUTZ™

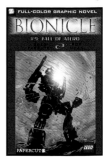

BIONICLE®

#8 Legends of Bara Magna

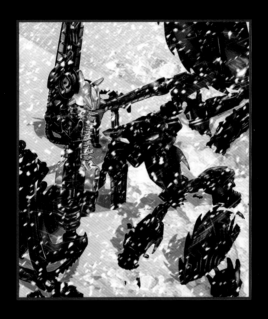

GREG FARSHTEY
Writer
CHRISTIAN ZANIER
STUART SAYGER
Artists

PAPERCUTZ™
NEW YORK

GREG FARSHTEY – WRITER
CHRISTIAN ZANIER – "FALL AND RISE OF THE SKRALL"
& "THE EXILE'S TALE" ARTIST AND COLORIST
STUART SAYGER – "ALL OUR SINS REMEMBERED" ARTIST
GARRY HENDERSON – "THE EXILE'S TALE" CO-COLORIST,
"ALL OUR SINS REMEMBERED" COLORIST
BRYAN SENKA – LETTERER
CHRIS NELSON and SHELLY DUTCHAK – PRODUCTION
MICHAEL PETRANEK – EDITORIAL ASSISTANT
JIM SALICRUP
EDITOR-IN-CHIEF

ISBN: 978-1-59707-180-2 PAPERBACK EDITION
ISBN: 978-1-59707-181-9 HARDCOVER EDITION

PRINTED IN HONG KONG
FEBRUARY 2010 BY NEW ERA PRINTING LTD.
TREND CENTRE, 29-31, CHEUNG LEE ST.
CHAIWAN

DISTRIBUTED BY MACMILLAN.
10 9 8 7 6 5 4 3 2 1

LEGENDS OF BARA MAGNA

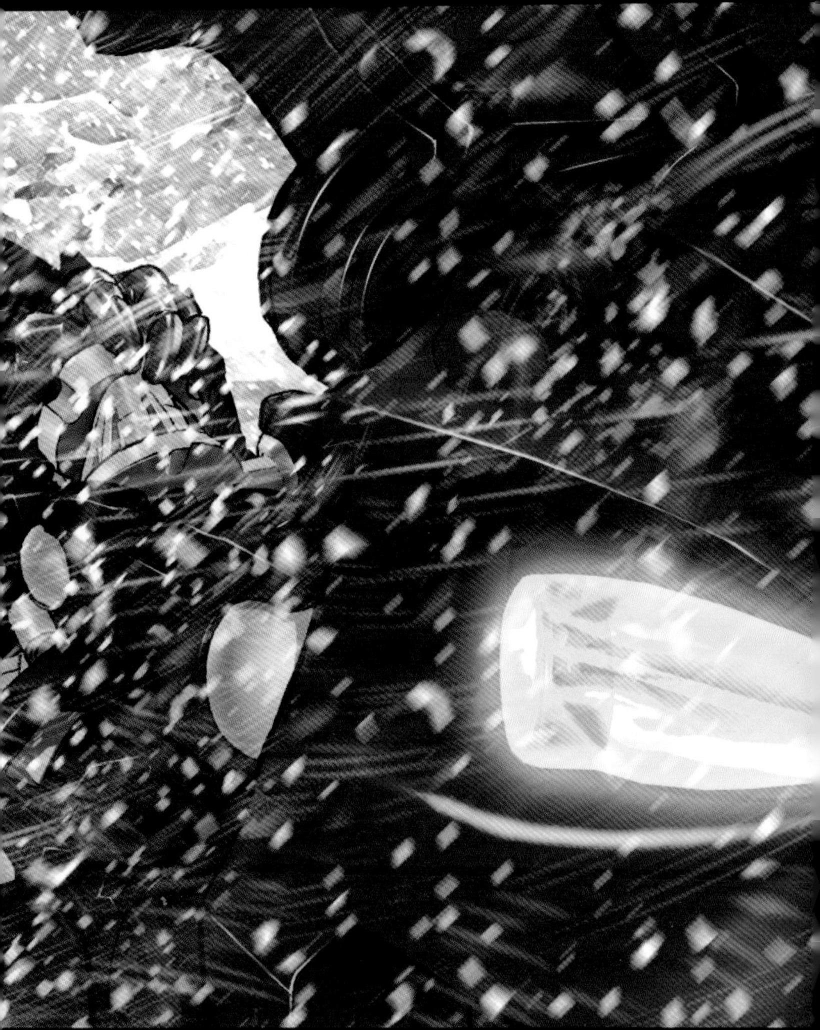

ALL AND RISE OF THE SKRALL

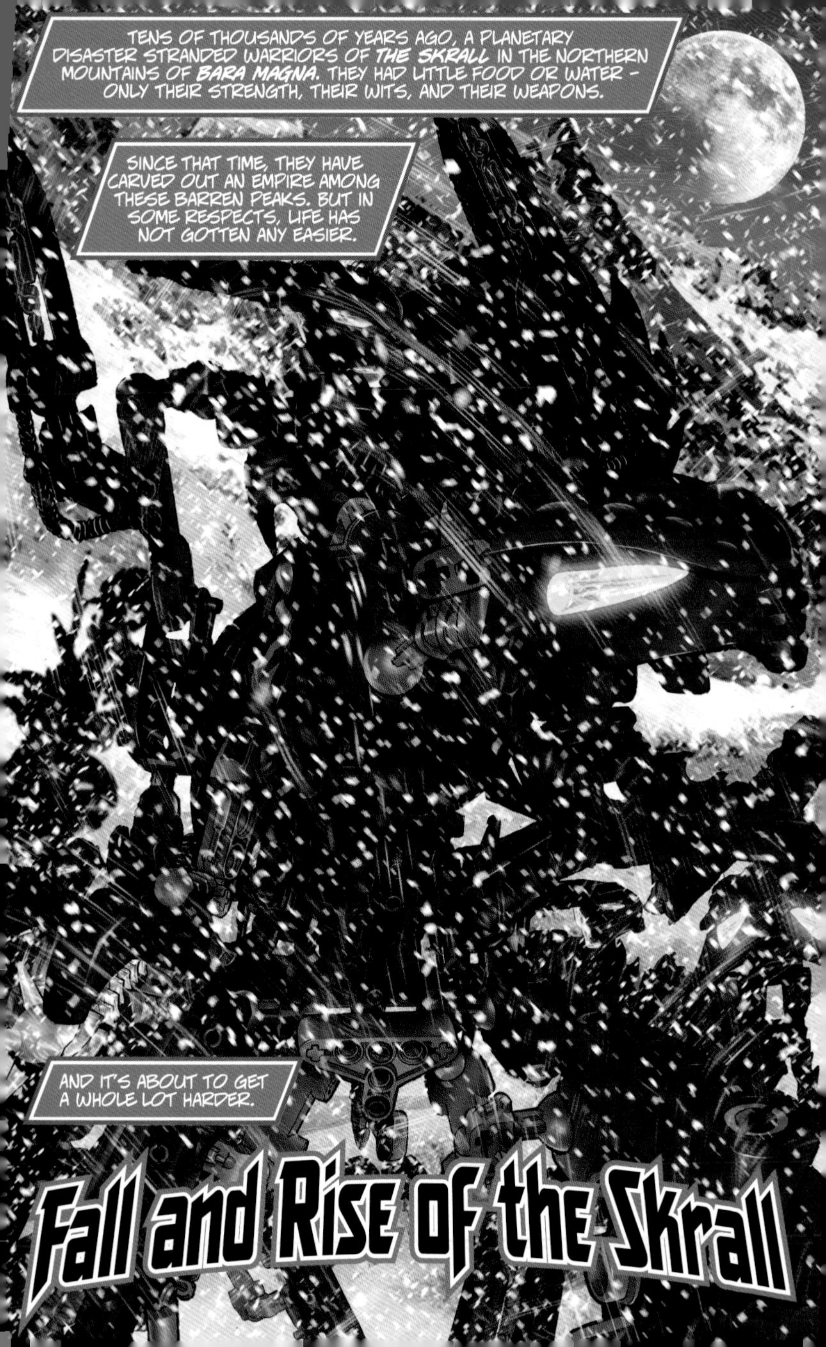
TENS OF THOUSANDS OF YEARS AGO, A PLANETARY DISASTER STRANDED WARRIORS OF THE SKRALL IN THE NORTHERN MOUNTAINS OF BARA MAGNA. THEY HAD LITTLE FOOD OR WATER - ONLY THEIR STRENGTH, THEIR WITS, AND THEIR WEAPONS.
SINCE THAT TIME, THEY HAVE CARVED OUT AN EMPIRE AMONG THESE BARREN PEAKS. BUT IN SOME RESPECTS, LIFE HAS NOT GOTTEN ANY EASIER.
AND IT'S ABOUT TO GET A WHOLE LOT HARDER.
Fall and Rise of the Skrall

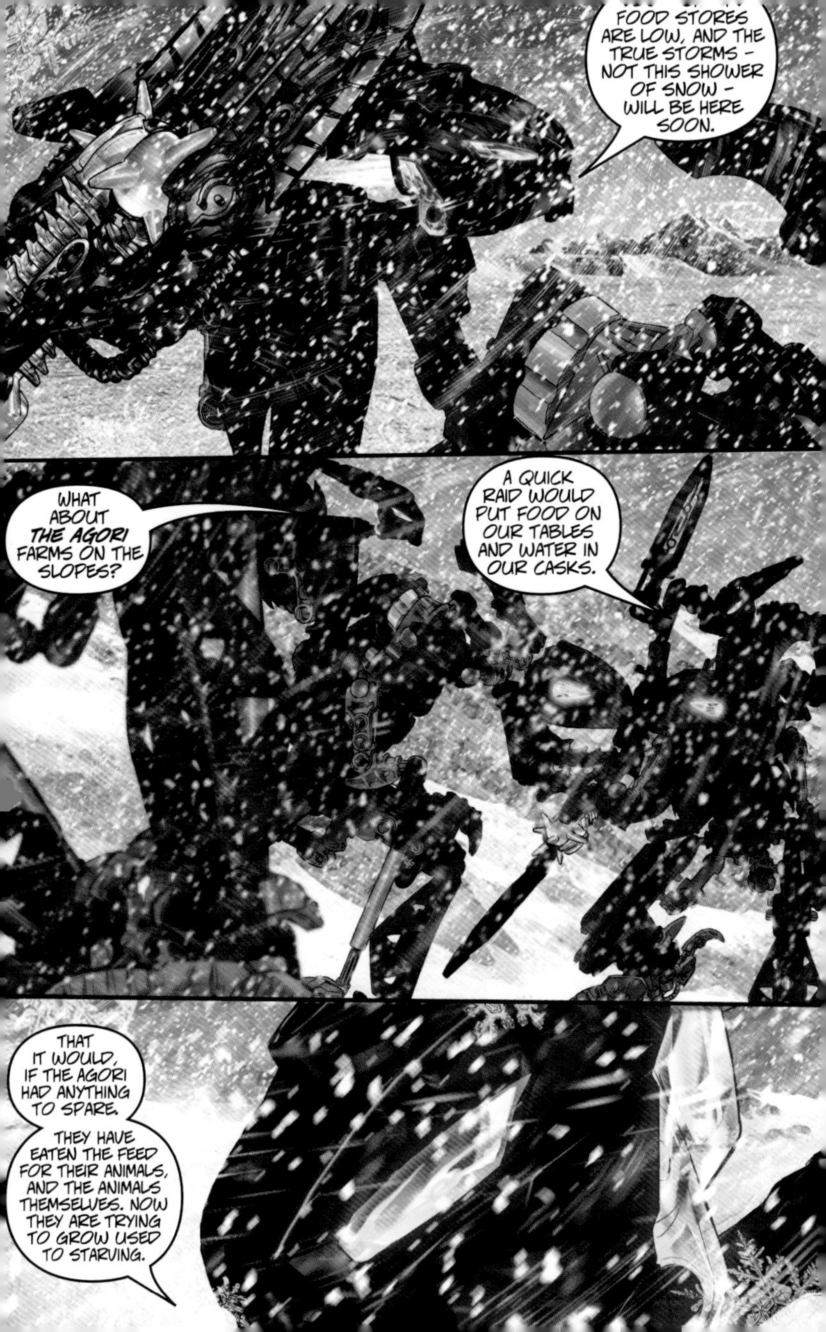
FOOD STORES ARE LOW, AND THE TRUE STORMS - NOT THIS SHOWER OF SNOW - WILL BE HERE SOON.
WHAT ABOUT THE AGORI FARMS ON THE SLOPES?
A QUICK RAID WOULD PUT FOOD ON OUR TABLES AND WATER IN OUR CASKS.
THAT IT WOULD, IF THE AGORI HAD ANYTHING TO SPARE.
THEY HAVE EATEN THE FEED FOR THEIR ANIMALS, AND THE ANIMALS THEMSELVES. NOW THEY ARE TRYING TO GROW USED TO STARVING.

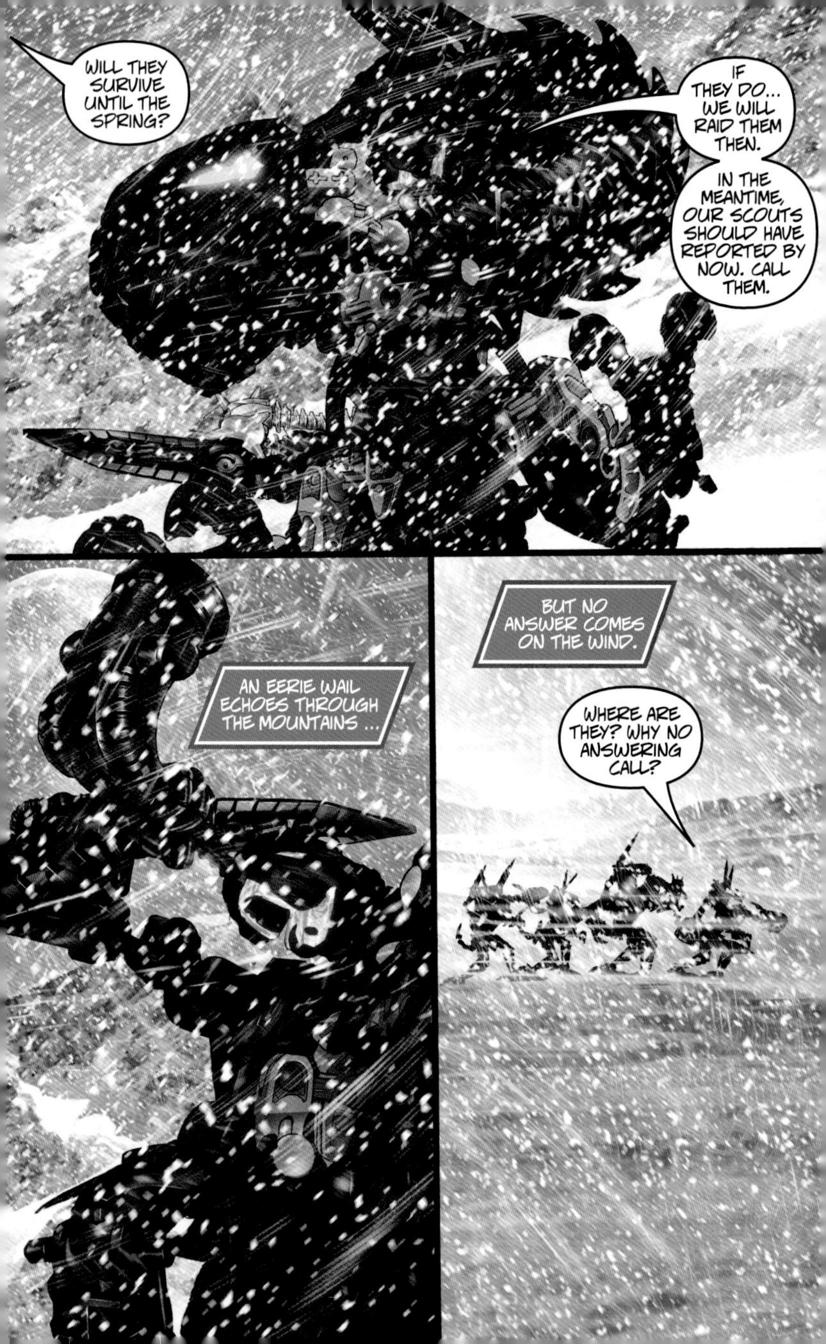

WILL THEY SURVIVE UNTIL THE SPRING?
IF THEY DO... WE WILL RAID THEM THEN.
IN THE MEANTIME, OUR SCOUTS SHOULD HAVE REPORTED BY NOW. CALL THEM.
AN EERIE WAIL ECHOES THROUGH THE MOUNTAINS ...
BUT NO ANSWER COMES ON THE WIND.
WHERE ARE THEY? WHY NO ANSWERING CALL?

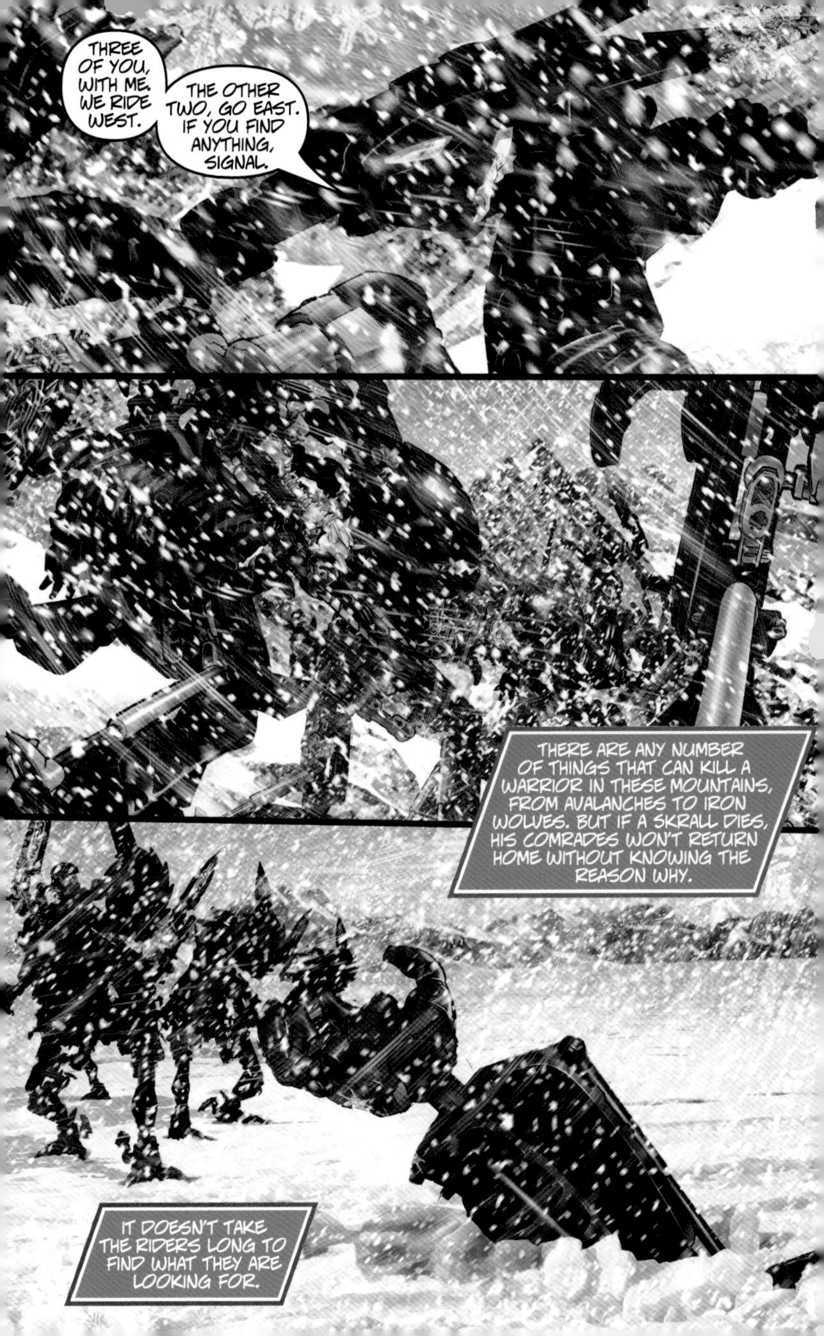
THREE OF YOU, WITH ME. WE RIDE WEST.
THE OTHER TWO, GO EAST. IF YOU FIND ANYTHING, SIGNAL.
THERE ARE ANY NUMBER OF THINGS THAT CAN KILL A WARRIOR IN THESE MOUNTAINS, FROM AVALANCHES TO IRON WOLVES. BUT IF A SKRALL DIES, HIS COMRADES WON'T RETURN HOME WITHOUT KNOWING THE REASON WHY.
IT DOESN'T TAKE THE RIDERS LONG TO FIND WHAT THEY ARE LOOKING FOR.

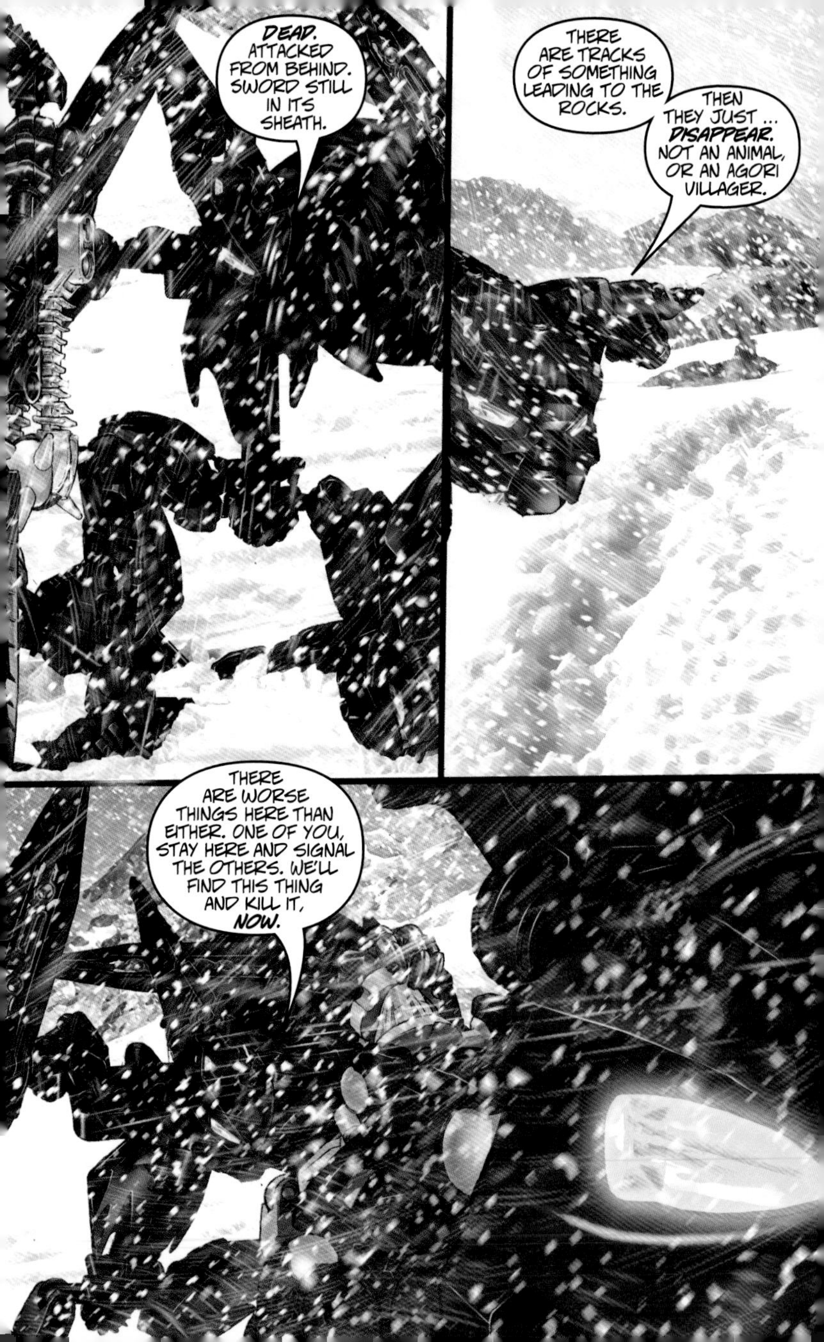
DEAD. ATTACKED FROM BEHIND. SWORD STILL IN ITS SHEATH.
THERE ARE TRACKS OF SOMETHING LEADING TO THE ROCKS.
THEN THEY JUST ... DISAPPEAR. NOT AN ANIMAL, OR AN AGORI VILLAGER.
THERE ARE WORSE THINGS HERE THAN EITHER. ONE OF YOU, STAY HERE AND SIGNAL THE OTHERS. WE'LL FIND THIS THING AND KILL IT, NOW.

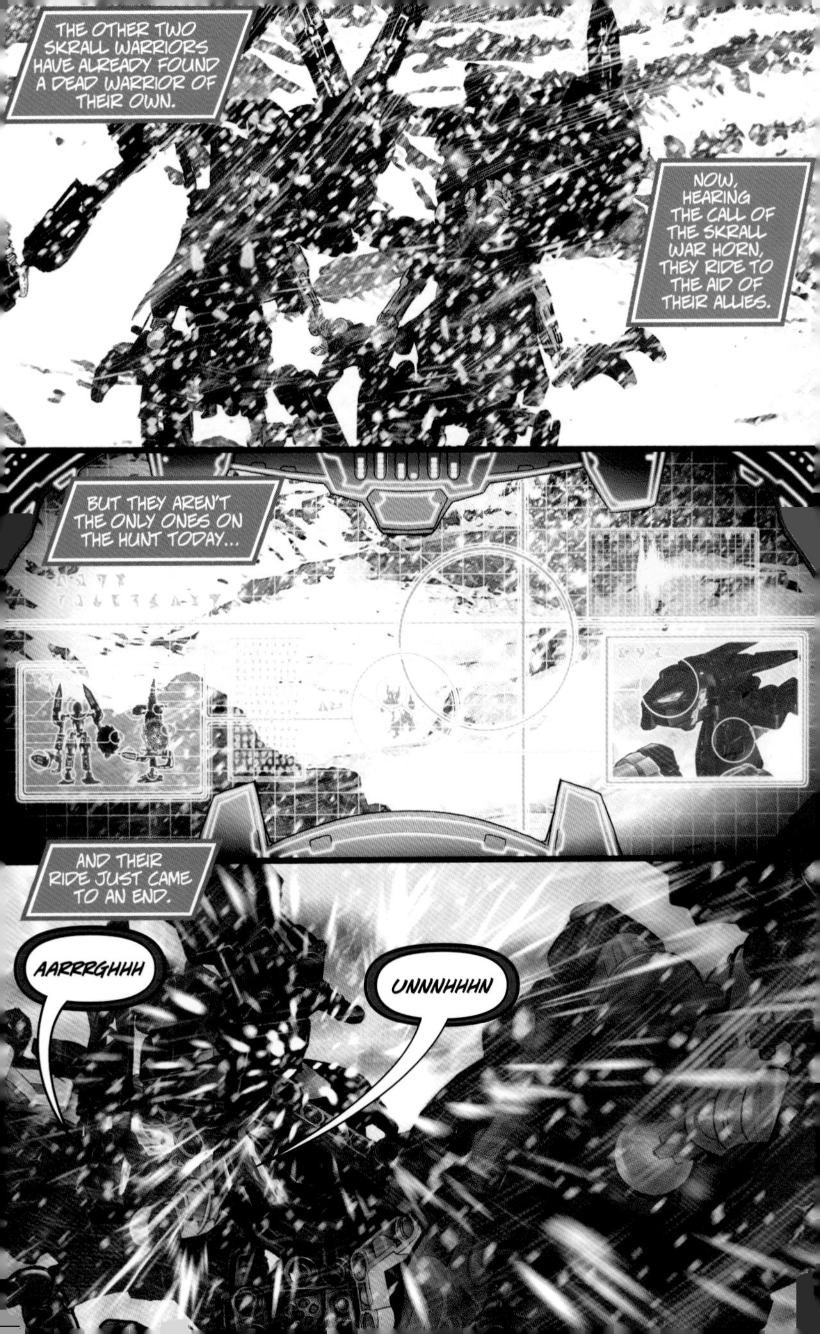
THE OTHER TWO SKRALL WARRIORS HAVE ALREADY FOUND A DEAD WARRIOR OF THEIR OWN.
NOW, HEARING THE CALL OF THE SKRALL WAR HORN, THEY RIDE TO THE AID OF THEIR ALLIES.
BUT THEY AREN'T THE ONLY ONES ON THE HUNT TODAY...
AND THEIR RIDE JUST CAME TO AN END.
AARRRGHHH
UNNNHHHN

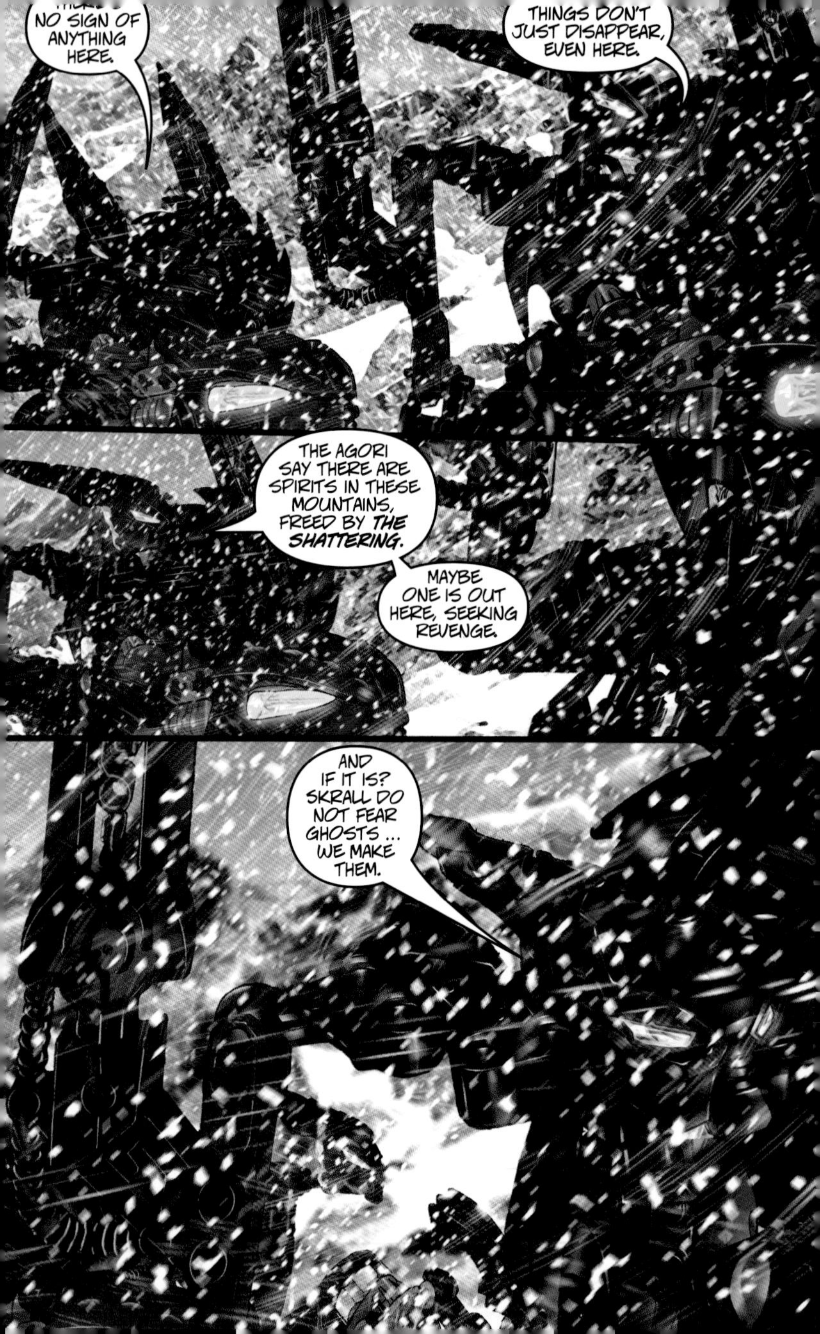
NO SIGN OF ANYTHING HERE.
THINGS DON'T JUST DISAPPEAR, EVEN HERE.
THE AGORI SAY THERE ARE SPIRITS IN THESE MOUNTAINS, FREED BY *THE SHATTERING*.
MAYBE ONE IS OUT HERE, SEEKING REVENGE.
AND IF IT IS? SKRALL DO NOT FEAR GHOSTS ... WE MAKE THEM.

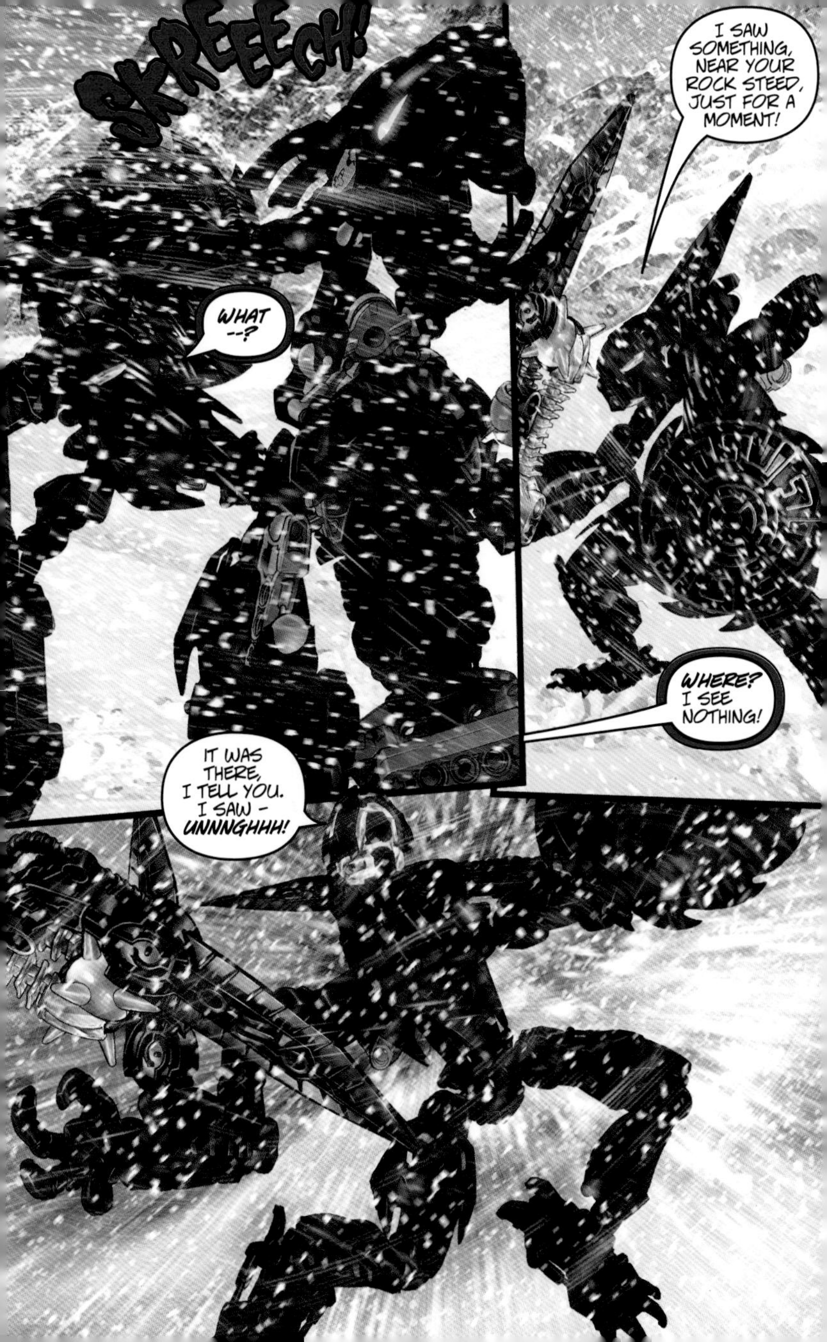
SKREEECH!
I SAW SOMETHING, NEAR YOUR ROCK STEED, JUST FOR A MOMENT!
WHAT --?
WHERE? I SEE NOTHING!
IT WAS THERE, I TELL YOU. I SAW - UNNNGHHH!

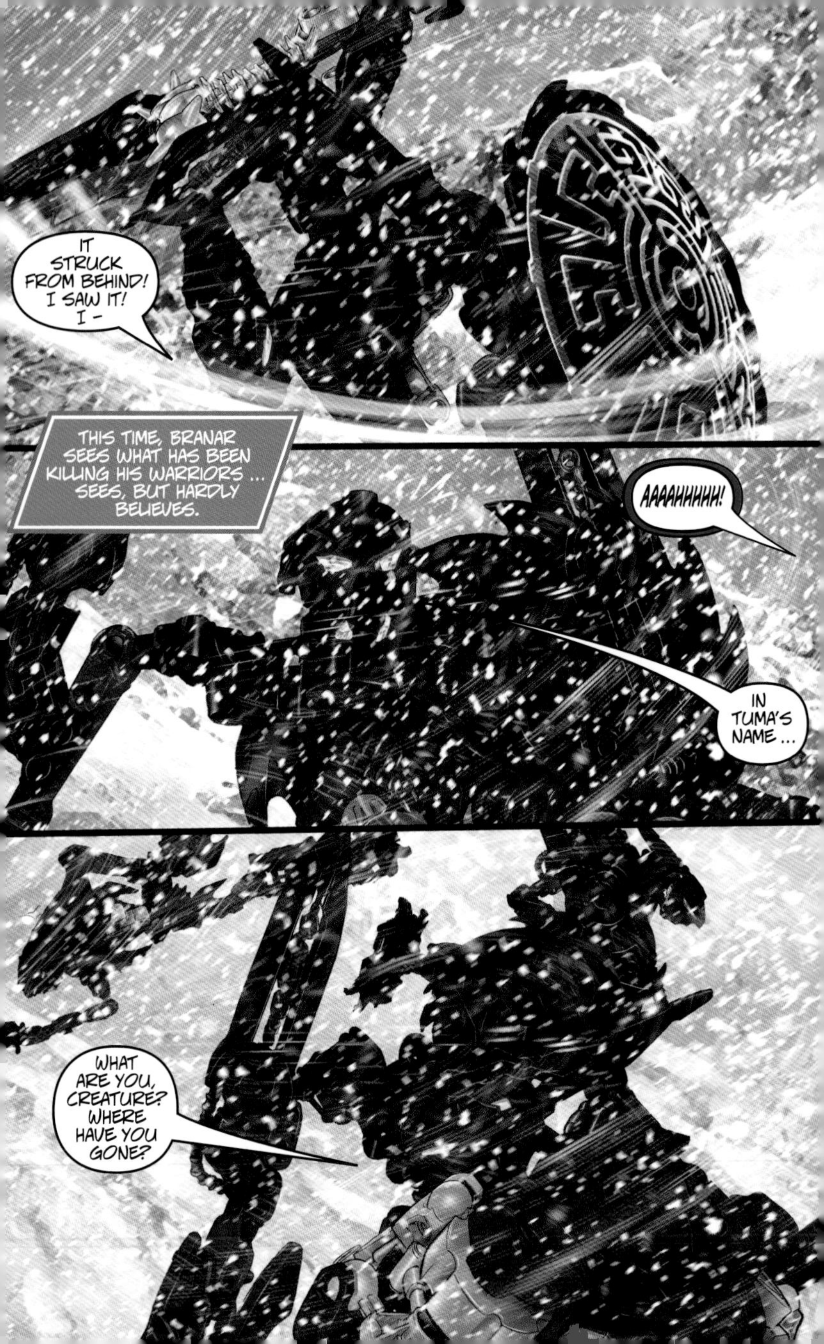
IT STRUCK FROM BEHIND! I SAW IT! I -
THIS TIME, BRANAR SEES WHAT HAS BEEN KILLING HIS WARRIORS ... SEES, BUT HARDLY BELIEVES.
AAAAHHHHH!
IN TUMA'S NAME ...
WHAT ARE YOU, CREATURE? WHERE HAVE YOU GONE?

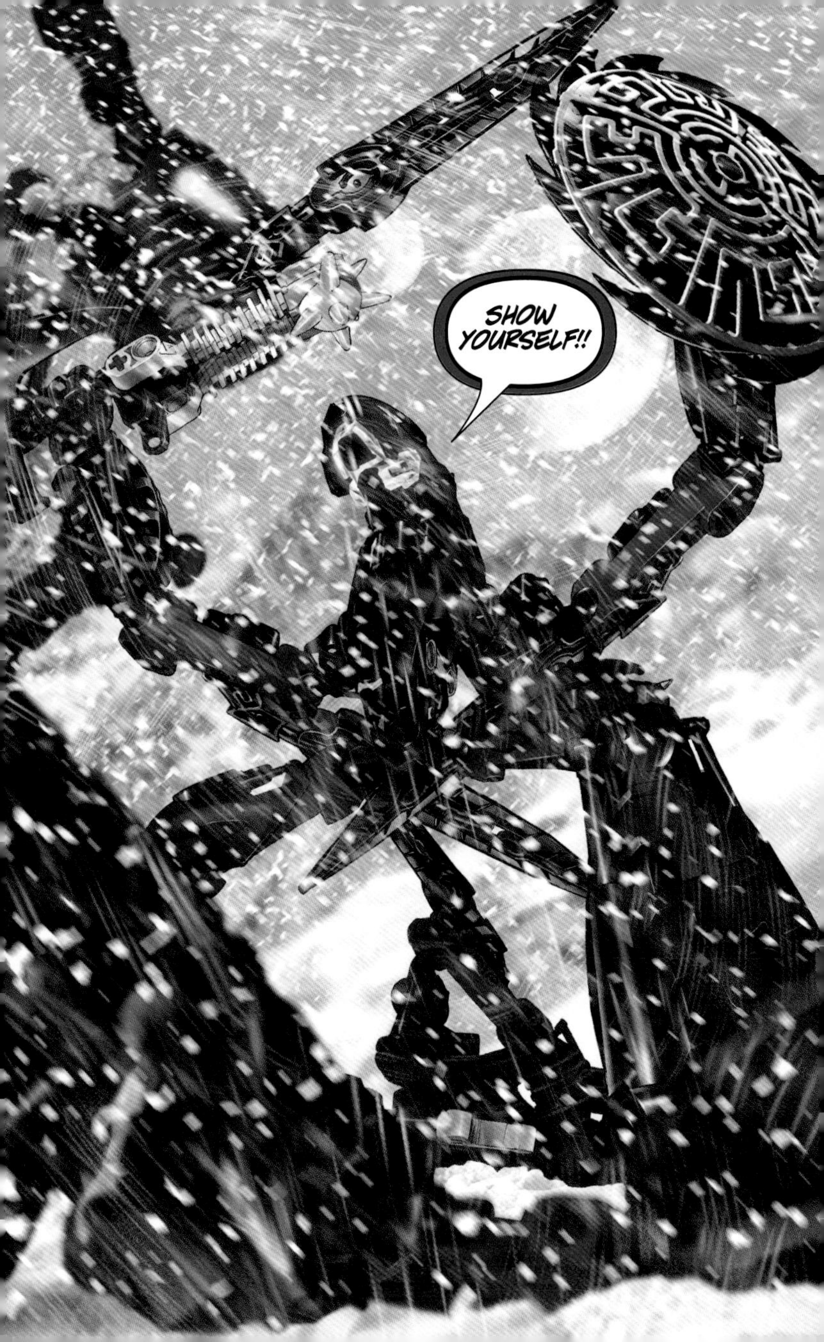
SHOW YOURSELF!!

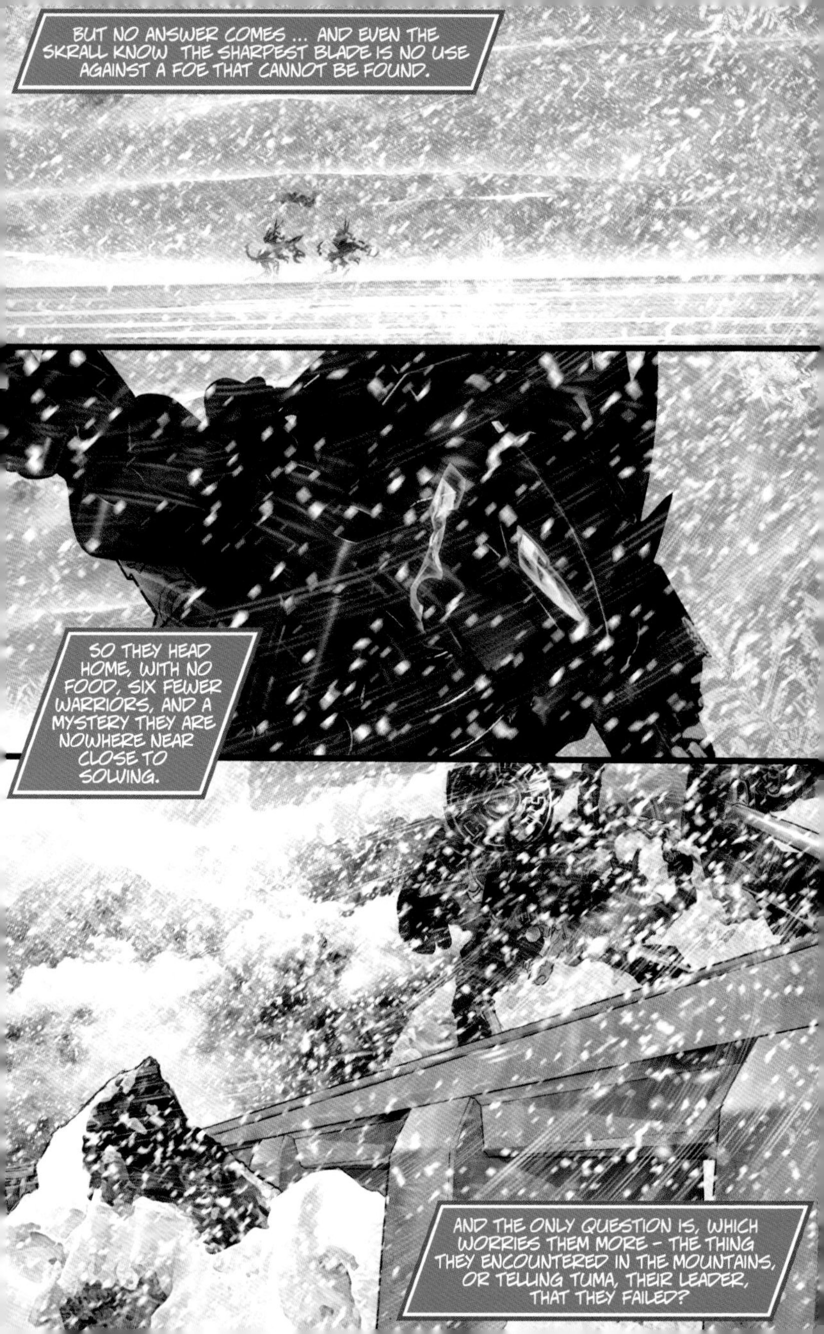
BUT NO ANSWER COMES ... AND EVEN THE SKRALL KNOW THE SHARPEST BLADE IS NO USE AGAINST A FOE THAT CANNOT BE FOUND.
SO THEY HEAD HOME, WITH NO FOOD, SIX FEWER WARRIORS, AND A MYSTERY THEY ARE NOWHERE NEAR CLOSE TO SOLVING.
AND THE ONLY QUESTION IS, WHICH WORRIES THEM MORE - THE THING THEY ENCOUNTERED IN THE MOUNTAINS, OR TELLING TUMA, THEIR LEADER, THAT THEY FAILED?

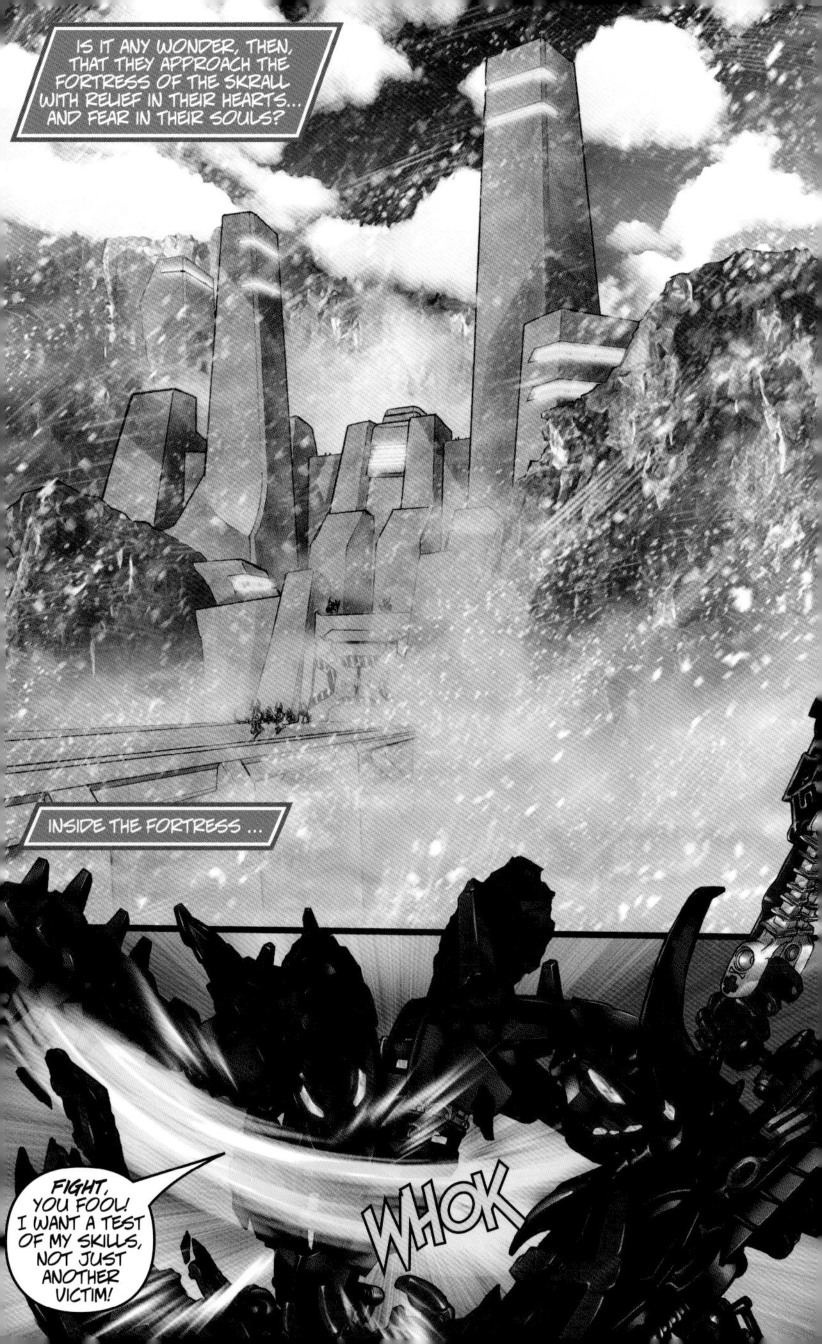
IS IT ANY WONDER, THEN, THAT THEY APPROACH THE FORTRESS OF THE SKRALL WITH RELIEF IN THEIR HEARTS... AND FEAR IN THEIR SOULS?
INSIDE THE FORTRESS ...
FIGHT, YOU FOOL! I WANT A TEST OF MY SKILLS, NOT JUST ANOTHER VICTIM!
WHOK

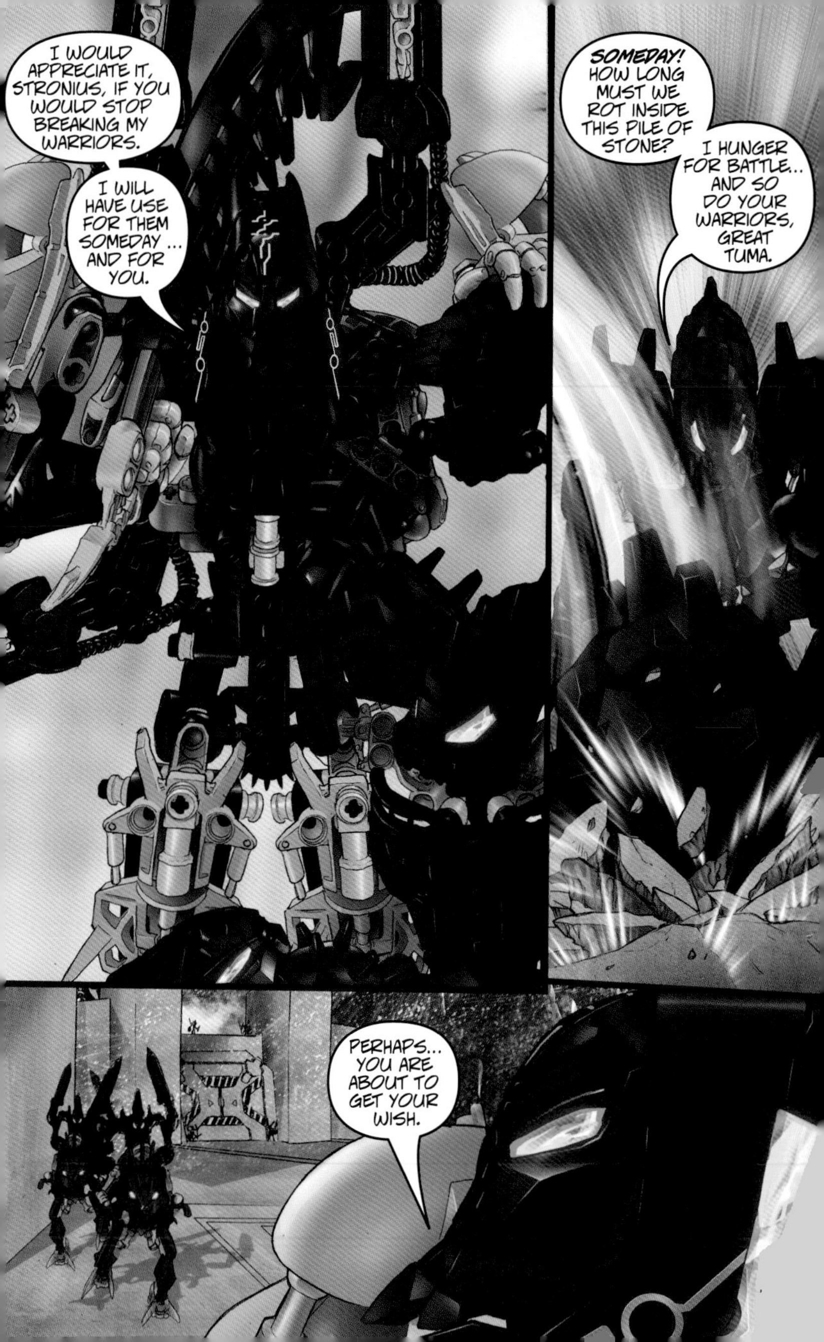
I WOULD APPRECIATE IT, STRONIUS, IF YOU WOULD STOP BREAKING MY WARRIORS.
I WILL HAVE USE FOR THEM SOMEDAY ... AND FOR YOU.
SOMEDAY! HOW LONG MUST WE ROT INSIDE THIS PILE OF STONE?
I HUNGER FOR BATTLE... AND SO DO YOUR WARRIORS, GREAT TUMA.
PERHAPS... YOU ARE ABOUT TO GET YOUR WISH.

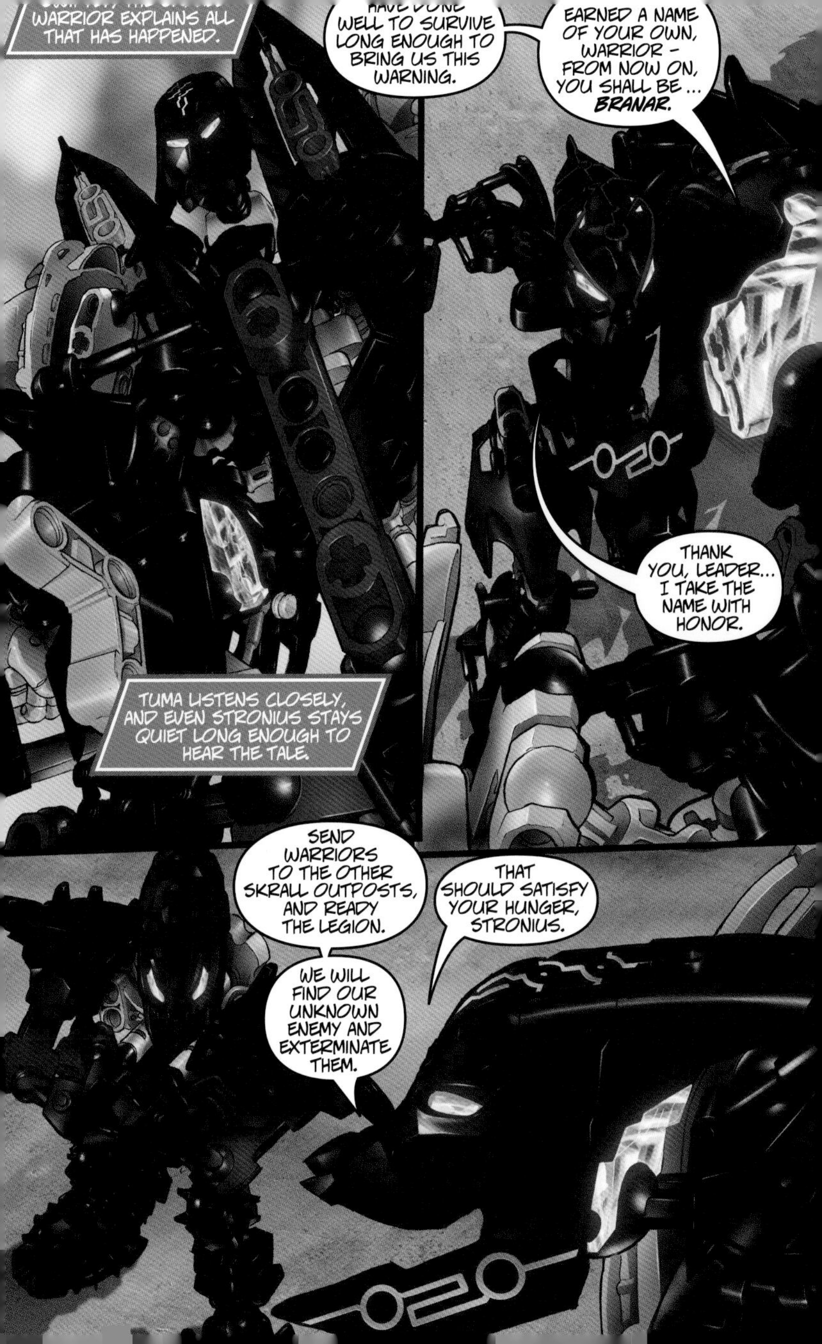
WARRIOR EXPLAINS ALL THAT HAS HAPPENED.
WELL TO SURVIVE LONG ENOUGH TO BRING US THIS WARNING.
EARNED A NAME OF YOUR OWN, WARRIOR - FROM NOW ON, YOU SHALL BE ... BRANAR.
TUMA LISTENS CLOSELY, AND EVEN STRONIUS STAYS QUIET LONG ENOUGH TO HEAR THE TALE.
THANK YOU, LEADER... I TAKE THE NAME WITH HONOR.
SEND WARRIORS TO THE OTHER SKRALL OUTPOSTS, AND READY THE LEGION.
WE WILL FIND OUR UNKNOWN ENEMY AND EXTERMINATE THEM.
THAT SHOULD SATISFY YOUR HUNGER, STRONIUS.

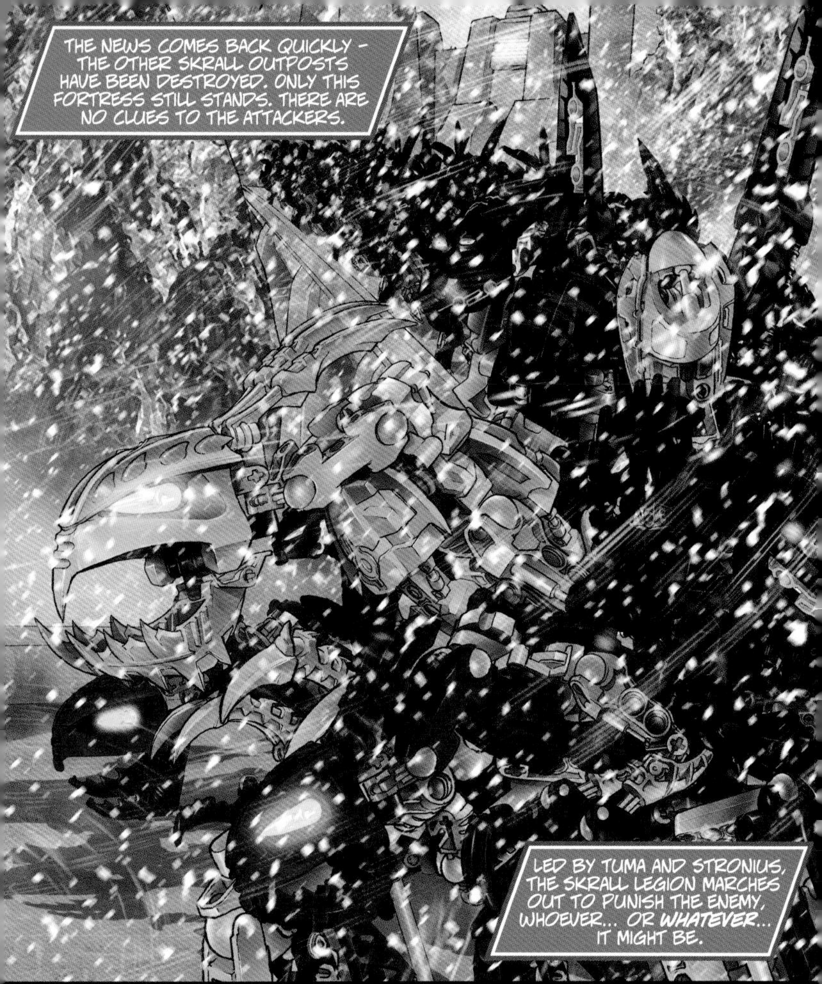
THE NEWS COMES BACK QUICKLY - THE OTHER SKRALL OUTPOSTS HAVE BEEN DESTROYED. ONLY THIS FORTRESS STILL STANDS. THERE ARE NO CLUES TO THE ATTACKERS.
LED BY TUMA AND STRONIUS, THE SKRALL LEGION MARCHES OUT TO PUNISH THE ENEMY, WHOEVER... OR *WHATEVER*... IT MIGHT BE.
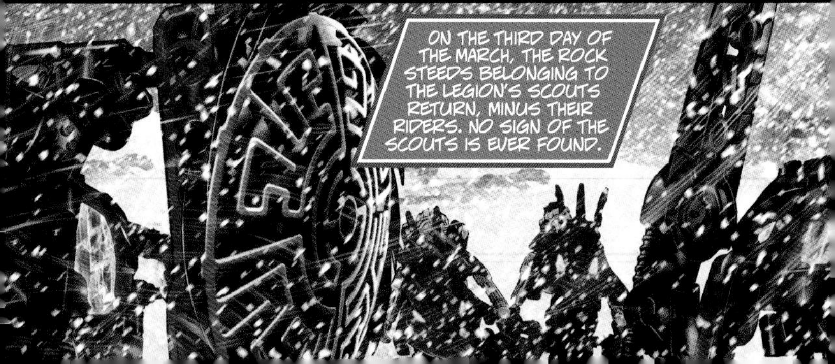
ON THE THIRD DAY OF THE MARCH, THE ROCK STEEDS BELONGING TO THE LEGION'S SCOUTS RETURN, MINUS THEIR RIDERS. NO SIGN OF THE SCOUTS IS EVER FOUND.

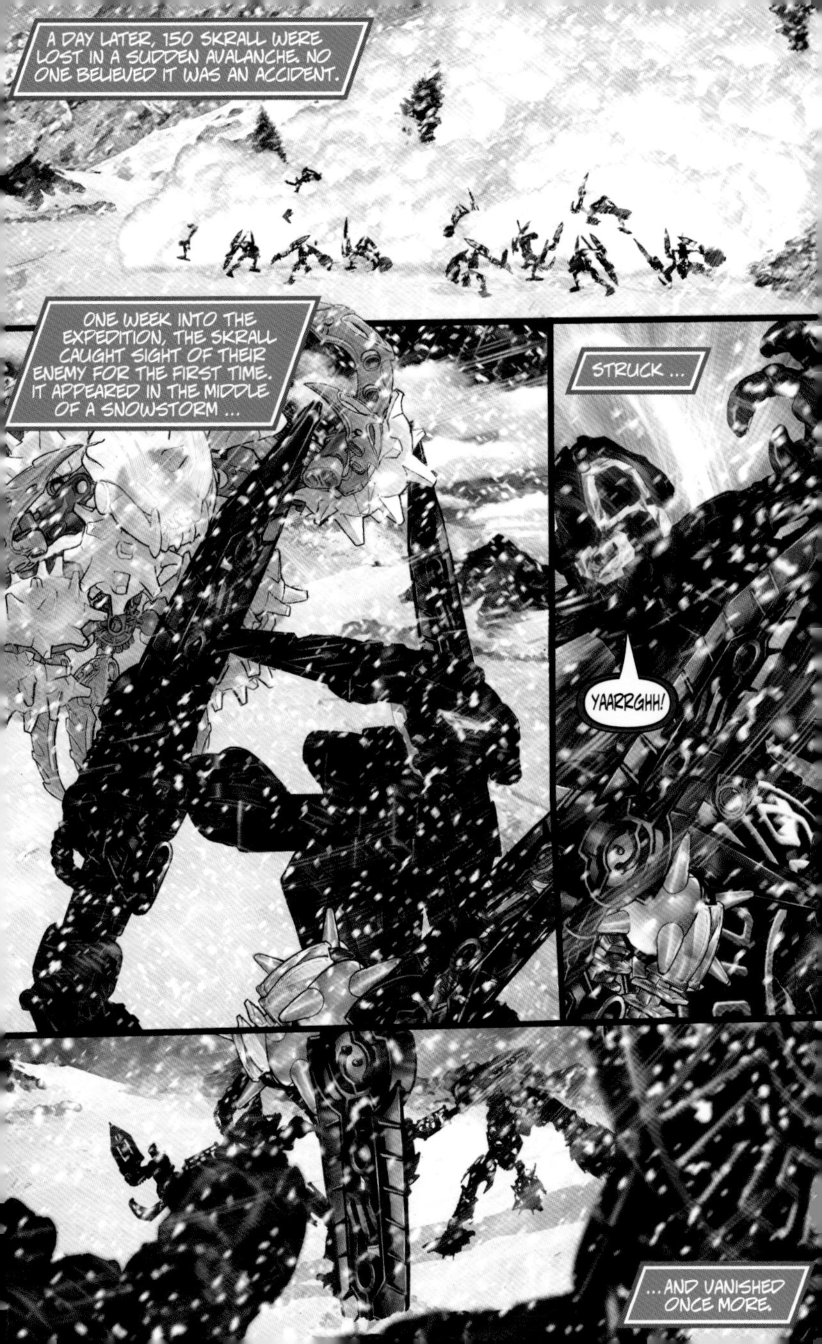
A DAY LATER, 150 SKRALL WERE LOST IN A SUDDEN AVALANCHE. NO ONE BELIEVED IT WAS AN ACCIDENT.
ONE WEEK INTO THE EXPEDITION, THE SKRALL CAUGHT SIGHT OF THEIR ENEMY FOR THE FIRST TIME. IT APPEARED IN THE MIDDLE OF A SNOWSTORM ...
STRUCK ...
YAARRGHH!
... AND VANISHED ONCE MORE.

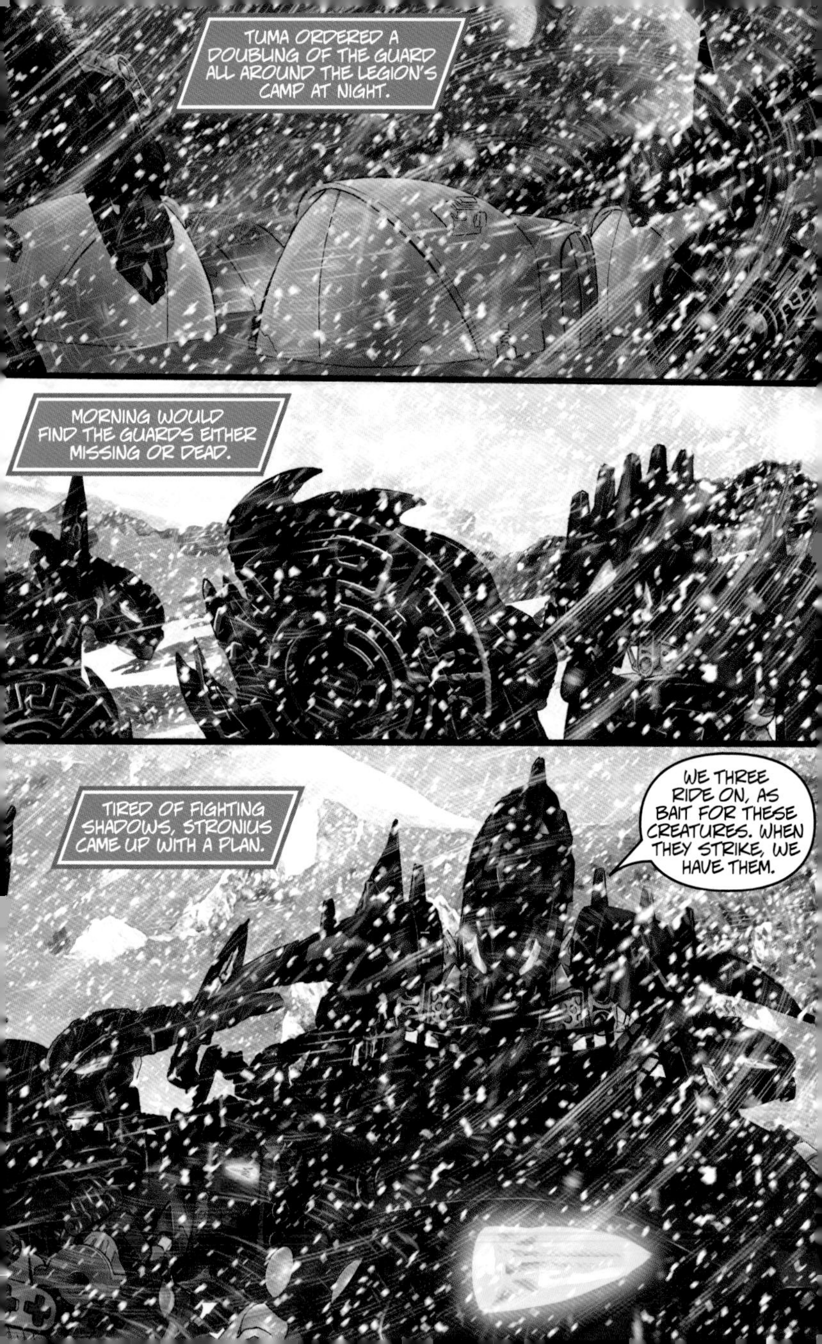
TUMA ORDERED A DOUBLING OF THE GUARD ALL AROUND THE LEGION'S CAMP AT NIGHT.
MORNING WOULD FIND THE GUARDS EITHER MISSING OR DEAD.
TIRED OF FIGHTING SHADOWS, STRONIUS CAME UP WITH A PLAN.
WE THREE RIDE ON, AS BAIT FOR THESE CREATURES. WHEN THEY STRIKE, WE HAVE THEM.

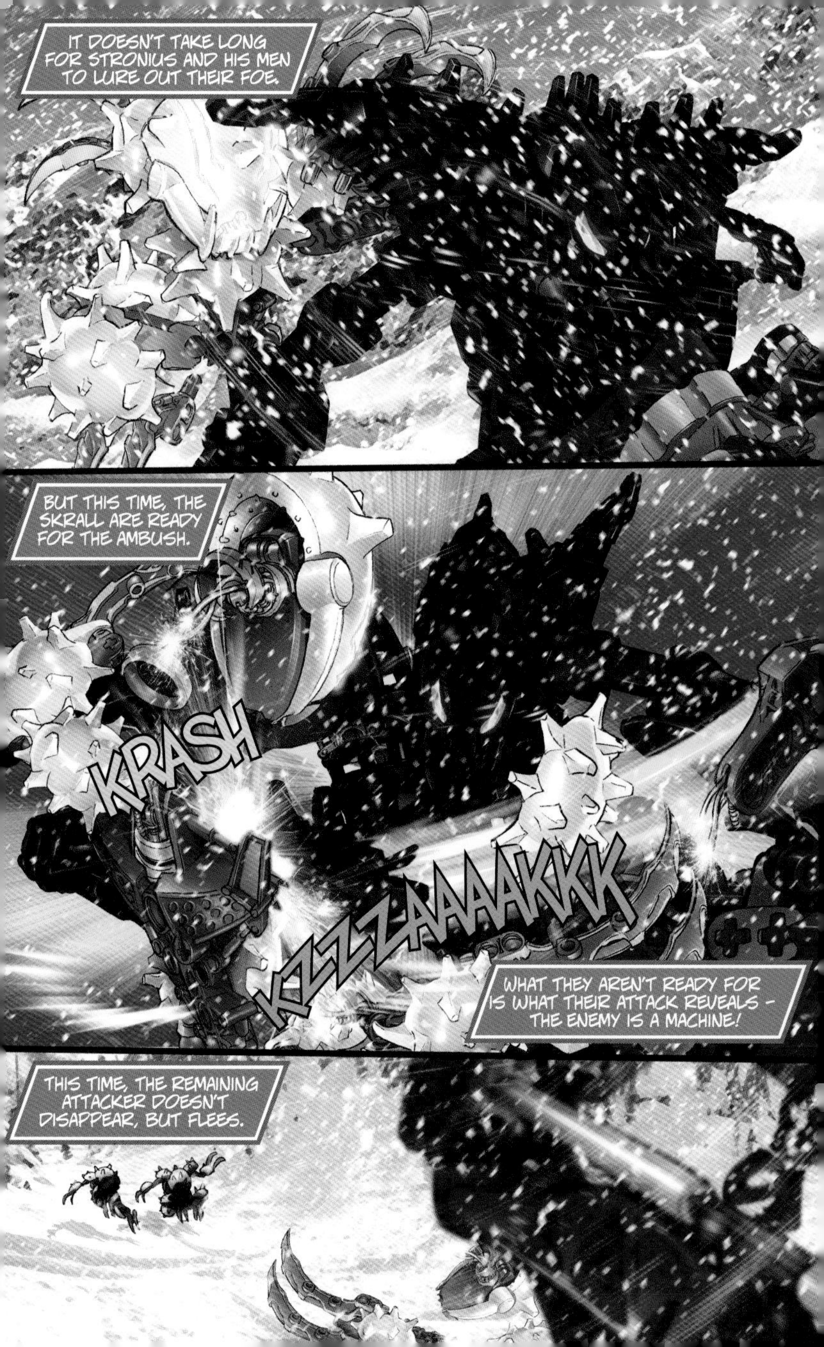
IT DOESN'T TAKE LONG FOR STRONIUS AND HIS MEN TO LURE OUT THEIR FOE.
BUT THIS TIME, THE SKRALL ARE READY FOR THE AMBUSH.
KRASH
KZZZZAAAAKKK
WHAT THEY AREN'T READY FOR IS WHAT THEIR ATTACK REVEALS - THE ENEMY IS A MACHINE!
THIS TIME, THE REMAINING ATTACKER DOESN'T DISAPPEAR, BUT FLEES.

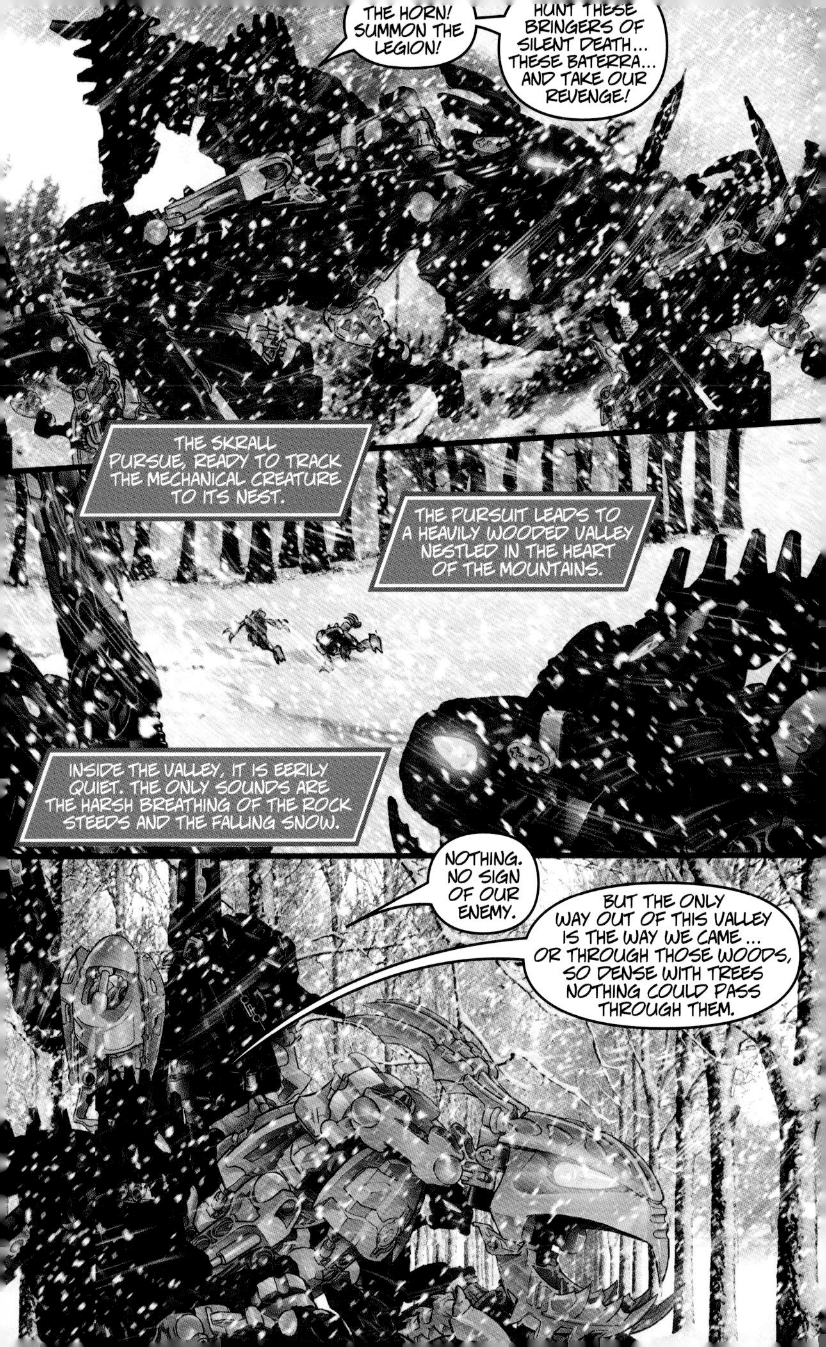
THE HORN! SUMMON THE LEGION!
HUNT THESE BRINGERS OF SILENT DEATH... THESE BATERRA... AND TAKE OUR REVENGE!
THE SKRALL PURSUE, READY TO TRACK THE MECHANICAL CREATURE TO ITS NEST.
THE PURSUIT LEADS TO A HEAVILY WOODED VALLEY NESTLED IN THE HEART OF THE MOUNTAINS.
INSIDE THE VALLEY, IT IS EERILY QUIET. THE ONLY SOUNDS ARE THE HARSH BREATHING OF THE ROCK STEEDS AND THE FALLING SNOW.
NOTHING. NO SIGN OF OUR ENEMY.
BUT THE ONLY WAY OUT OF THIS VALLEY IS THE WAY WE CAME... OR THROUGH THOSE WOODS, SO DENSE WITH TREES NOTHING COULD PASS THROUGH THEM.

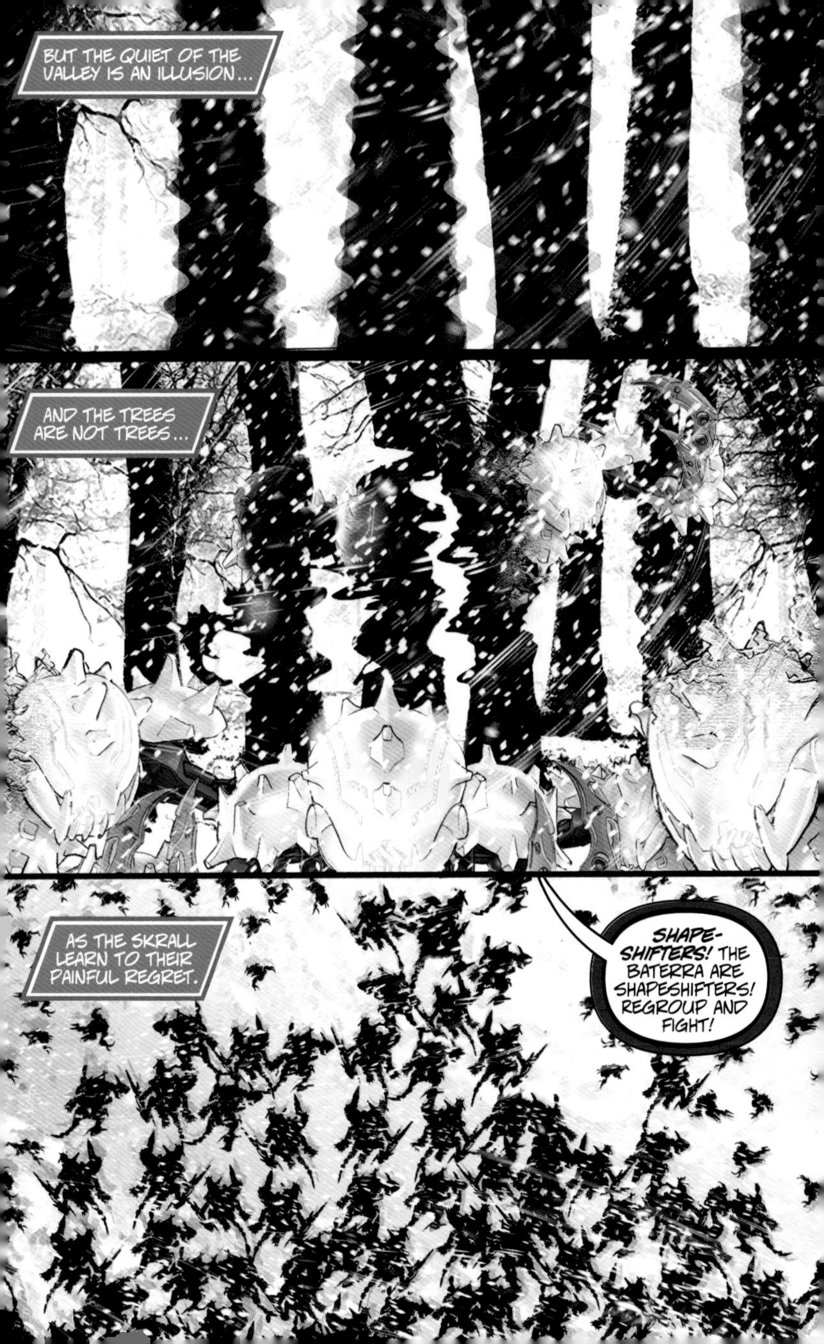
BUT THE QUIET OF THE VALLEY IS AN ILLUSION...
AND THE TREES ARE NOT TREES...
AS THE SKRALL LEARN TO THEIR PAINFUL REGRET.
SHAPE-SHIFTERS! THE BATERRA ARE SHAPESHIFTERS! REGROUP AND FIGHT!

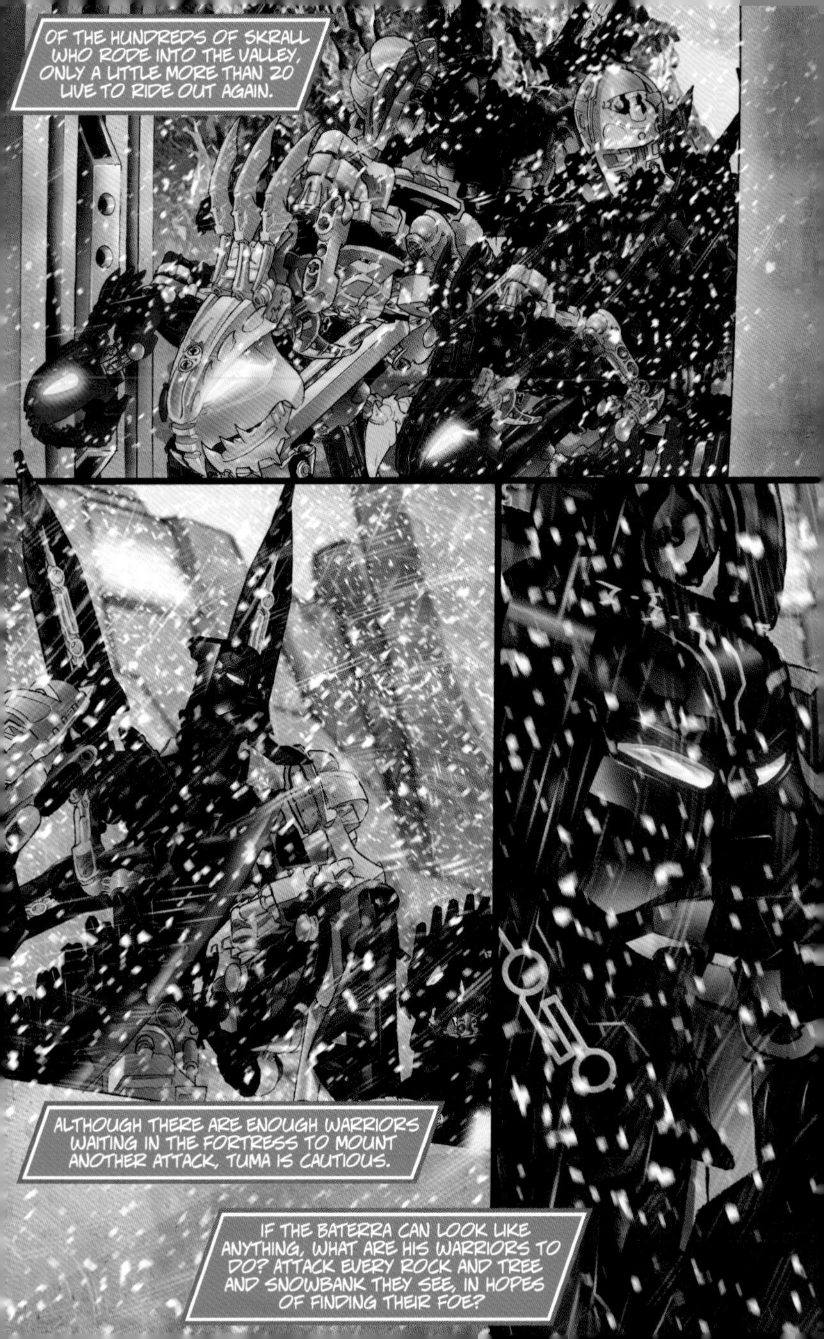
OF THE HUNDREDS OF SKRALL WHO RODE INTO THE VALLEY, ONLY A LITTLE MORE THAN 20 LIVE TO RIDE OUT AGAIN.
ALTHOUGH THERE ARE ENOUGH WARRIORS WAITING IN THE FORTRESS TO MOUNT ANOTHER ATTACK, TUMA IS CAUTIOUS.
IF THE BATERRA CAN LOOK LIKE ANYTHING, WHAT ARE HIS WARRIORS TO DO? ATTACK EVERY ROCK AND TREE AND SNOWBANK THEY SEE, IN HOPES OF FINDING THEIR FOE?

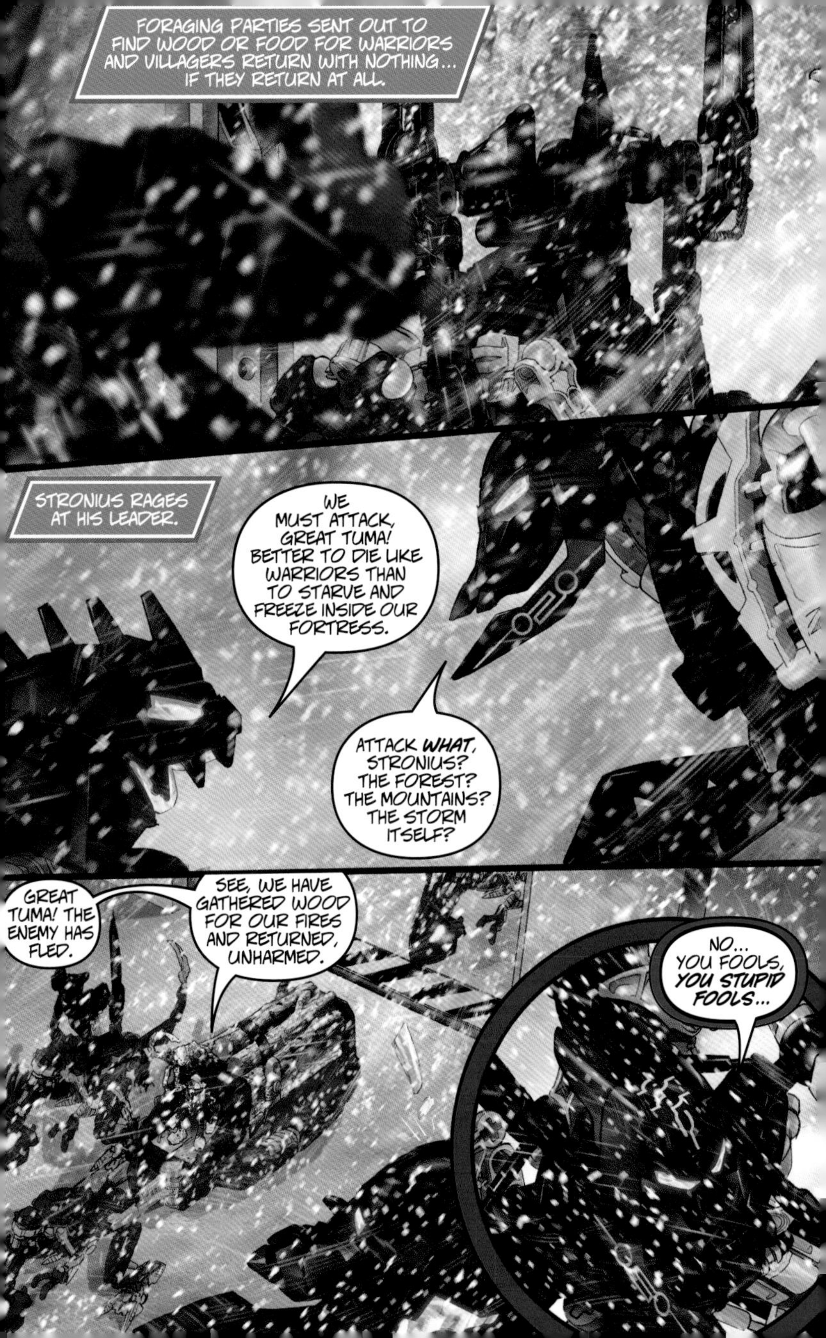
FORAGING PARTIES SENT OUT TO FIND WOOD OR FOOD FOR WARRIORS AND VILLAGERS RETURN WITH NOTHING... IF THEY RETURN AT ALL.
STRONIUS RAGES AT HIS LEADER.
WE MUST ATTACK, GREAT TUMA! BETTER TO DIE LIKE WARRIORS THAN TO STARVE AND FREEZE INSIDE OUR FORTRESS.
ATTACK WHAT, STRONIUS? THE FOREST? THE MOUNTAINS? THE STORM ITSELF?
GREAT TUMA! THE ENEMY HAS FLED.
SEE, WE HAVE GATHERED WOOD FOR OUR FIRES AND RETURNED, UNHARMED.
NO... YOU FOOLS, YOU STUPID FOOLS...

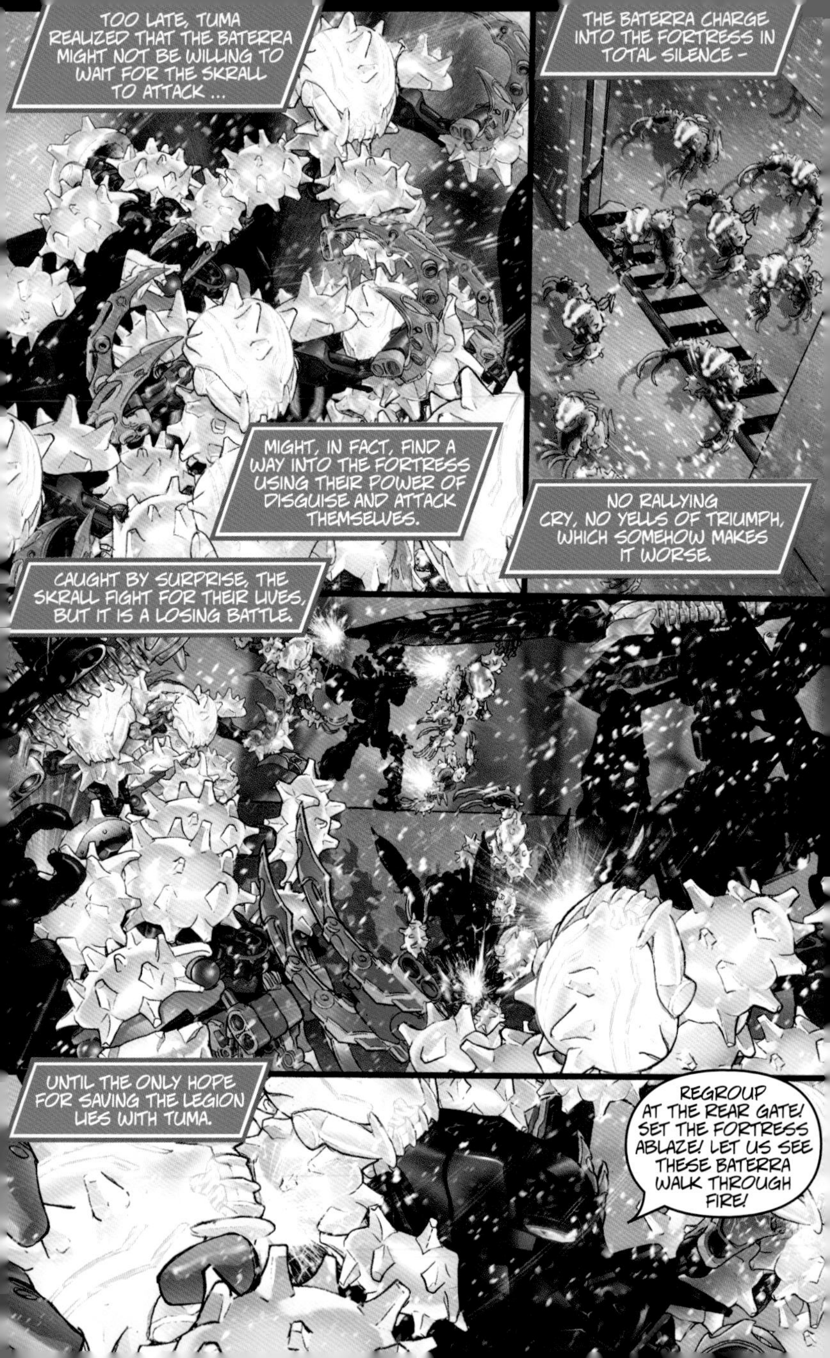
TOO LATE, TUMA REALIZED THAT THE BATERRA MIGHT NOT BE WILLING TO WAIT FOR THE SKRALL TO ATTACK ...
MIGHT, IN FACT, FIND A WAY INTO THE FORTRESS USING THEIR POWER OF DISGUISE AND ATTACK THEMSELVES.
THE BATERRA CHARGE INTO THE FORTRESS IN TOTAL SILENCE –
NO RALLYING CRY, NO YELLS OF TRIUMPH, WHICH SOMEHOW MAKES IT WORSE.
CAUGHT BY SURPRISE, THE SKRALL FIGHT FOR THEIR LIVES, BUT IT IS A LOSING BATTLE.
UNTIL THE ONLY HOPE FOR SAVING THE LEGION LIES WITH TUMA.
REGROUP AT THE REAR GATE! SET THE FORTRESS ABLAZE! LET US SEE THESE BATERRA WALK THROUGH FIRE!

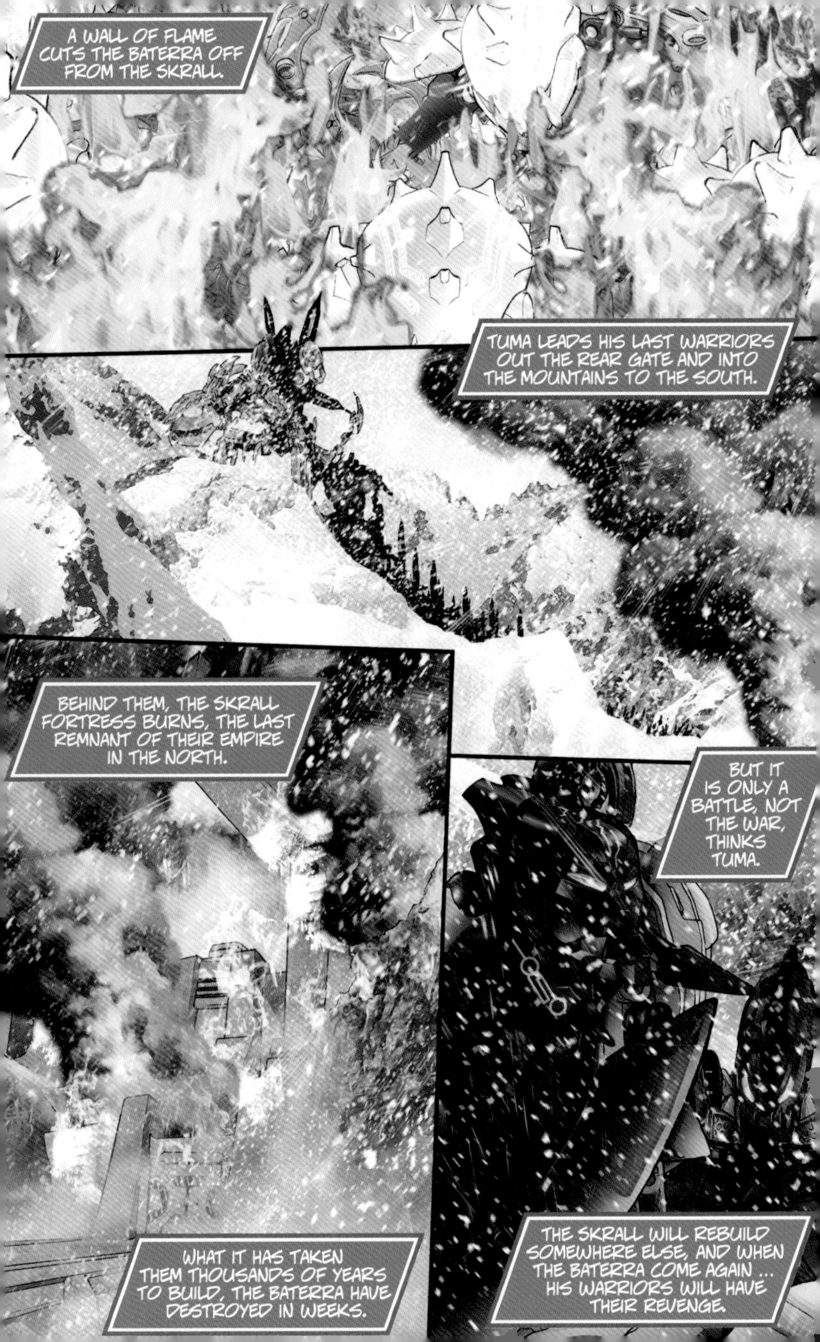
A WALL OF FLAME CUTS THE BATERRA OFF FROM THE SKRALL.
TUMA LEADS HIS LAST WARRIORS OUT THE REAR GATE AND INTO THE MOUNTAINS TO THE SOUTH.
BEHIND THEM, THE SKRALL FORTRESS BURNS, THE LAST REMNANT OF THEIR EMPIRE IN THE NORTH.
WHAT IT HAS TAKEN THEM THOUSANDS OF YEARS TO BUILD, THE BATERRA HAVE DESTROYED IN WEEKS.
BUT IT IS ONLY A BATTLE, NOT THE WAR, THINKS TUMA.
THE SKRALL WILL REBUILD SOMEWHERE ELSE, AND WHEN THE BATERRA COME AGAIN ... HIS WARRIORS WILL HAVE THEIR REVENGE.

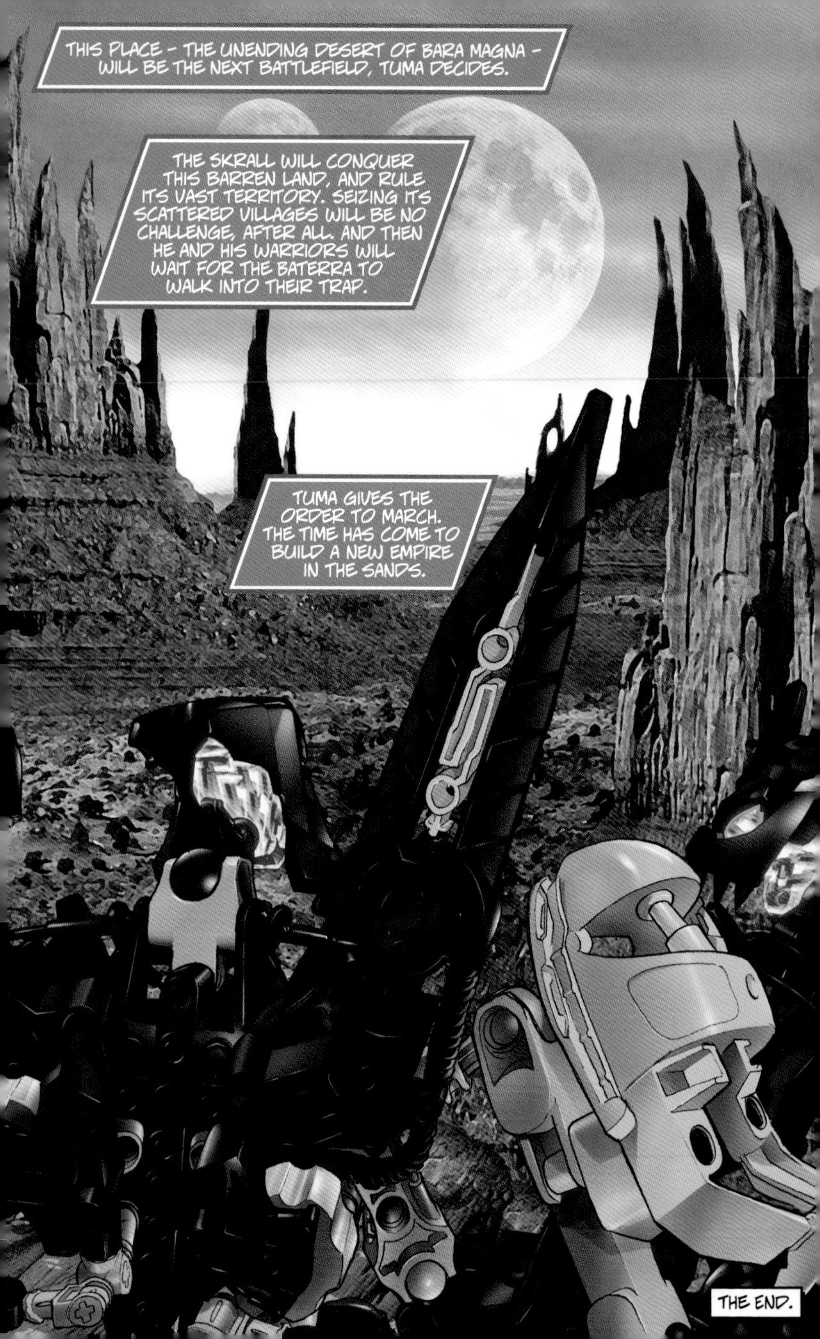
THIS PLACE - THE UNENDING DESERT OF BARA MAGNA - WILL BE THE NEXT BATTLEFIELD, TUMA DECIDES.
THE SKRALL WILL CONQUER THIS BARREN LAND, AND RULE ITS VAST TERRITORY. SEIZING ITS SCATTERED VILLAGES WILL BE NO CHALLENGE, AFTER ALL. AND THEN HE AND HIS WARRIORS WILL WAIT FOR THE BATERRA TO WALK INTO THEIR TRAP.
TUMA GIVES THE ORDER TO MARCH. THE TIME HAS COME TO BUILD A NEW EMPIRE IN THE SANDS.
THE END.

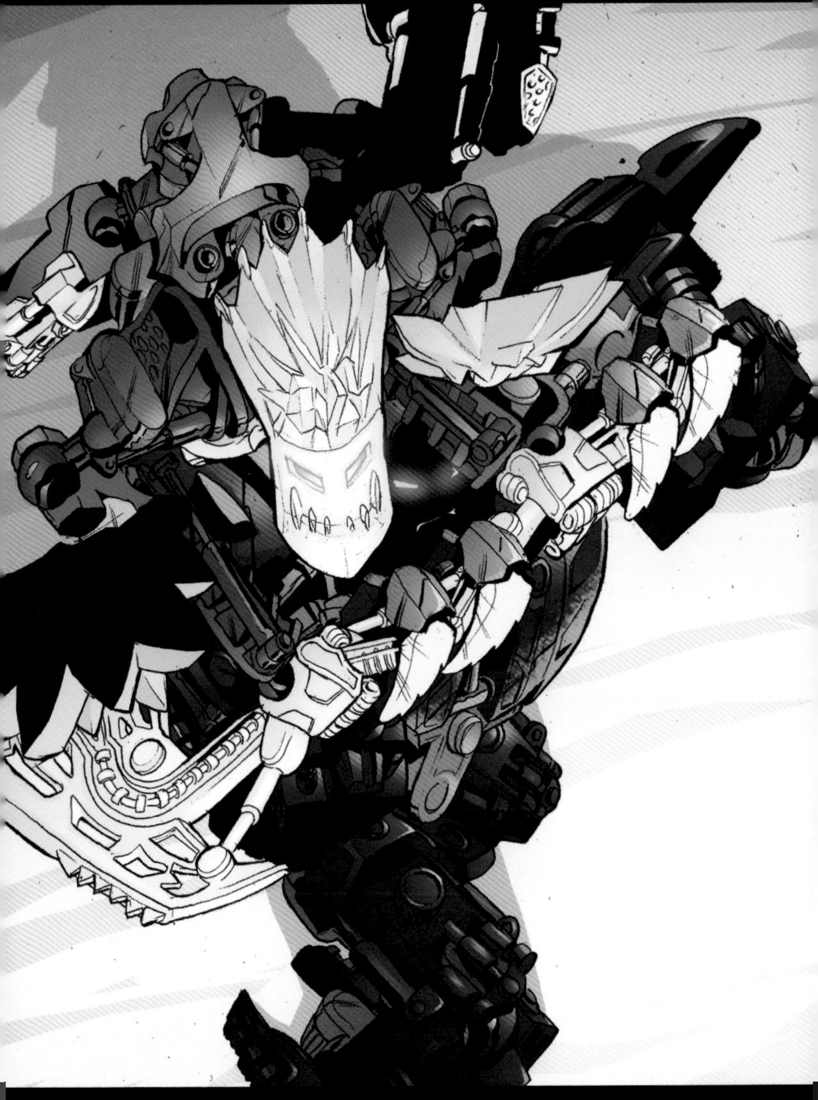

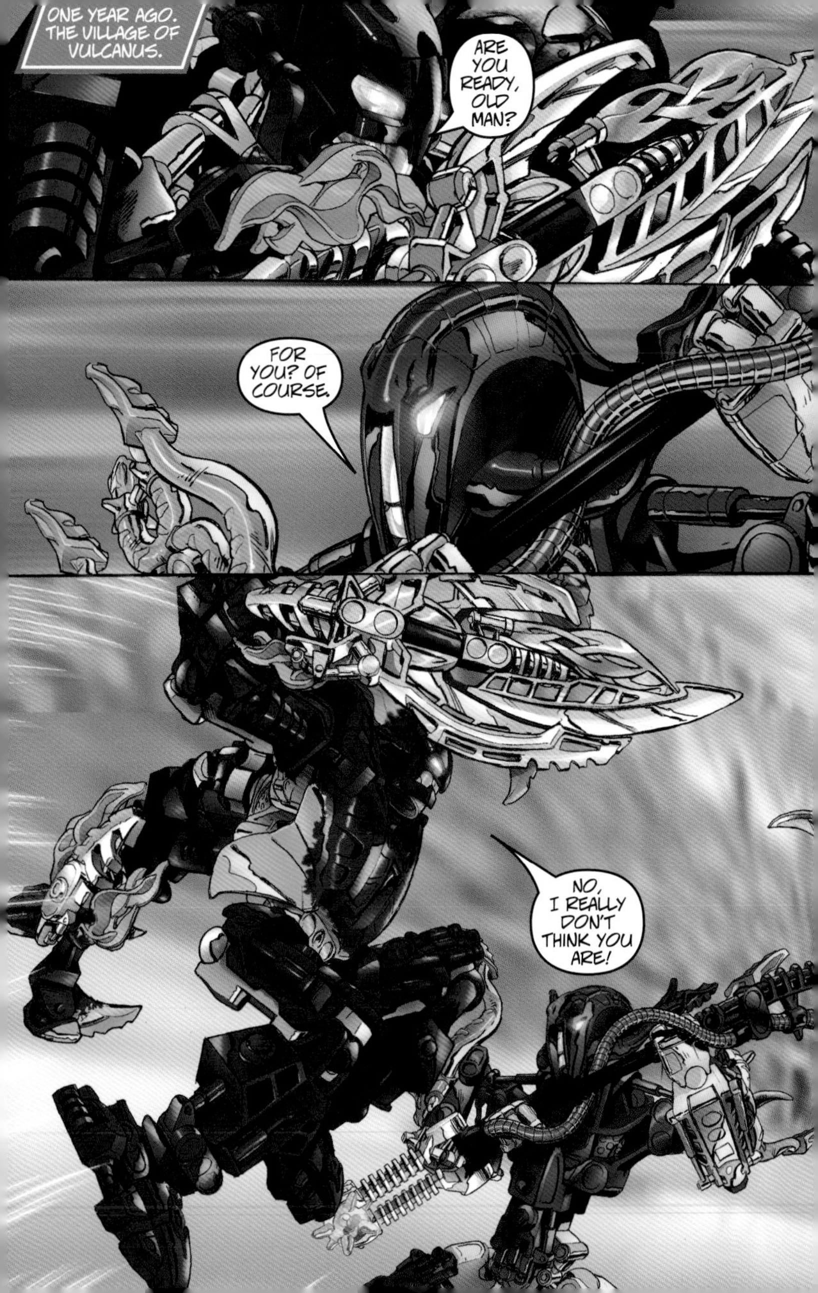
ONE YEAR AGO. THE VILLAGE OF VULCANUS.
ARE YOU READY, OLD MAN?
FOR YOU? OF COURSE.
NO, I REALLY DON'T THINK YOU ARE!

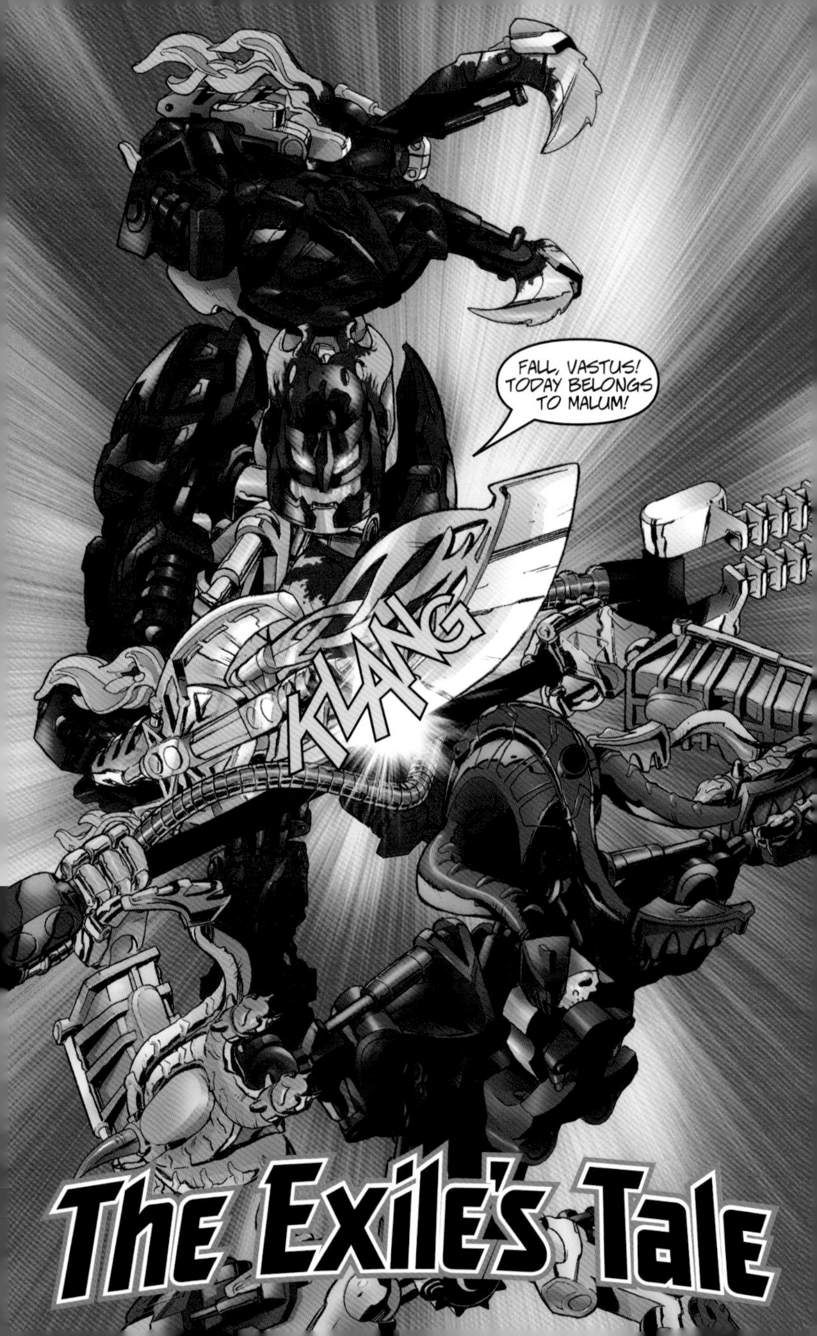
FALL, VASTUS! TODAY BELONGS TO MALUM!
KLANG
The Exile's Tale

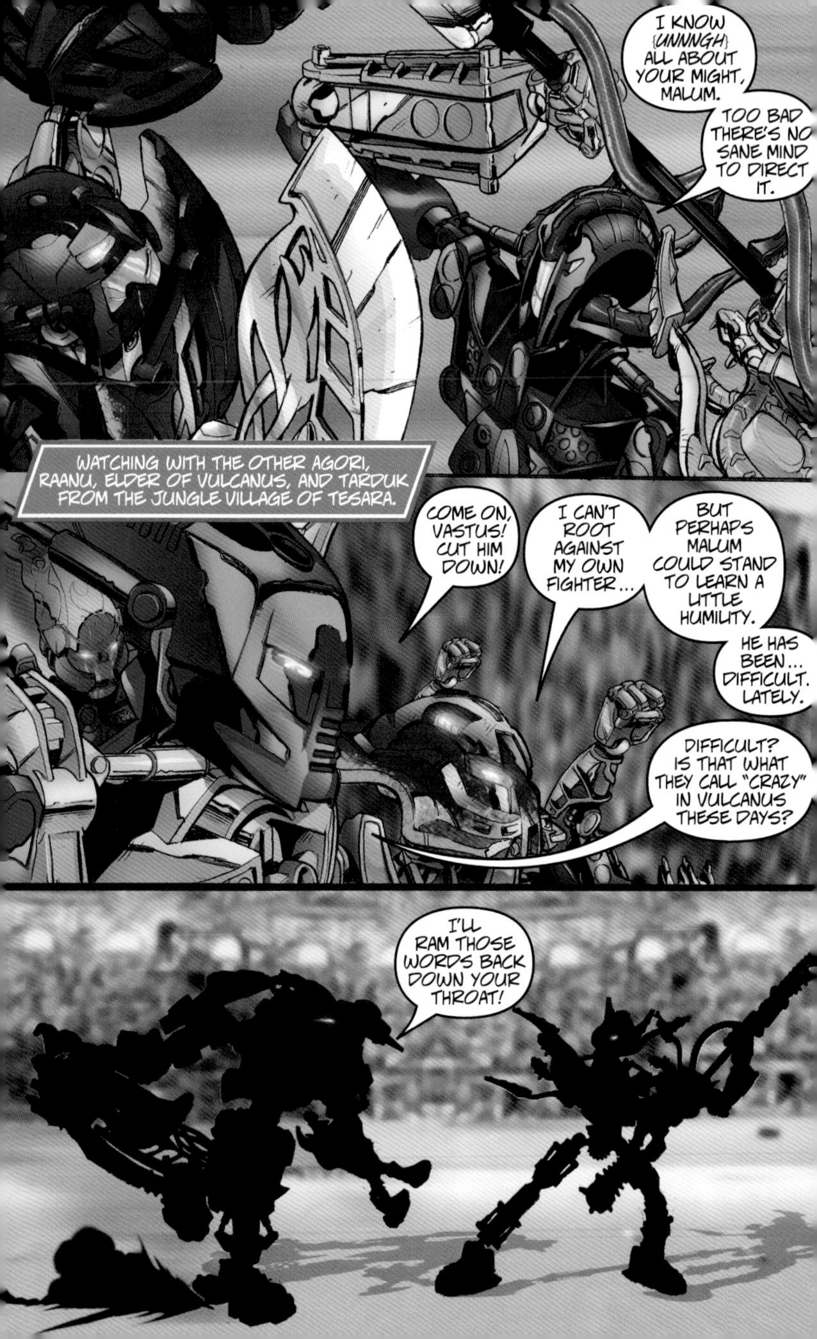
I KNOW {UNNNGH} ALL ABOUT YOUR MIGHT, MALUM.
TOO BAD THERE'S NO SANE MIND TO DIRECT IT.
WATCHING WITH THE OTHER AGORI, RAANU, ELDER OF VULCANUS, AND TARDUK FROM THE JUNGLE VILLAGE OF TESARA.
COME ON, VASTUS! CUT HIM DOWN!
I CAN'T ROOT AGAINST MY OWN FIGHTER...
BUT PERHAPS MALUM COULD STAND TO LEARN A LITTLE HUMILITY.
HE HAS BEEN... DIFFICULT. LATELY.
DIFFICULT? IS THAT WHAT THEY CALL "CRAZY" IN VULCANUS THESE DAYS?
I'LL RAM THOSE WORDS BACK DOWN YOUR THROAT!

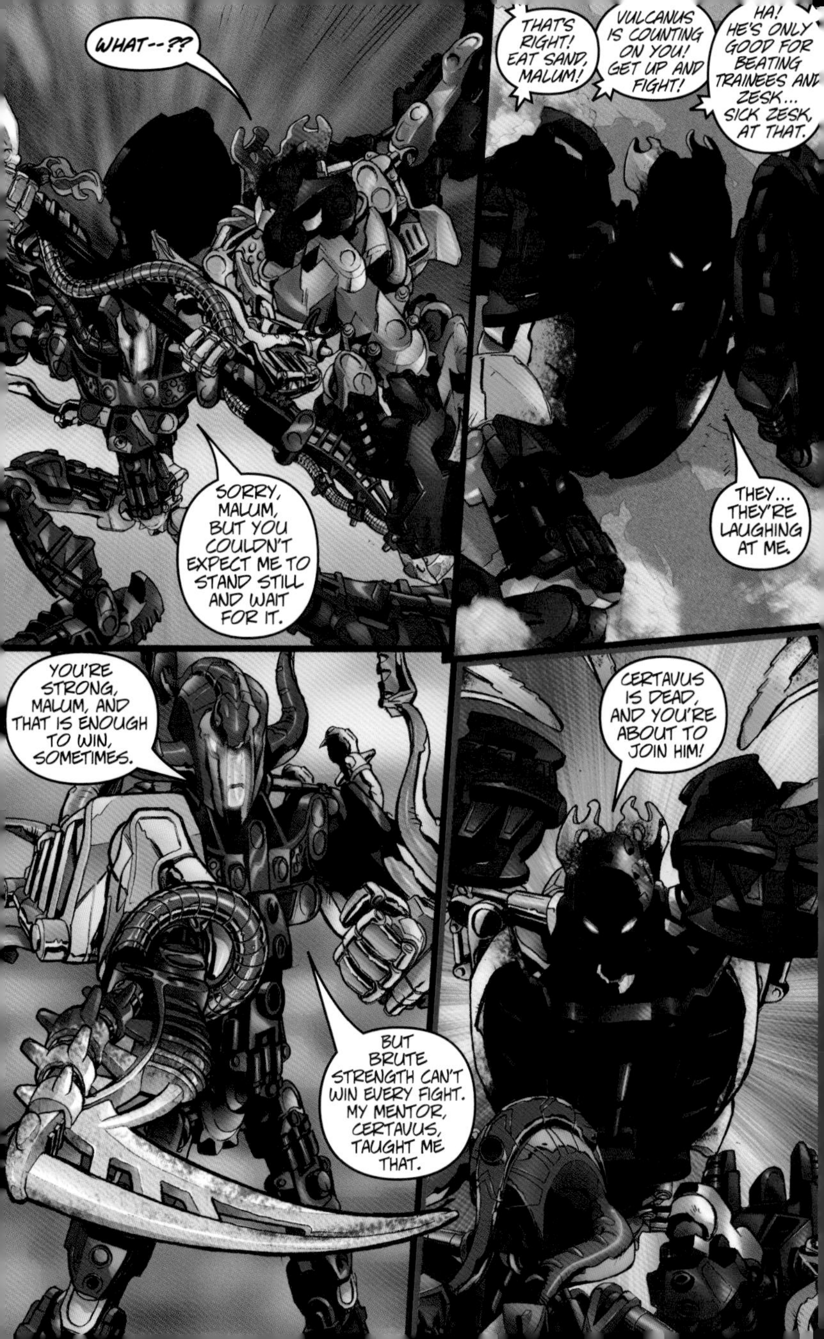
WHAT--??
SORRY, MALUM, BUT YOU COULDN'T EXPECT ME TO STAND STILL AND WAIT FOR IT.
THAT'S RIGHT! EAT SAND, MALUM!
VULCANUS IS COUNTING ON YOU! GET UP AND FIGHT!
HA! HE'S ONLY GOOD FOR BEATING TRAINEES AND ZESK... SICK ZESK, AT THAT.
THEY... THEY'RE LAUGHING AT ME.
YOU'RE STRONG, MALUM, AND THAT IS ENOUGH TO WIN, SOMETIMES.
BUT BRUTE STRENGTH CAN'T WIN EVERY FIGHT. MY MENTOR, CERTAVUS, TAUGHT ME THAT.
CERTAVUS IS DEAD, AND YOU'RE ABOUT TO JOIN HIM!

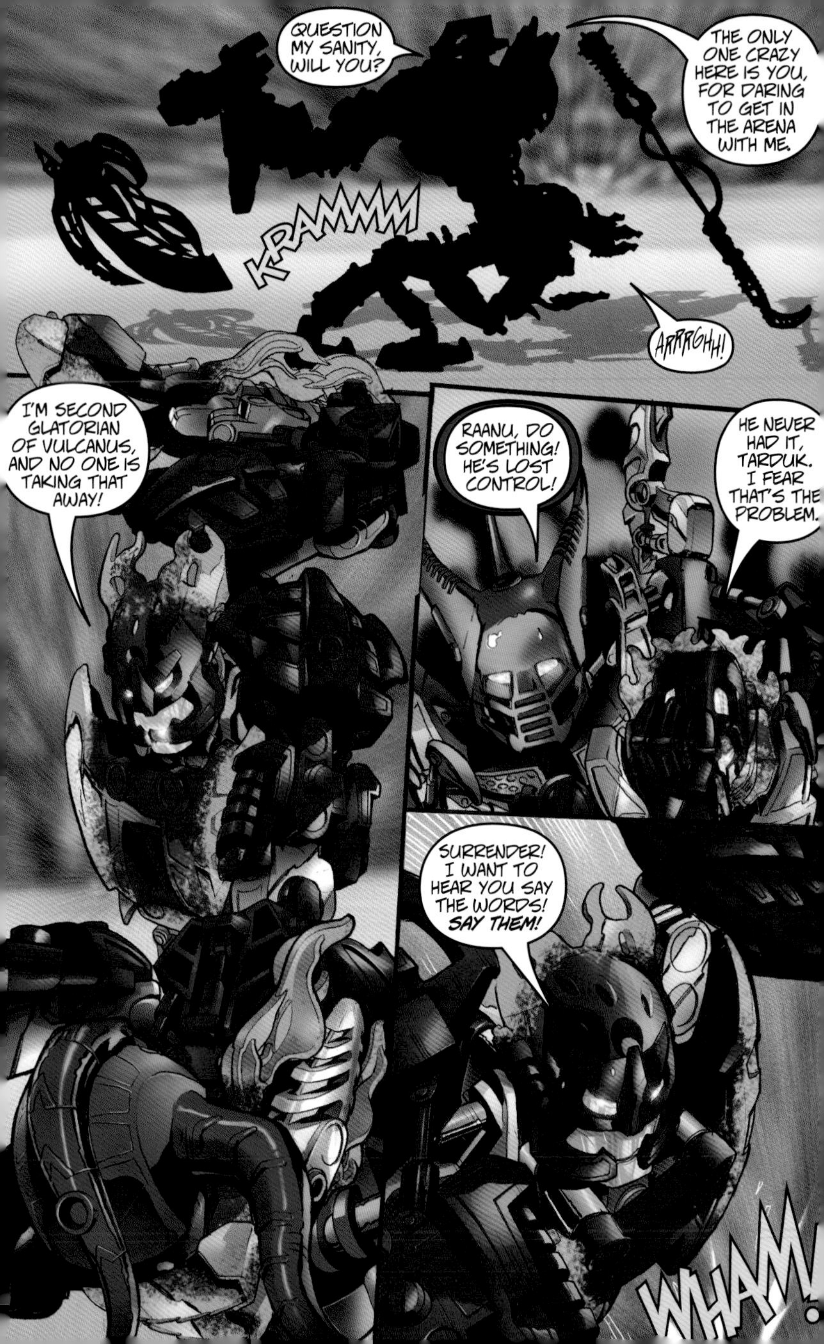
QUESTION MY SANITY, WILL YOU?
THE ONLY ONE CRAZY HERE IS YOU, FOR DARING TO GET IN THE ARENA WITH ME.
KRAMMMM
ARRRGHH!
I'M SECOND GLATORIAN OF VULCANUS, AND NO ONE IS TAKING THAT AWAY!
RAANU, DO SOMETHING! HE'S LOST CONTROL!
HE NEVER HAD IT, TARDUK. I FEAR THAT'S THE PROBLEM.
SURRENDER! I WANT TO HEAR YOU SAY THE WORDS! SAY THEM!
WHAM!

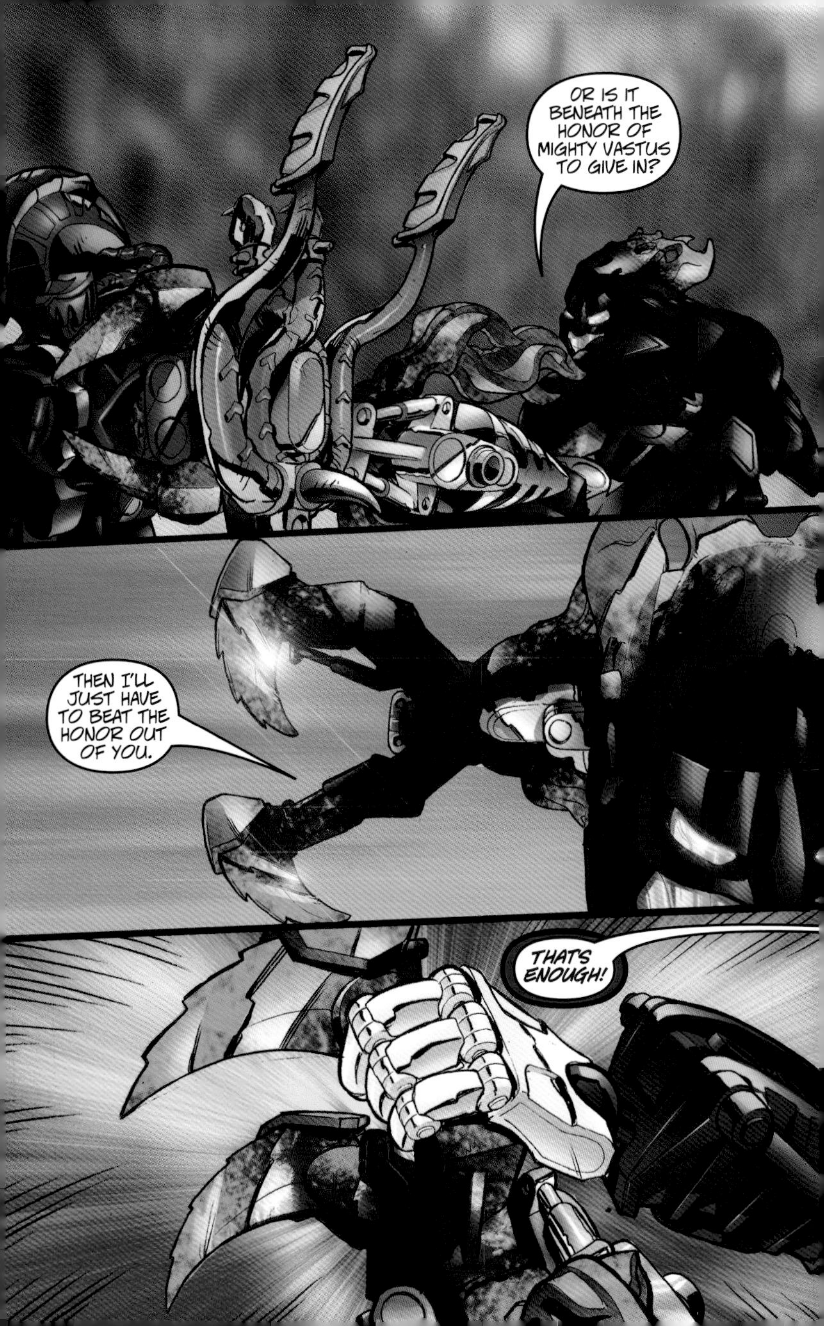
OR IS IT BENEATH THE HONOR OF MIGHTY VASTUS TO GIVE IN?
THEN I'LL JUST HAVE TO BEAT THE HONOR OUT OF YOU.
THAT'S ENOUGH!

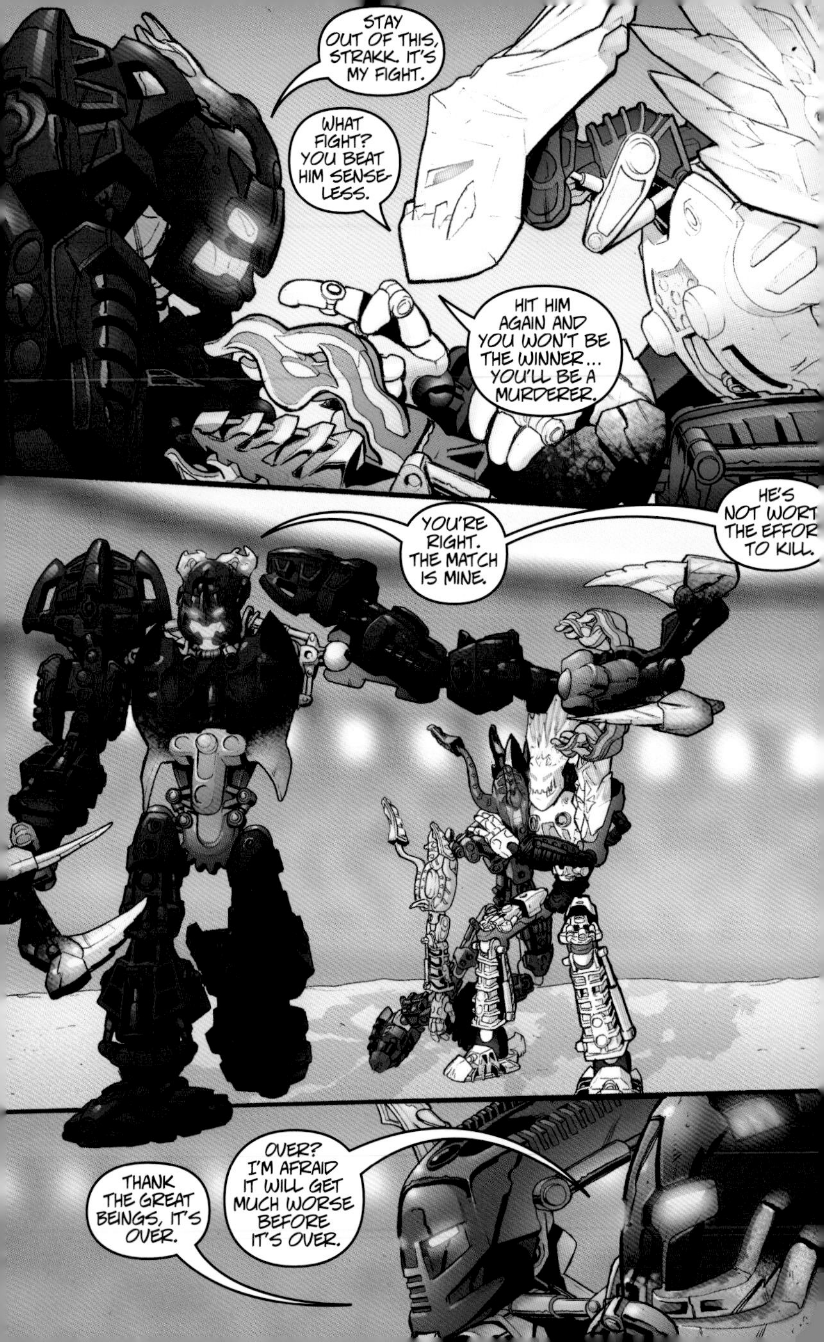
STAY OUT OF THIS, STRAKK. IT'S MY FIGHT.
WHAT FIGHT? YOU BEAT HIM SENSELESS.
HIT HIM AGAIN AND YOU WON'T BE THE WINNER... YOU'LL BE A MURDERER.
YOU'RE RIGHT. THE MATCH IS MINE.
HE'S NOT WORT THE EFFOR TO KILL.
THANK THE GREAT BEINGS, IT'S OVER.
OVER? I'M AFRAID IT WILL GET MUCH WORSE BEFORE IT'S OVER.

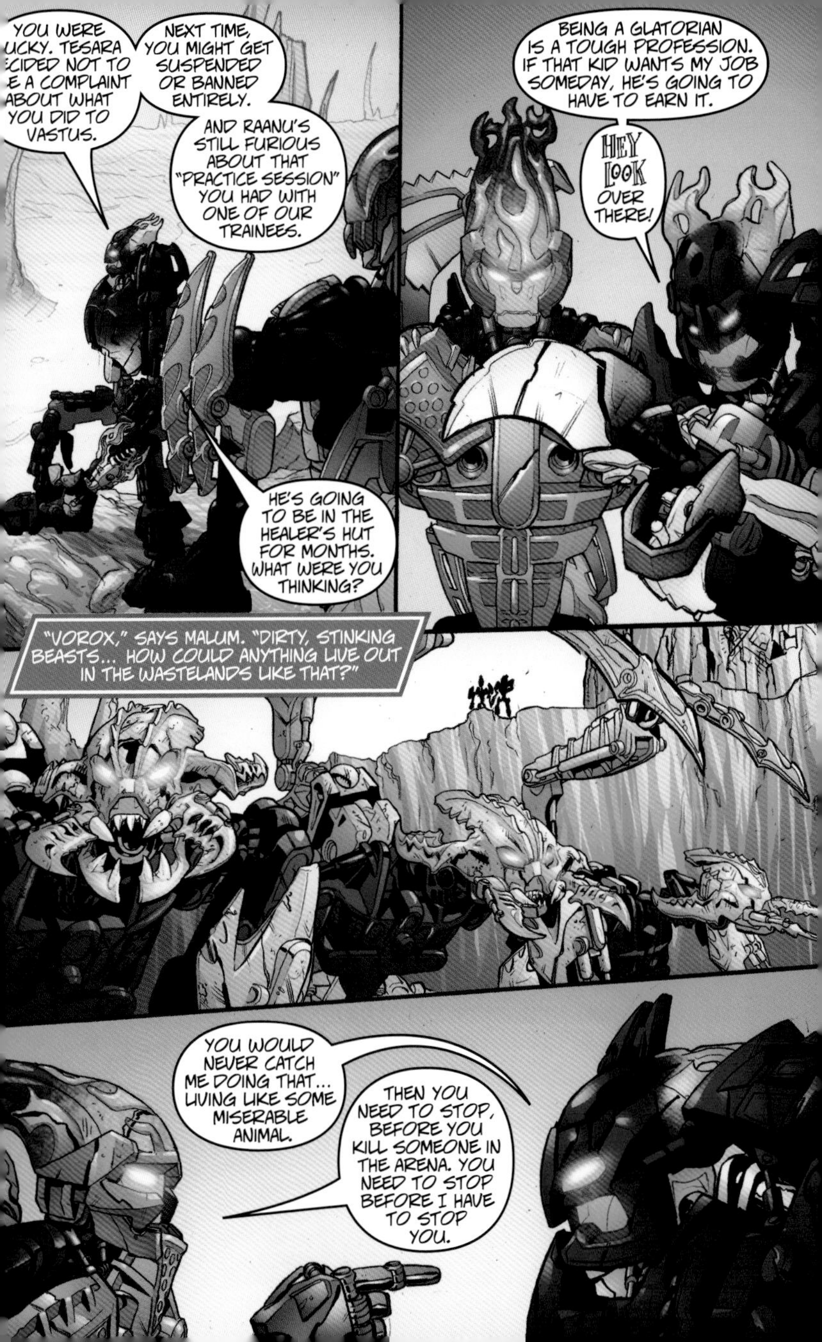
YOU WERE UCKY. TESARA ECIDED NOT TO E A COMPLAINT ABOUT WHAT YOU DID TO VASTUS.
NEXT TIME, YOU MIGHT GET SUSPENDED OR BANNED ENTIRELY.
AND RAANU'S STILL FURIOUS ABOUT THAT "PRACTICE SESSION" YOU HAD WITH ONE OF OUR TRAINEES.
HE'S GOING TO BE IN THE HEALER'S HUT FOR MONTHS. WHAT WERE YOU THINKING?
BEING A GLATORIAN IS A TOUGH PROFESSION. IF THAT KID WANTS MY JOB SOMEDAY, HE'S GOING TO HAVE TO EARN IT.
HEY LOOK OVER THERE!
"VOROX," SAYS MALUM. "DIRTY, STINKING BEASTS... HOW COULD ANYTHING LIVE OUT IN THE WASTELANDS LIKE THAT?"
YOU WOULD NEVER CATCH ME DOING THAT... LIVING LIKE SOME MISERABLE ANIMAL.
THEN YOU NEED TO STOP, BEFORE YOU KILL SOMEONE IN THE ARENA. YOU NEED TO STOP BEFORE I HAVE TO STOP YOU.

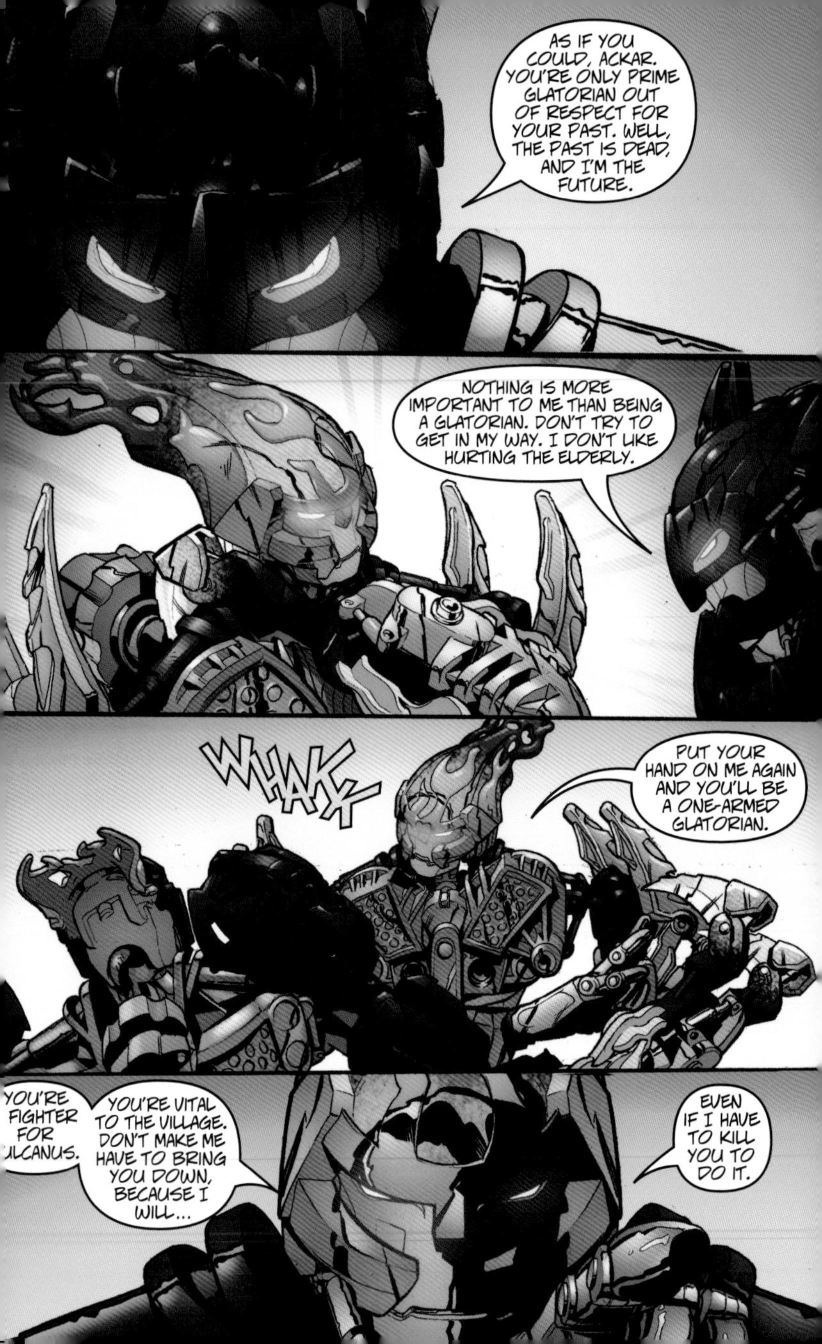
AS IF YOU COULD, ACKAR. YOU'RE ONLY PRIME GLATORIAN OUT OF RESPECT FOR YOUR PAST. WELL, THE PAST IS DEAD, AND I'M THE FUTURE.
NOTHING IS MORE IMPORTANT TO ME THAN BEING A GLATORIAN. DON'T TRY TO GET IN MY WAY. I DON'T LIKE HURTING THE ELDERLY.
WHAKK
PUT YOUR HAND ON ME AGAIN AND YOU'LL BE A ONE-ARMED GLATORIAN.
YOU'RE FIGHTER FOR LCANUS.
YOU'RE VITAL TO THE VILLAGE. DON'T MAKE ME HAVE TO BRING YOU DOWN, BECAUSE I WILL...
EVEN IF I HAVE TO KILL YOU TO DO IT.

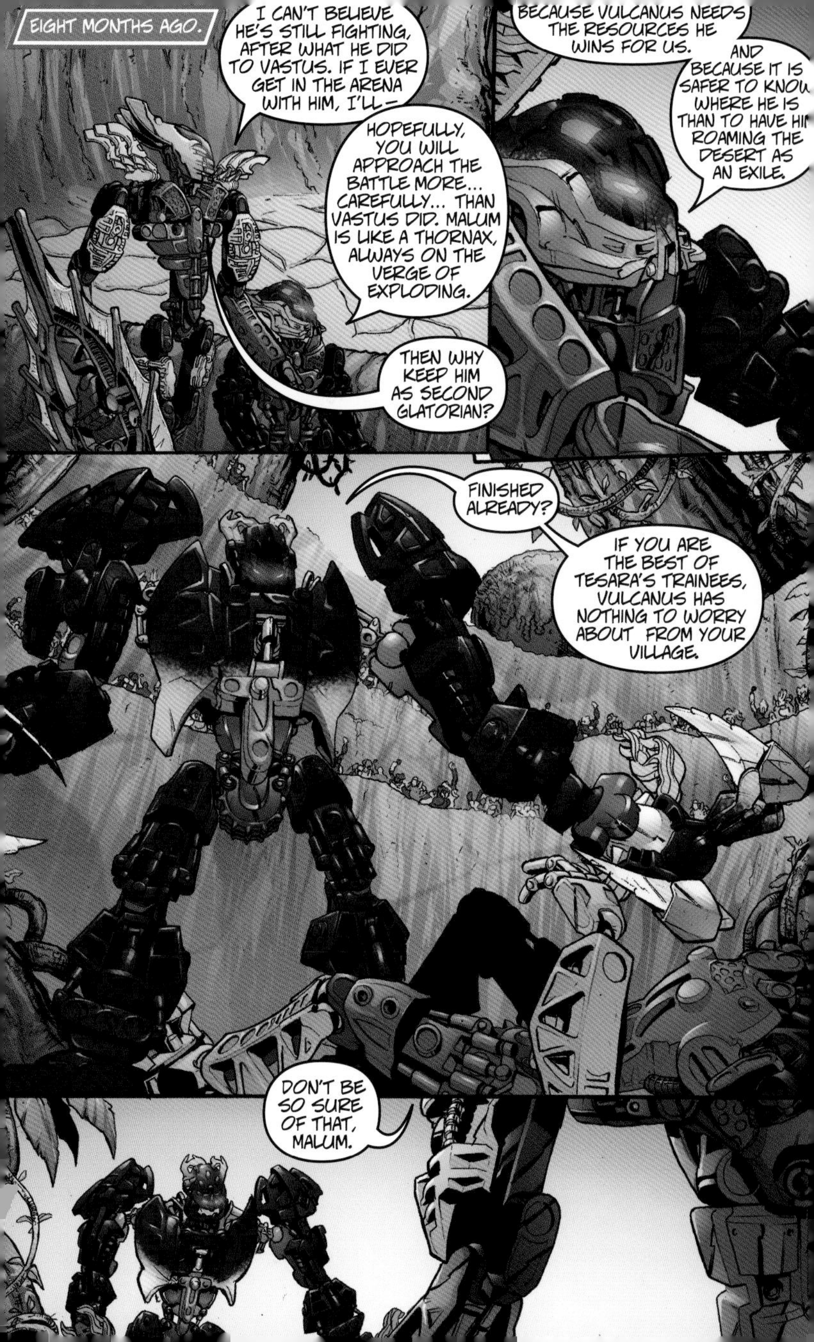
EIGHT MONTHS AGO.
I CAN'T BELIEVE HE'S STILL FIGHTING, AFTER WHAT HE DID TO VASTUS. IF I EVER GET IN THE ARENA WITH HIM, I'LL—
HOPEFULLY, YOU WILL APPROACH THE BATTLE MORE... CAREFULLY... THAN VASTUS DID. MALUM IS LIKE A THORNAX, ALWAYS ON THE VERGE OF EXPLODING.
THEN WHY KEEP HIM AS SECOND GLATORIAN?
BECAUSE VULCANUS NEEDS THE RESOURCES HE WINS FOR US.
AND BECAUSE IT IS SAFER TO KNOW WHERE HE IS THAN TO HAVE HIM ROAMING THE DESERT AS AN EXILE.
FINISHED ALREADY?
IF YOU ARE THE BEST OF TESARA'S TRAINEES, VULCANUS HAS NOTHING TO WORRY ABOUT FROM YOUR VILLAGE.
DON'T BE SO SURE OF THAT, MALUM.

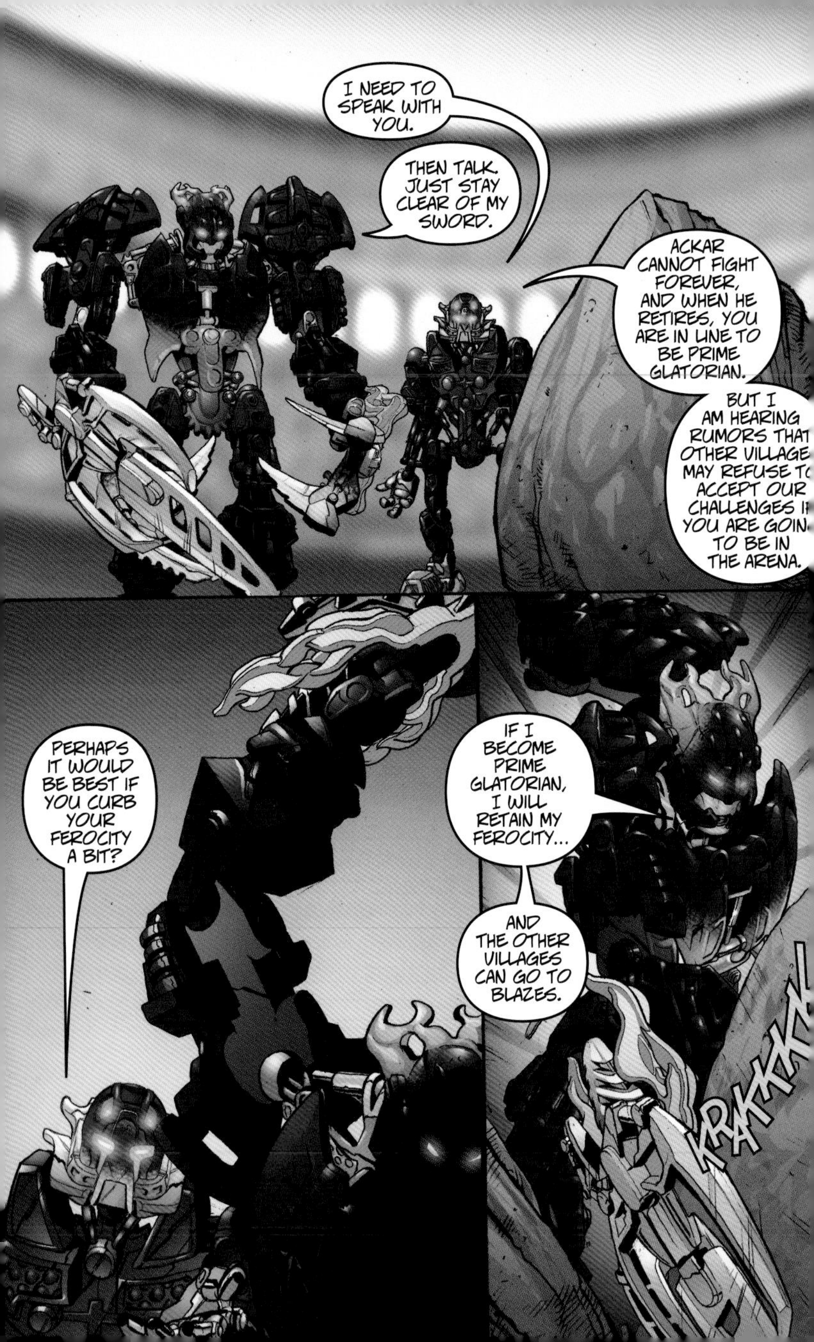
I NEED TO SPEAK WITH YOU.
THEN TALK. JUST STAY CLEAR OF MY SWORD.
ACKAR CANNOT FIGHT FOREVER, AND WHEN HE RETIRES, YOU ARE IN LINE TO BE PRIME GLATORIAN.
BUT I AM HEARING RUMORS THAT OTHER VILLAGE MAY REFUSE T ACCEPT OUR CHALLENGES I YOU ARE GOIN TO BE IN THE ARENA.
PERHAPS IT WOULD BE BEST IF YOU CURB YOUR FEROCITY A BIT?
IF I BECOME PRIME GLATORIAN, I WILL RETAIN MY FEROCITY...
AND THE OTHER VILLAGES CAN GO TO BLAZES.
KRAKKKK!

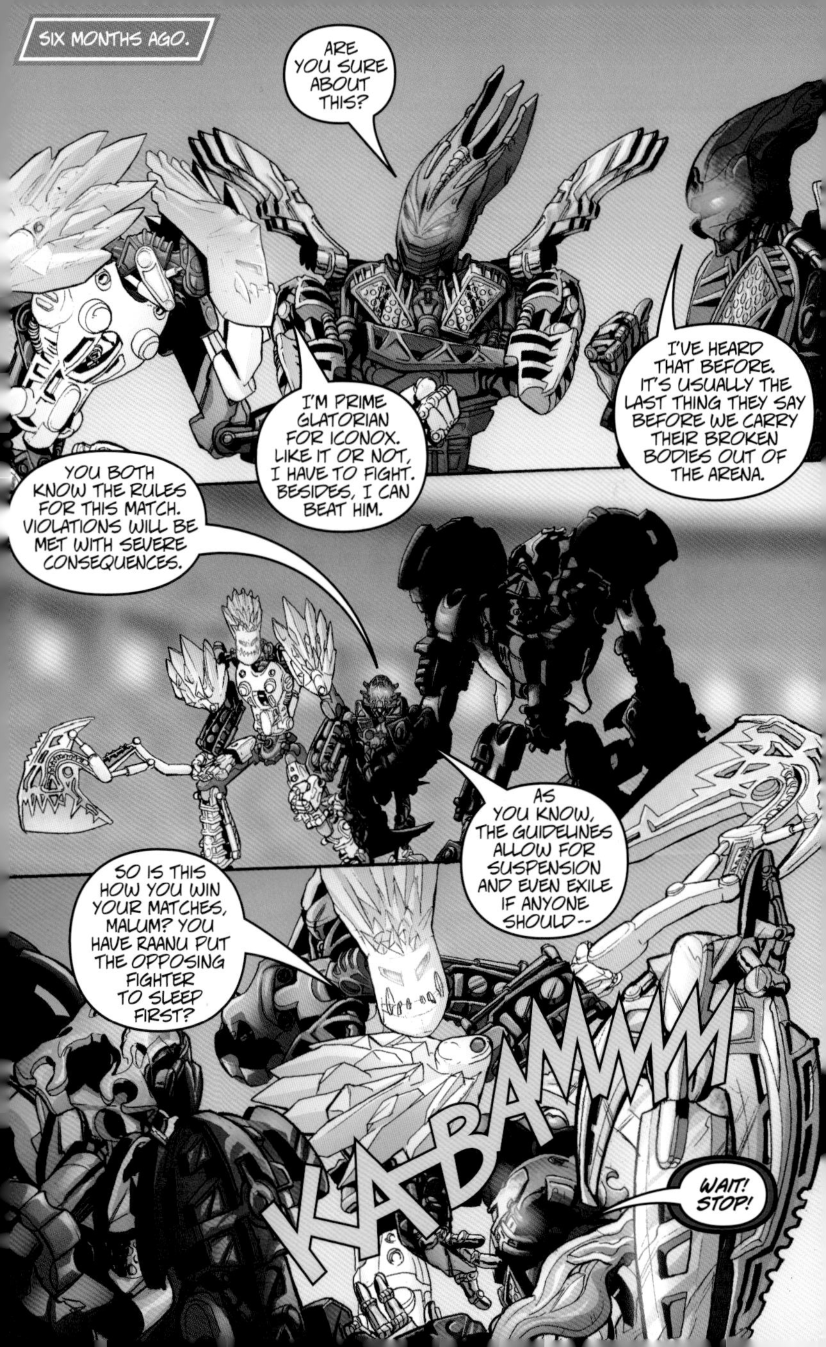
SIX MONTHS AGO.
ARE YOU SURE ABOUT THIS?
I'M PRIME GLATORIAN FOR ICONOX. LIKE IT OR NOT, I HAVE TO FIGHT. BESIDES, I CAN BEAT HIM.
I'VE HEARD THAT BEFORE. IT'S USUALLY THE LAST THING THEY SAY BEFORE WE CARRY THEIR BROKEN BODIES OUT OF THE ARENA.
YOU BOTH KNOW THE RULES FOR THIS MATCH. VIOLATIONS WILL BE MET WITH SEVERE CONSEQUENCES.
AS YOU KNOW, THE GUIDELINES ALLOW FOR SUSPENSION AND EVEN EXILE IF ANYONE SHOULD--
SO IS THIS HOW YOU WIN YOUR MATCHES, MALUM? YOU HAVE RAANU PUT THE OPPOSING FIGHTER TO SLEEP FIRST?
KA-BAMMM
WAIT! STOP!

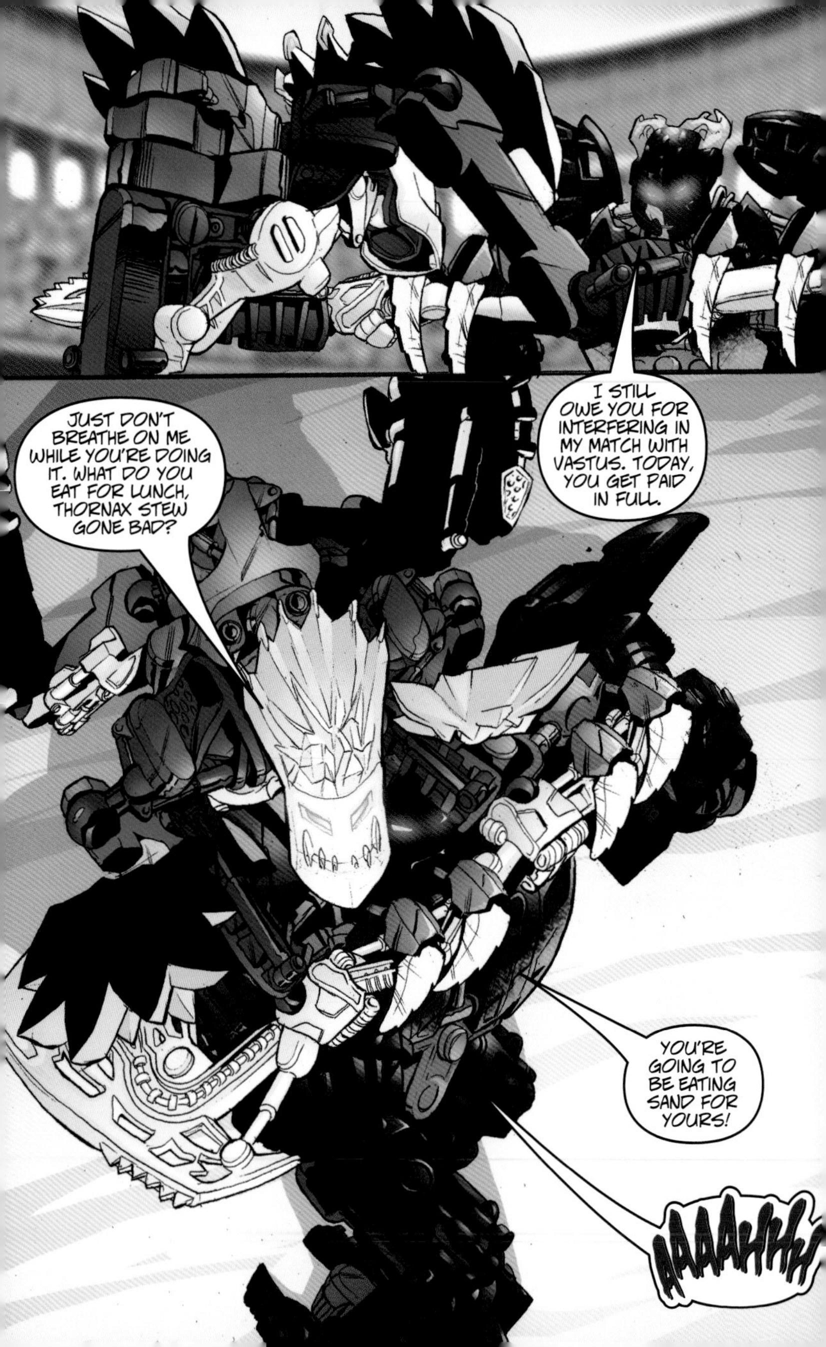
I STILL OWE YOU FOR INTERFERING IN MY MATCH WITH VASTUS. TODAY, YOU GET PAID IN FULL.
JUST DON'T BREATHE ON ME WHILE YOU'RE DOING IT. WHAT DO YOU EAT FOR LUNCH, THORNAX STEW GONE BAD?
YOU'RE GOING TO BE EATING SAND FOR YOURS!
AAAAHHH!

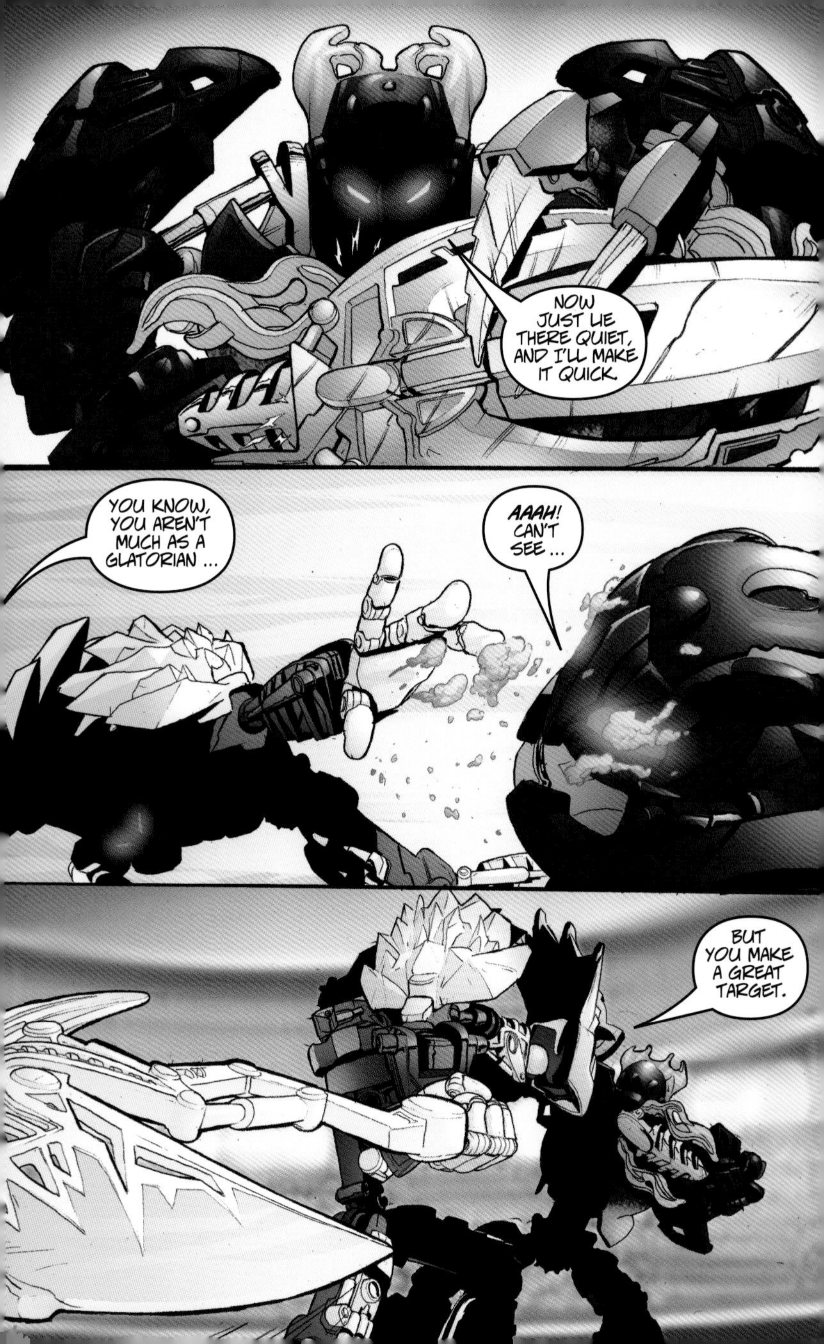
NOW JUST LIE THERE QUIET, AND I'LL MAKE IT QUICK.
YOU KNOW, YOU AREN'T MUCH AS A GLATORIAN ...
AAAH! CAN'T SEE ...
BUT YOU MAKE A GREAT TARGET.

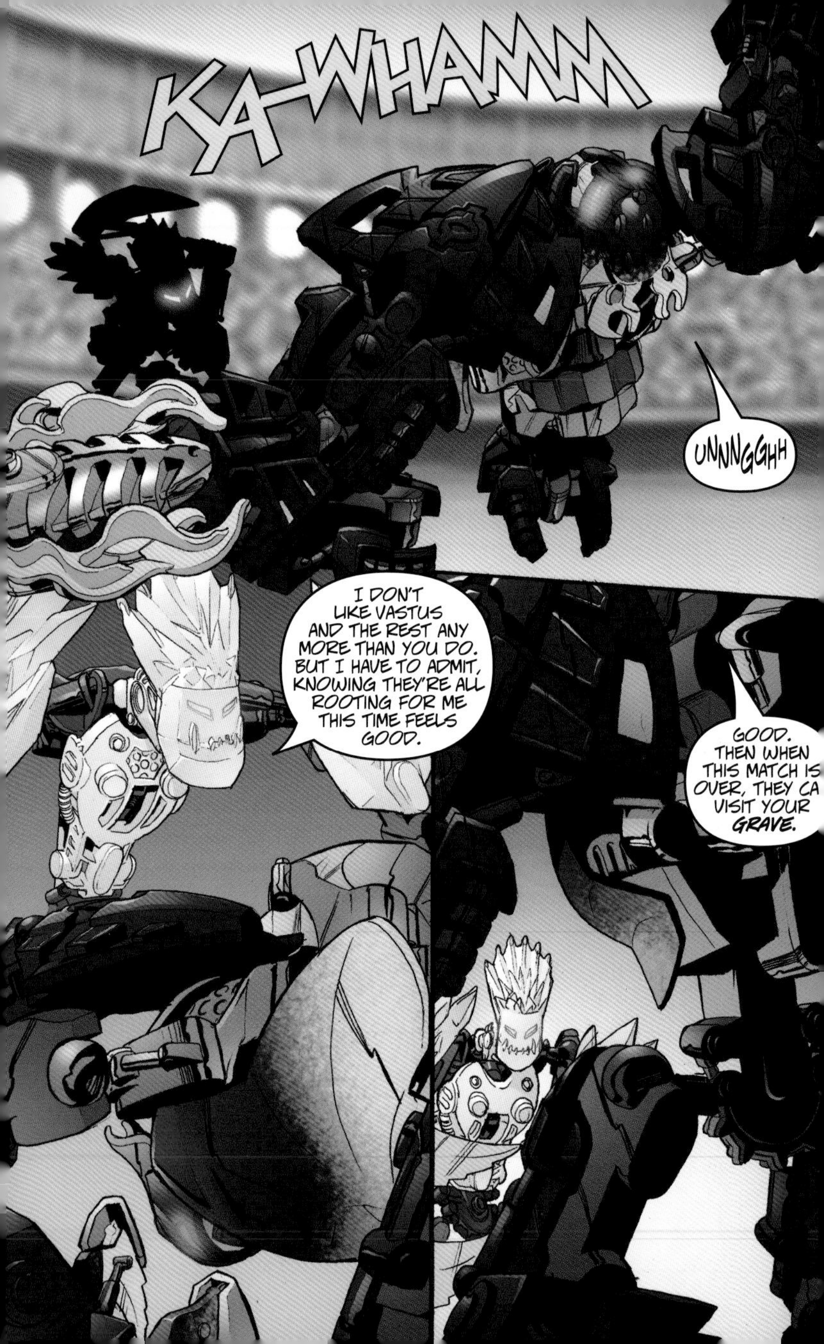
KA-WHAMM
UNNNGGHH
I DON'T LIKE VASTUS AND THE REST ANY MORE THAN YOU DO. BUT I HAVE TO ADMIT, KNOWING THEY'RE ALL ROOTING FOR ME THIS TIME FEELS GOOD.
GOOD. THEN WHEN THIS MATCH IS OVER, THEY CA VISIT YOUR *GRAVE*.

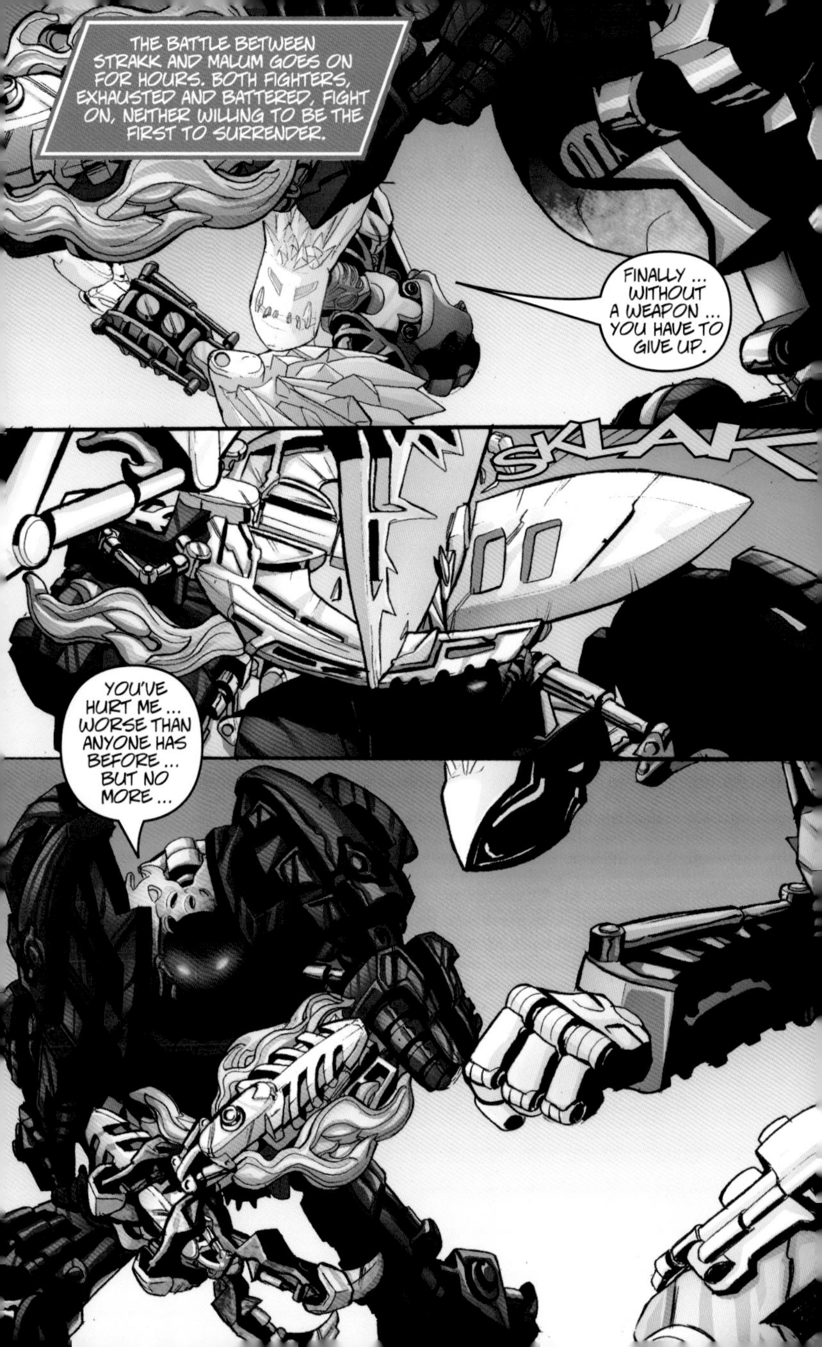
THE BATTLE BETWEEN STRAKK AND MALUM GOES ON FOR HOURS. BOTH FIGHTERS, EXHAUSTED AND BATTERED, FIGHT ON, NEITHER WILLING TO BE THE FIRST TO SURRENDER.
FINALLY ... WITHOUT A WEAPON ... YOU HAVE TO GIVE UP.
SKLAK
YOU'VE HURT ME ... WORSE THAN ANYONE HAS BEFORE ... BUT NO MORE ...

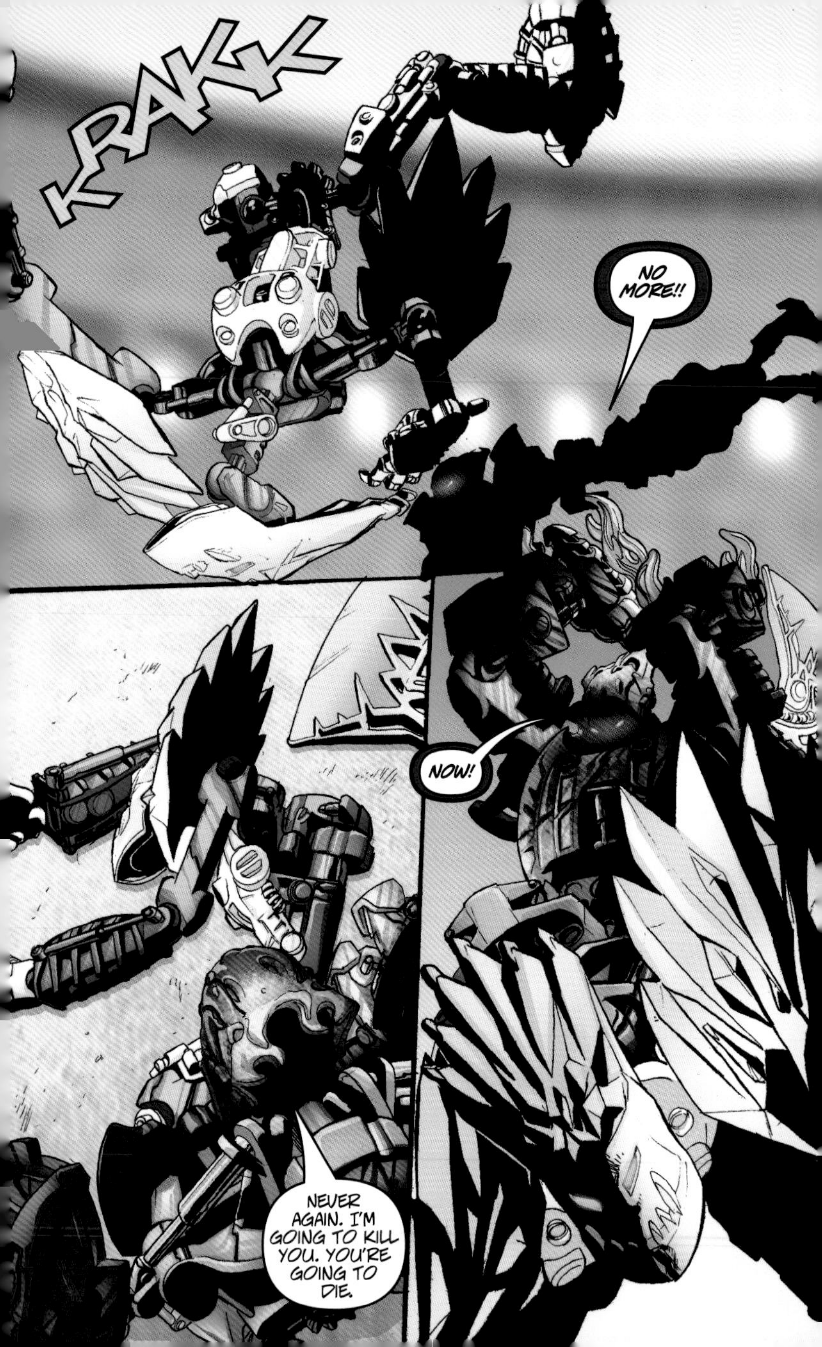
KRAKK
NO MORE!!
NOW!
NEVER AGAIN. I'M GOING TO KILL YOU. YOU'RE GOING TO DIE.

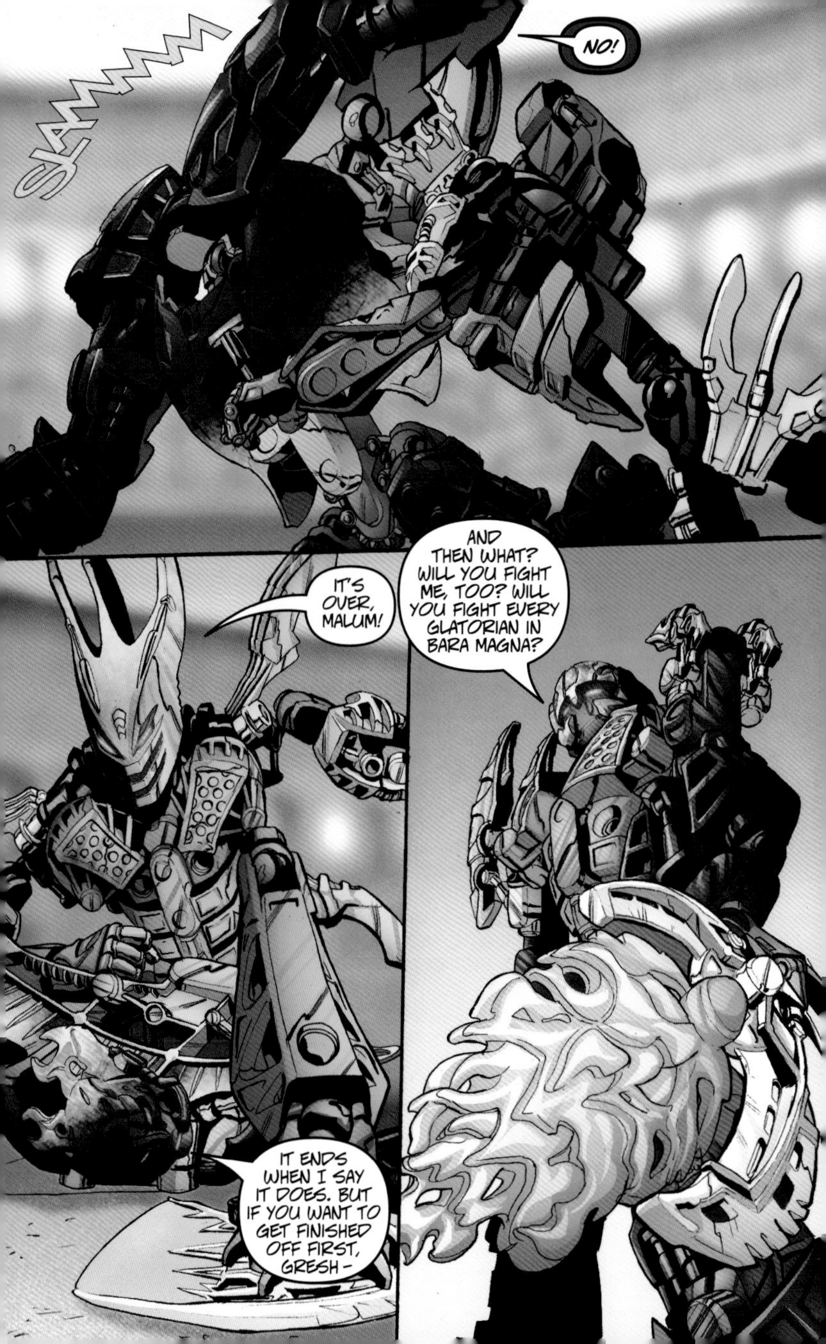
SLAMMM
NO!
IT'S OVER, MALUM!
AND THEN WHAT? WILL YOU FIGHT ME, TOO? WILL YOU FIGHT EVERY GLATORIAN IN BARA MAGNA?
IT ENDS WHEN I SAY IT DOES. BUT IF YOU WANT TO GET FINISHED OFF FIRST, GRESH -

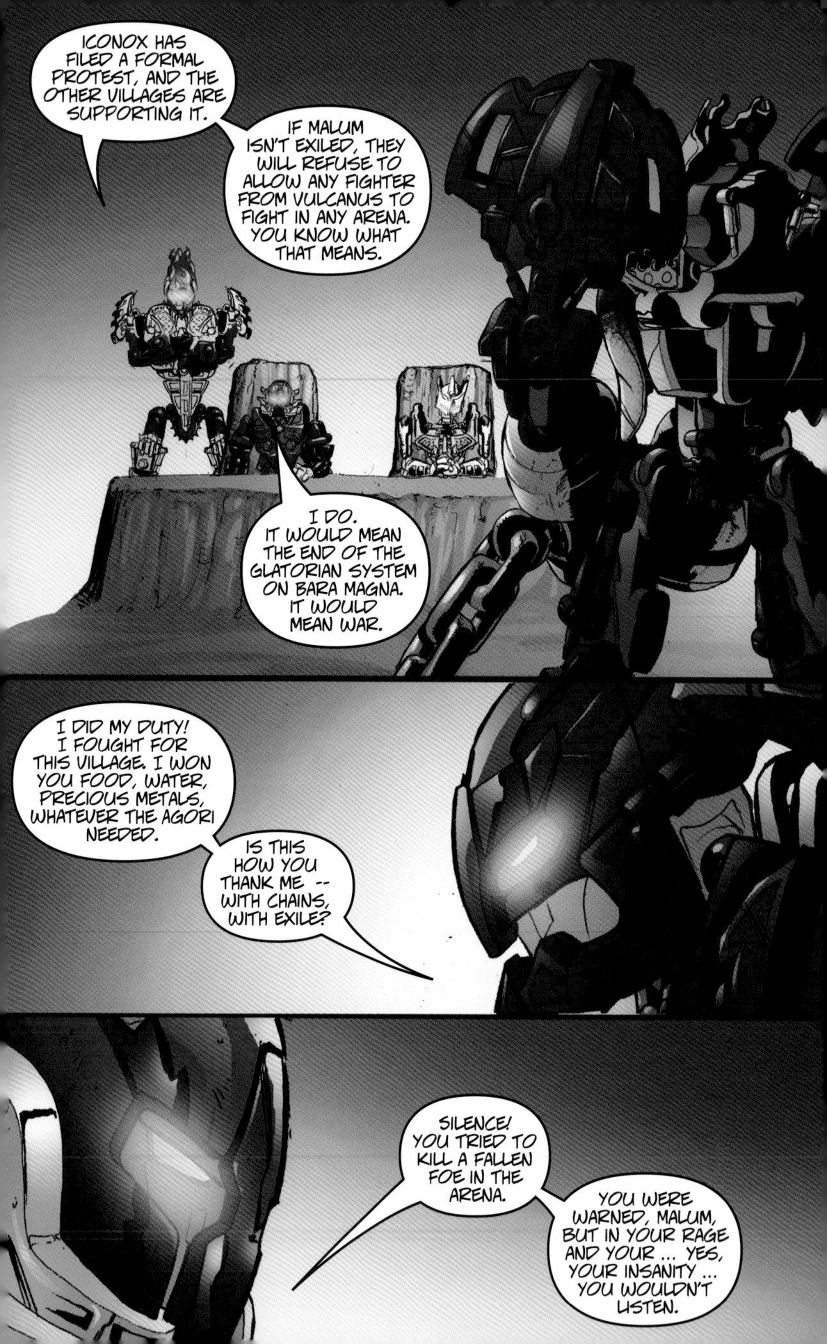
ICONOX HAS FILED A FORMAL PROTEST, AND THE OTHER VILLAGES ARE SUPPORTING IT.
IF MALUM ISN'T EXILED, THEY WILL REFUSE TO ALLOW ANY FIGHTER FROM VULCANUS TO FIGHT IN ANY ARENA. YOU KNOW WHAT THAT MEANS.
I DO. IT WOULD MEAN THE END OF THE GLATORIAN SYSTEM ON BARA MAGNA. IT WOULD MEAN WAR.
I DID MY DUTY! I FOUGHT FOR THIS VILLAGE. I WON YOU FOOD, WATER, PRECIOUS METALS, WHATEVER THE AGORI NEEDED.
IS THIS HOW YOU THANK ME -- WITH CHAINS, WITH EXILE?
SILENCE! YOU TRIED TO KILL A FALLEN FOE IN THE ARENA.
YOU WERE WARNED, MALUM, BUT IN YOUR RAGE AND YOUR ... YES, YOUR INSANITY ... YOU WOULDN'T LISTEN.

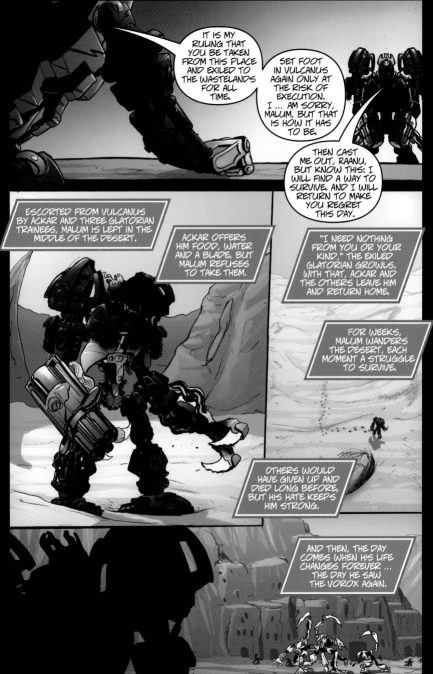

IT IS MY RULING THAT YOU BE TAKEN FROM THIS PLACE AND EXILED TO THE WASTELANDS FOR ALL TIME.

SET FOOT IN VULCANUS AGAIN ONLY AT THE RISK OF EXECUTION. I ... AM SORRY, MALUM, BUT THAT IS HOW IT HAS TO BE.

THEN CAST ME OUT, RAANU, BUT KNOW THIS: I WILL FIND A WAY TO SURVIVE. AND I WILL RETURN TO MAKE YOU REGRET THIS DAY.

ESCORTED FROM VULCANUS BY ACKAR AND THREE GLATORIAN TRAINEES, MALUM IS LEFT IN THE MIDDLE OF THE DESERT.

ACKAR OFFERS HIM FOOD, WATER AND A BLADE, BUT MALUM REFUSES TO TAKE THEM.

"I NEED NOTHING FROM YOU OR YOUR KIND," THE EXILED GLATORIAN GROWLS. WITH THAT, ACKAR AND THE OTHERS LEAVE HIM AND RETURN HOME.

FOR WEEKS, MALUM WANDERS THE DESERT, EACH MOMENT A STRUGGLE TO SURVIVE.

OTHERS WOULD HAVE GIVEN UP AND DIED LONG BEFORE, BUT HIS HATE KEEPS HIM STRONG.

AND THEN, THE DAY COMES WHEN HIS LIFE CHANGES FOREVER ... THE DAY HE SAW THE VOROX AGAIN.

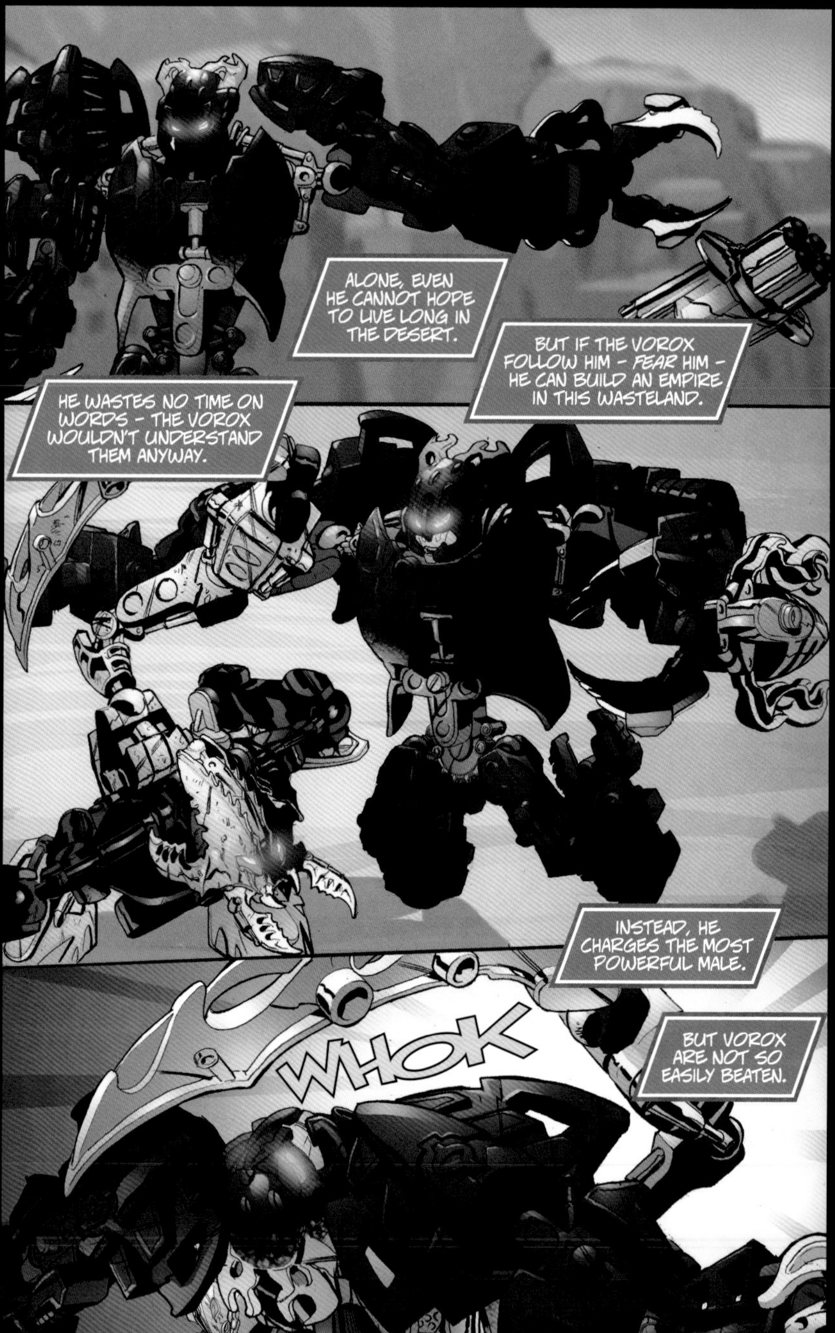
ALONE, EVEN HE CANNOT HOPE TO LIVE LONG IN THE DESERT.
BUT IF THE VOROX FOLLOW HIM - *FEAR* HIM - HE CAN BUILD AN EMPIRE IN THIS WASTELAND.
HE WASTES NO TIME ON WORDS - THE VOROX WOULDN'T UNDERSTAND THEM ANYWAY.
INSTEAD, HE CHARGES THE MOST POWERFUL MALE.
WHOK
BUT VOROX ARE NOT SO EASILY BEATEN.

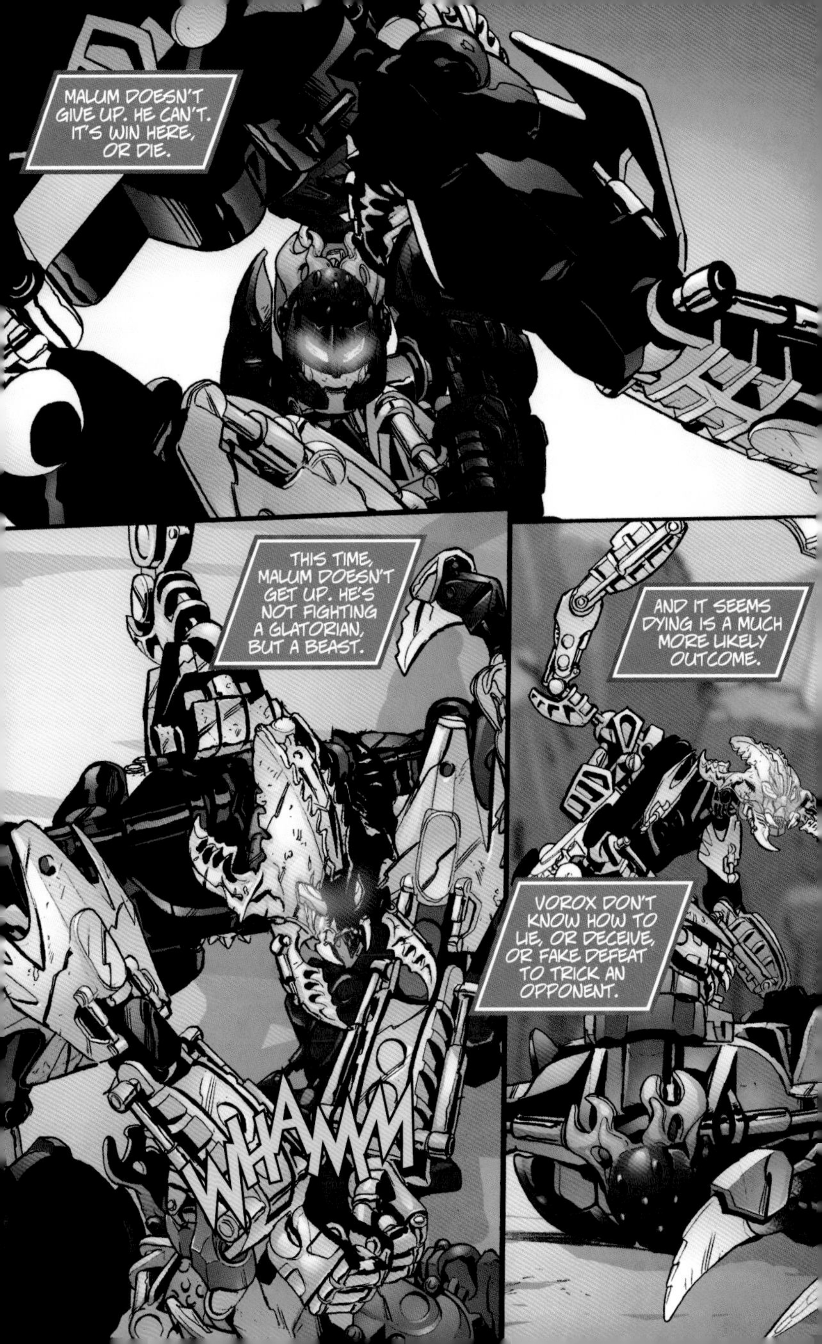
MALUM DOESN'T GIVE UP. HE CAN'T. IT'S WIN HERE, OR DIE.
THIS TIME, MALUM DOESN'T GET UP. HE'S NOT FIGHTING A GLATORIAN, BUT A BEAST.
WHAMM
AND IT SEEMS DYING IS A MUCH MORE LIKELY OUTCOME.
VOROX DON'T KNOW HOW TO LIE, OR DECEIVE, OR FAKE DEFEAT TO TRICK AN OPPONENT.

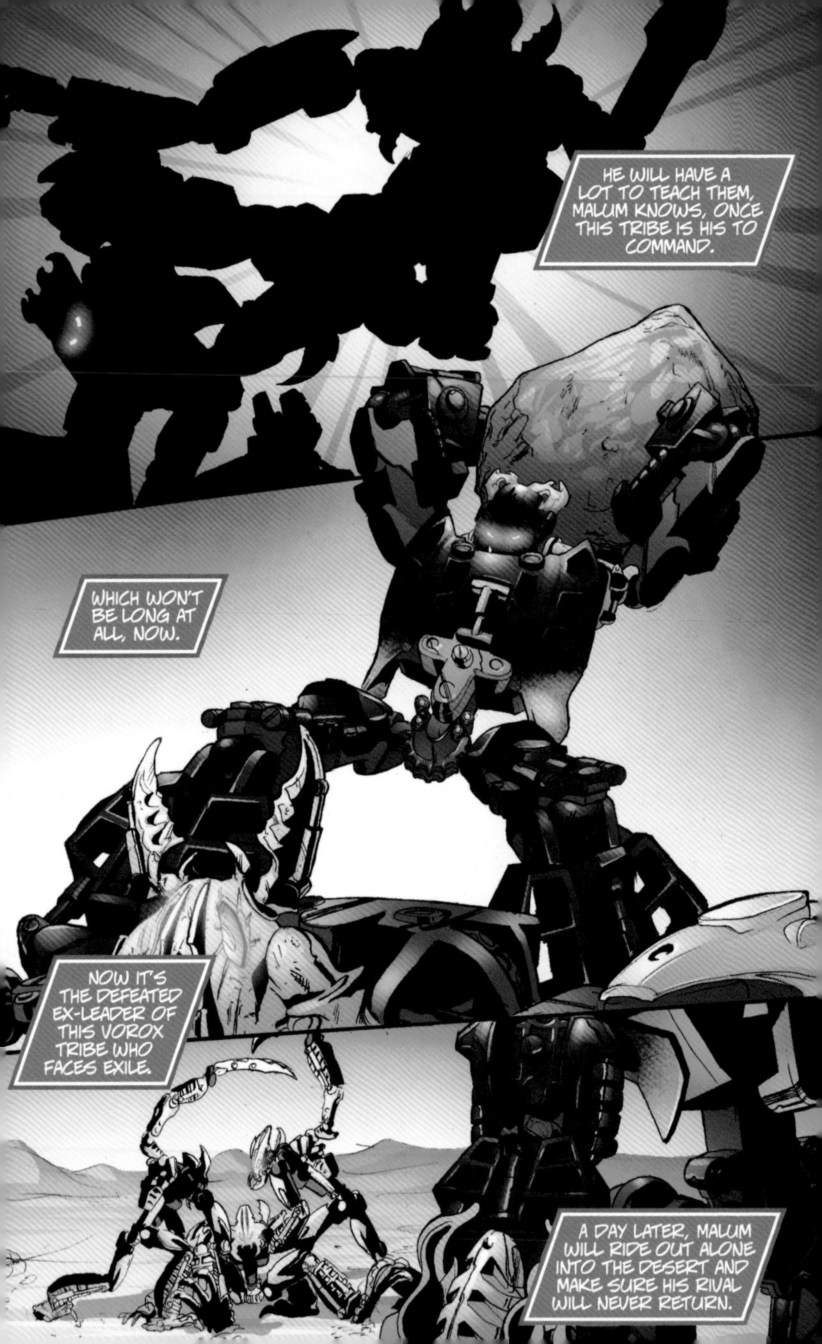
HE WILL HAVE A LOT TO TEACH THEM, MALUM KNOWS, ONCE THIS TRIBE IS HIS TO COMMAND.
WHICH WON'T BE LONG AT ALL, NOW.
NOW IT'S THE DEFEATED EX-LEADER OF THIS VOROX TRIBE WHO FACES EXILE.
A DAY LATER, MALUM WILL RIDE OUT ALONE INTO THE DESERT AND MAKE SURE HIS RIVAL WILL NEVER RETURN.

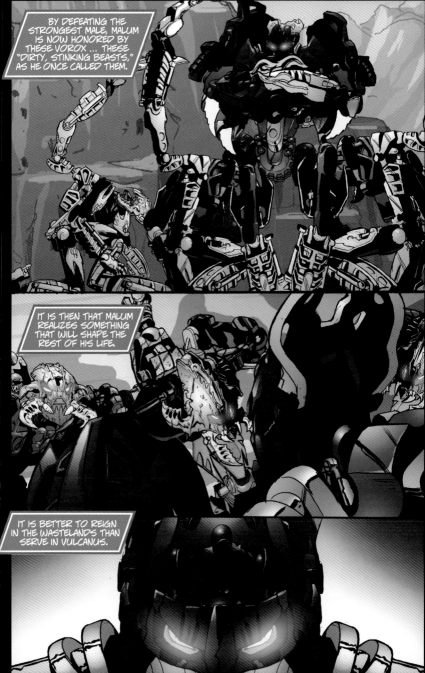

BY DEFEATING THE STRONGEST MALE, MALUM IS NOW HONORED BY THESE VOROX ... THESE "DIRTY, STINKING BEASTS," AS HE ONCE CALLED THEM.

IT IS THEN THAT MALUM REALIZES SOMETHING THAT WILL SHAPE THE REST OF HIS LIFE.

IT IS BETTER TO REIGN IN THE WASTELANDS THAN SERVE IN VULCANUS.

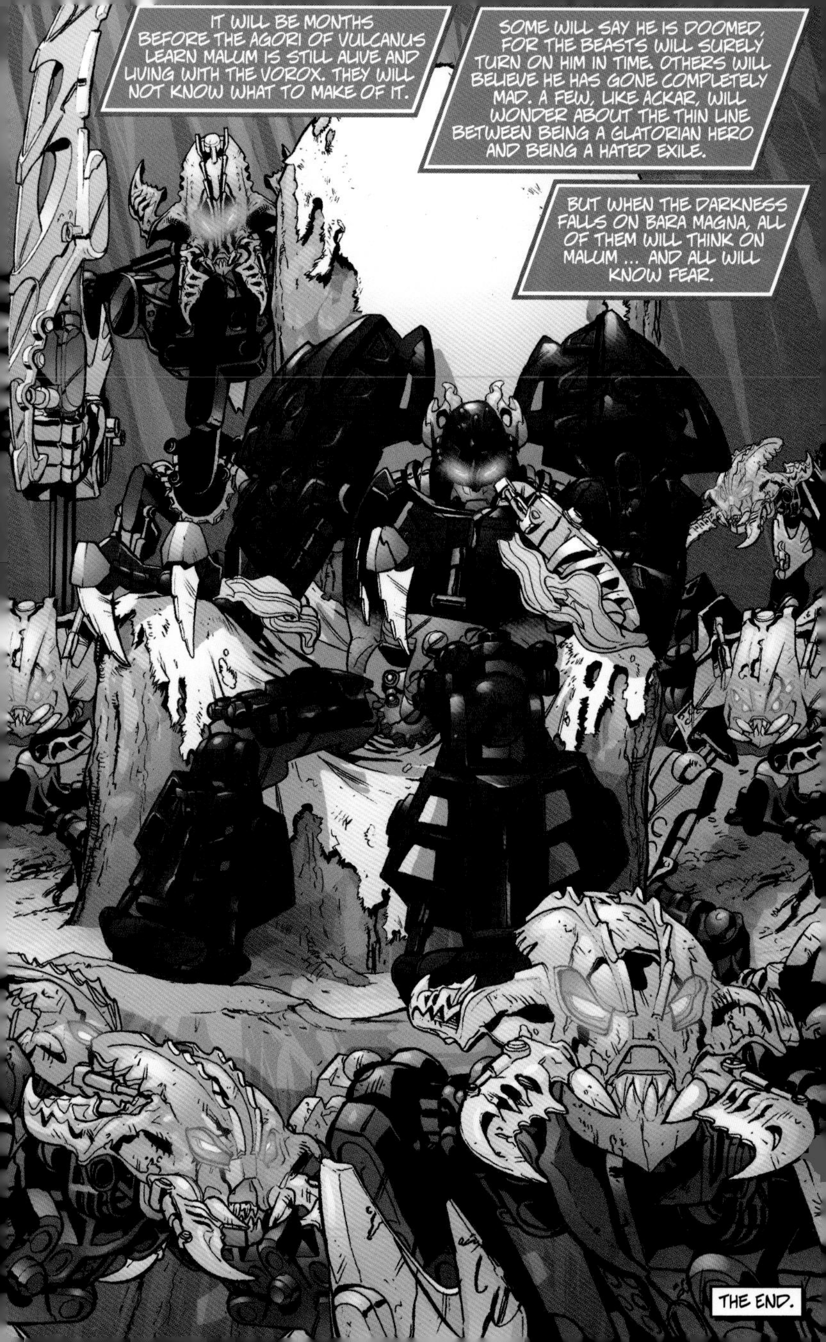
IT WILL BE MONTHS BEFORE THE AGORI OF VULCANUS LEARN MALUM IS STILL ALIVE AND LIVING WITH THE VOROX. THEY WILL NOT KNOW WHAT TO MAKE OF IT.
SOME WILL SAY HE IS DOOMED, FOR THE BEASTS WILL SURELY TURN ON HIM IN TIME. OTHERS WILL BELIEVE HE HAS GONE COMPLETELY MAD. A FEW, LIKE ACKAR, WILL WONDER ABOUT THE THIN LINE BETWEEN BEING A GLATORIAN HERO AND BEING A HATED EXILE.
BUT WHEN THE DARKNESS FALLS ON BARA MAGNA, ALL OF THEM WILL THINK ON MALUM ... AND ALL WILL KNOW FEAR.
THE END.

LEGENDS OF BARA MAGNA

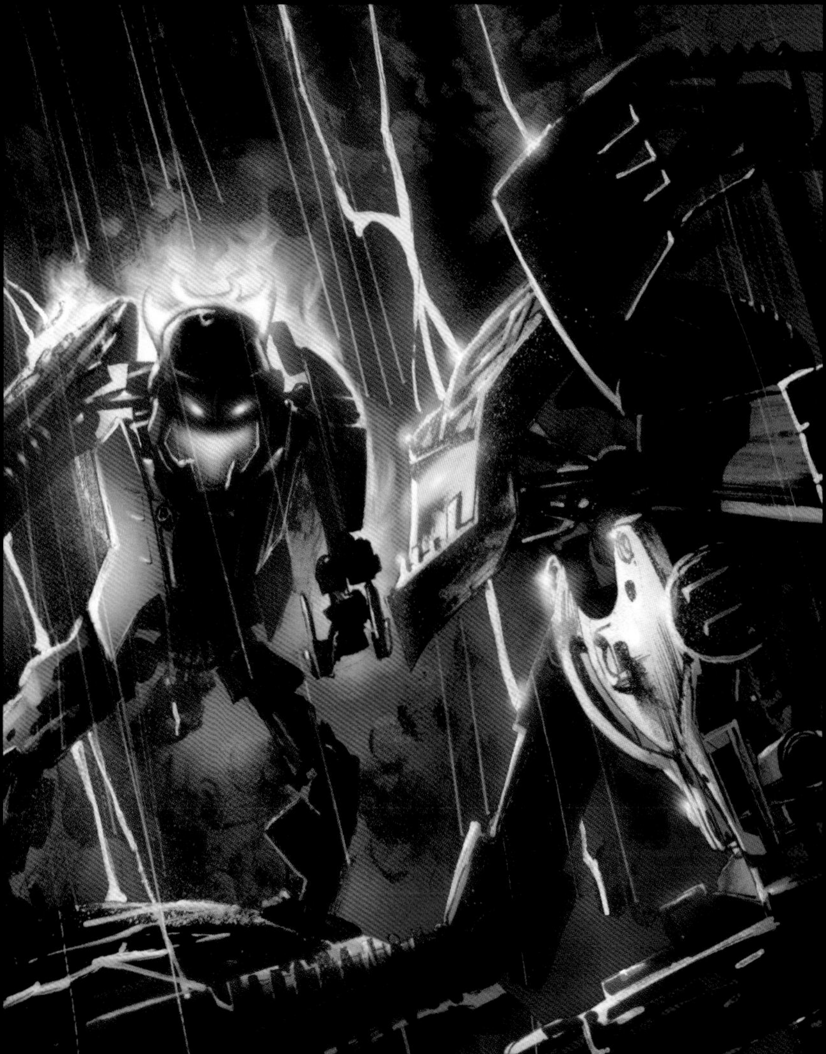

ALL OUR SI[redacted]S REMEMBERED

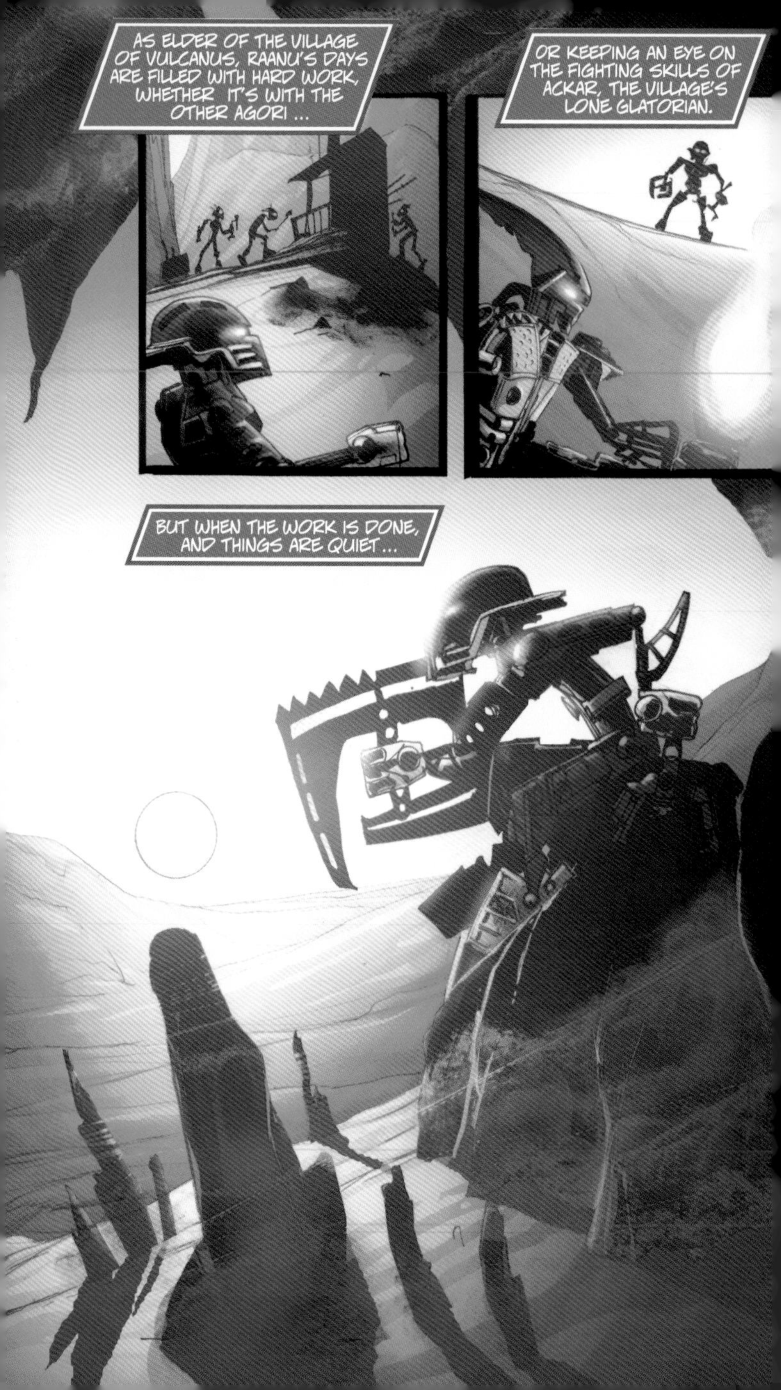
AS ELDER OF THE VILLAGE OF VULCANUS, RAANU'S DAYS ARE FILLED WITH HARD WORK, WHETHER IT'S WITH THE OTHER AGORI ...
OR KEEPING AN EYE ON THE FIGHTING SKILLS OF ACKAR, THE VILLAGE'S LONE GLATORIAN.
BUT WHEN THE WORK IS DONE, AND THINGS ARE QUIET ...

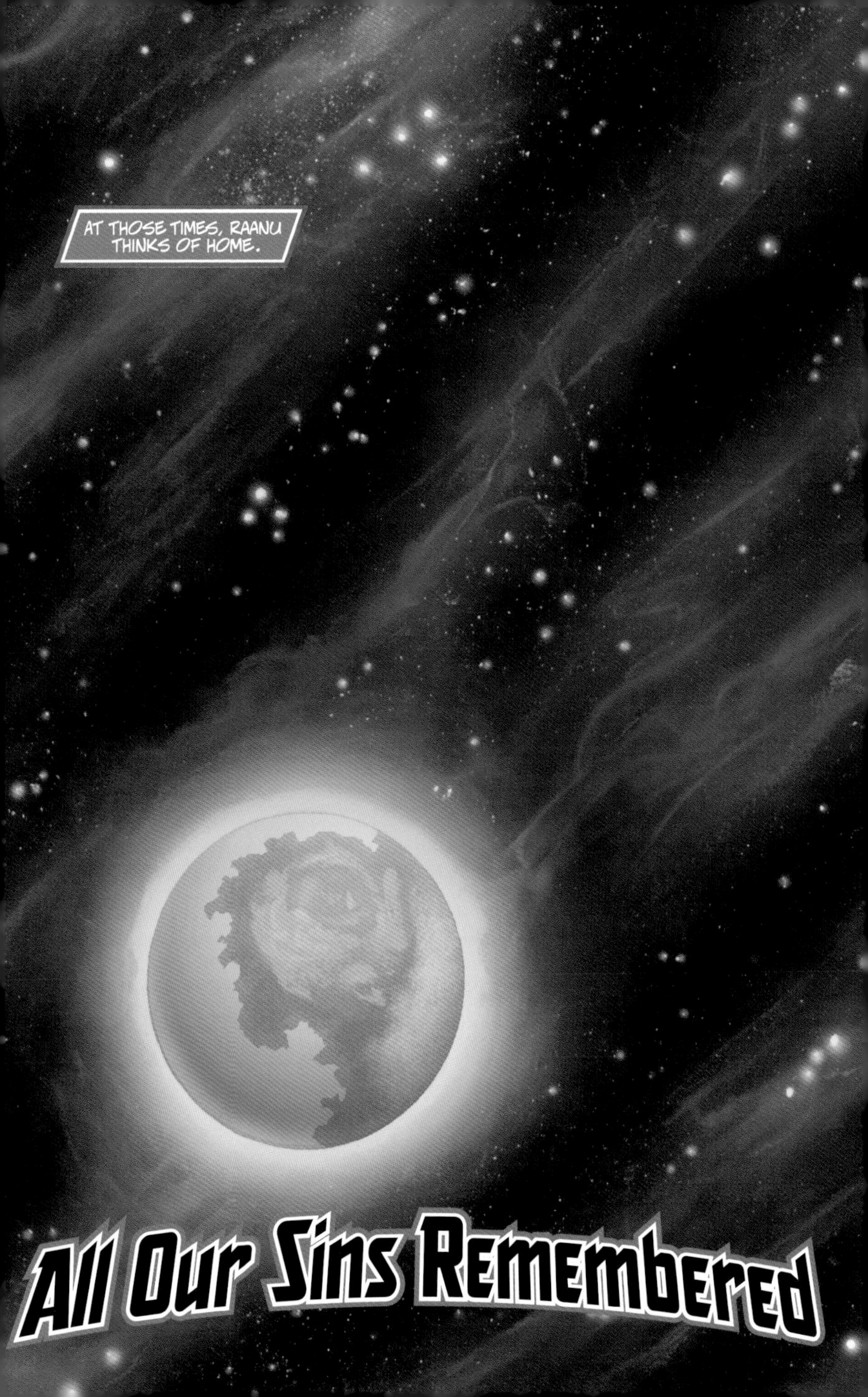
AT THOSE TIMES, RAANU THINKS OF HOME.
All Our Sins Remembered

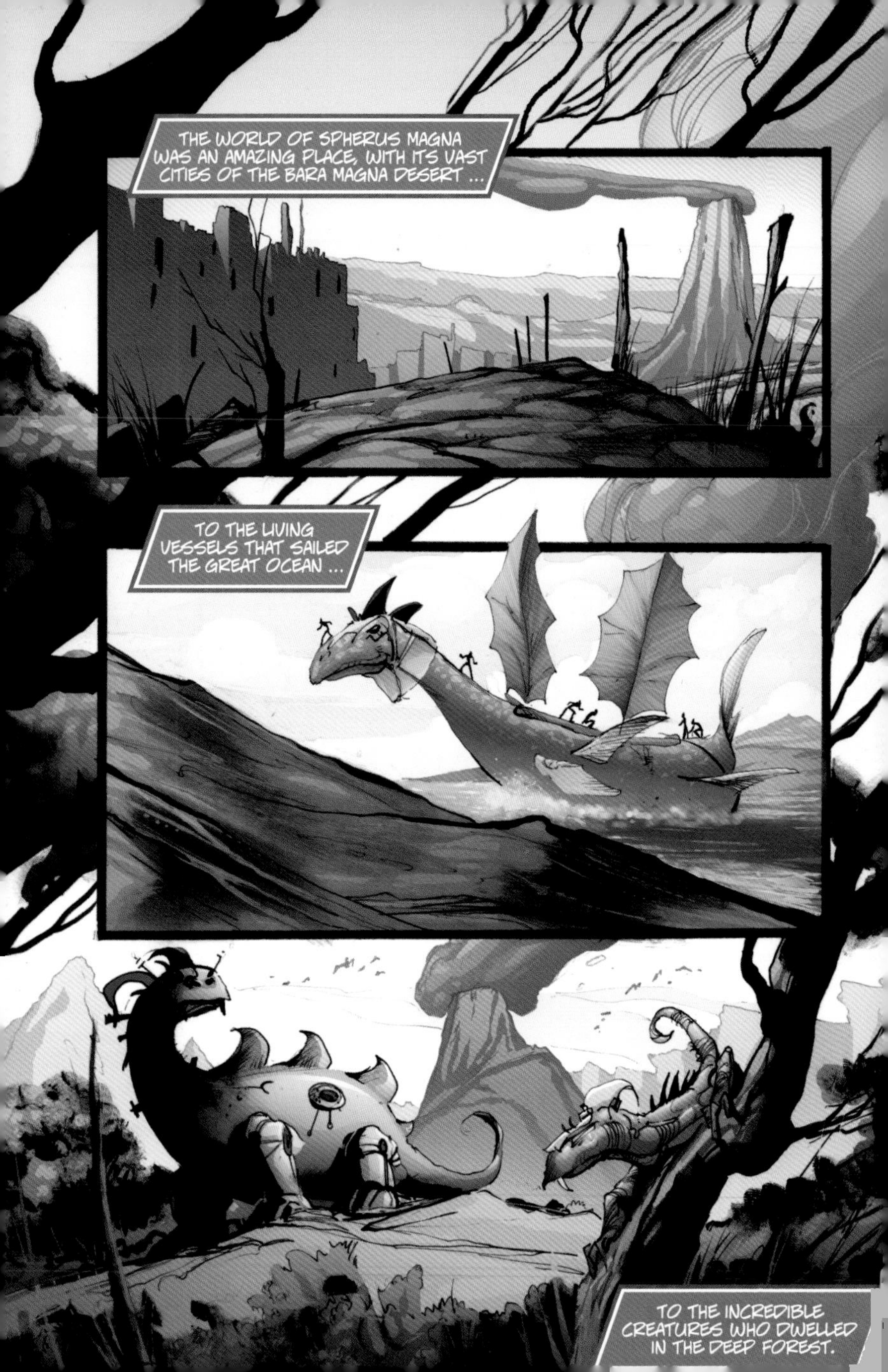
THE WORLD OF SPHERUS MAGNA WAS AN AMAZING PLACE, WITH ITS VAST CITIES OF THE BARA MAGNA DESERT ...
TO THE LIVING VESSELS THAT SAILED THE GREAT OCEAN ...
TO THE INCREDIBLE CREATURES WHO DWELLED IN THE DEEP FOREST.

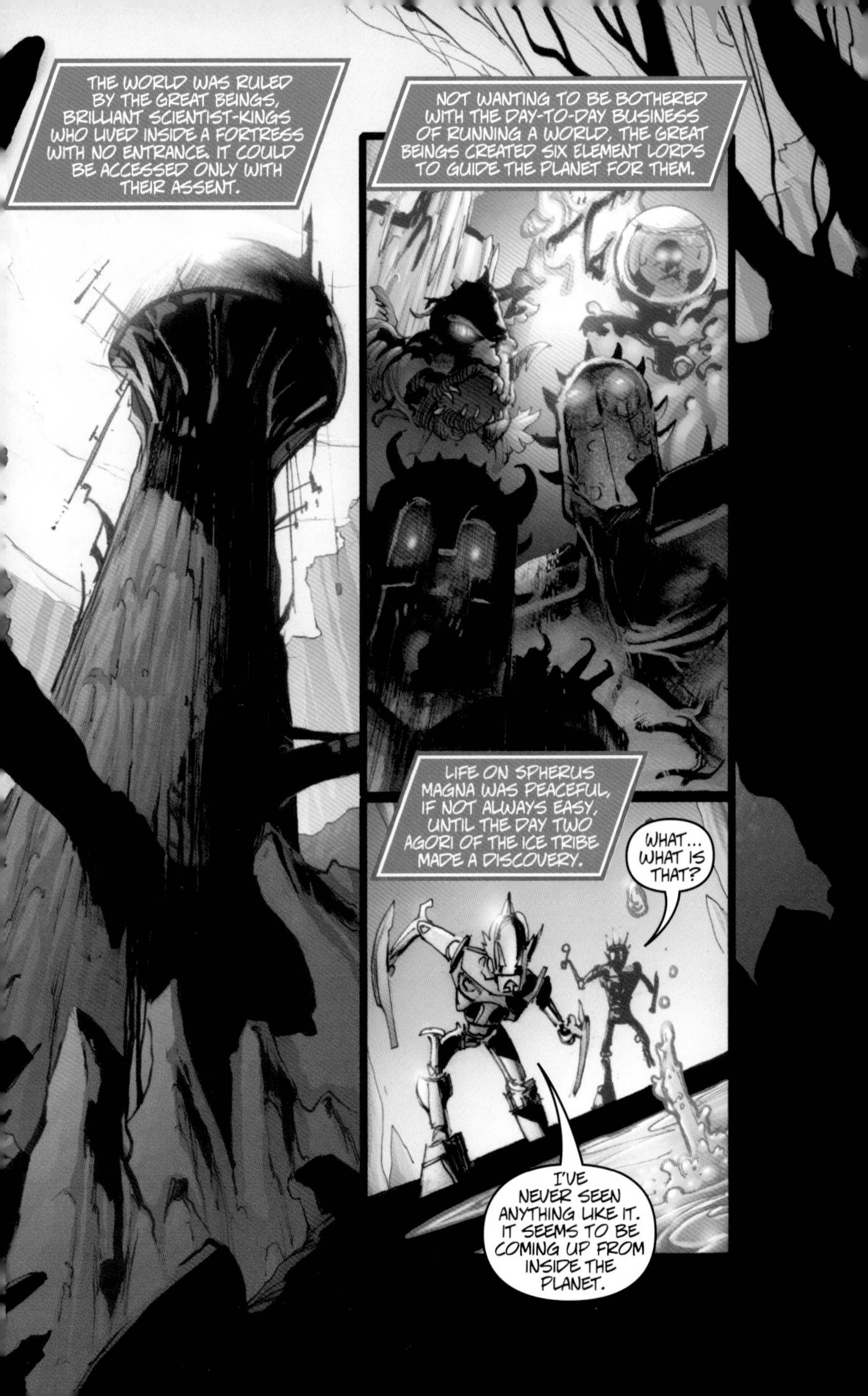
THE WORLD WAS RULED BY THE GREAT BEINGS, BRILLIANT SCIENTIST-KINGS WHO LIVED INSIDE A FORTRESS WITH NO ENTRANCE. IT COULD BE ACCESSED ONLY WITH THEIR ASSENT.
NOT WANTING TO BE BOTHERED WITH THE DAY-TO-DAY BUSINESS OF RUNNING A WORLD, THE GREAT BEINGS CREATED SIX ELEMENT LORDS TO GUIDE THE PLANET FOR THEM.
LIFE ON SPHERUS MAGNA WAS PEACEFUL, IF NOT ALWAYS EASY, UNTIL THE DAY TWO AGORI OF THE ICE TRIBE MADE A DISCOVERY.
WHAT... WHAT IS THAT?
I'VE NEVER SEEN ANYTHING LIKE IT. IT SEEMS TO BE COMING UP FROM INSIDE THE PLANET.

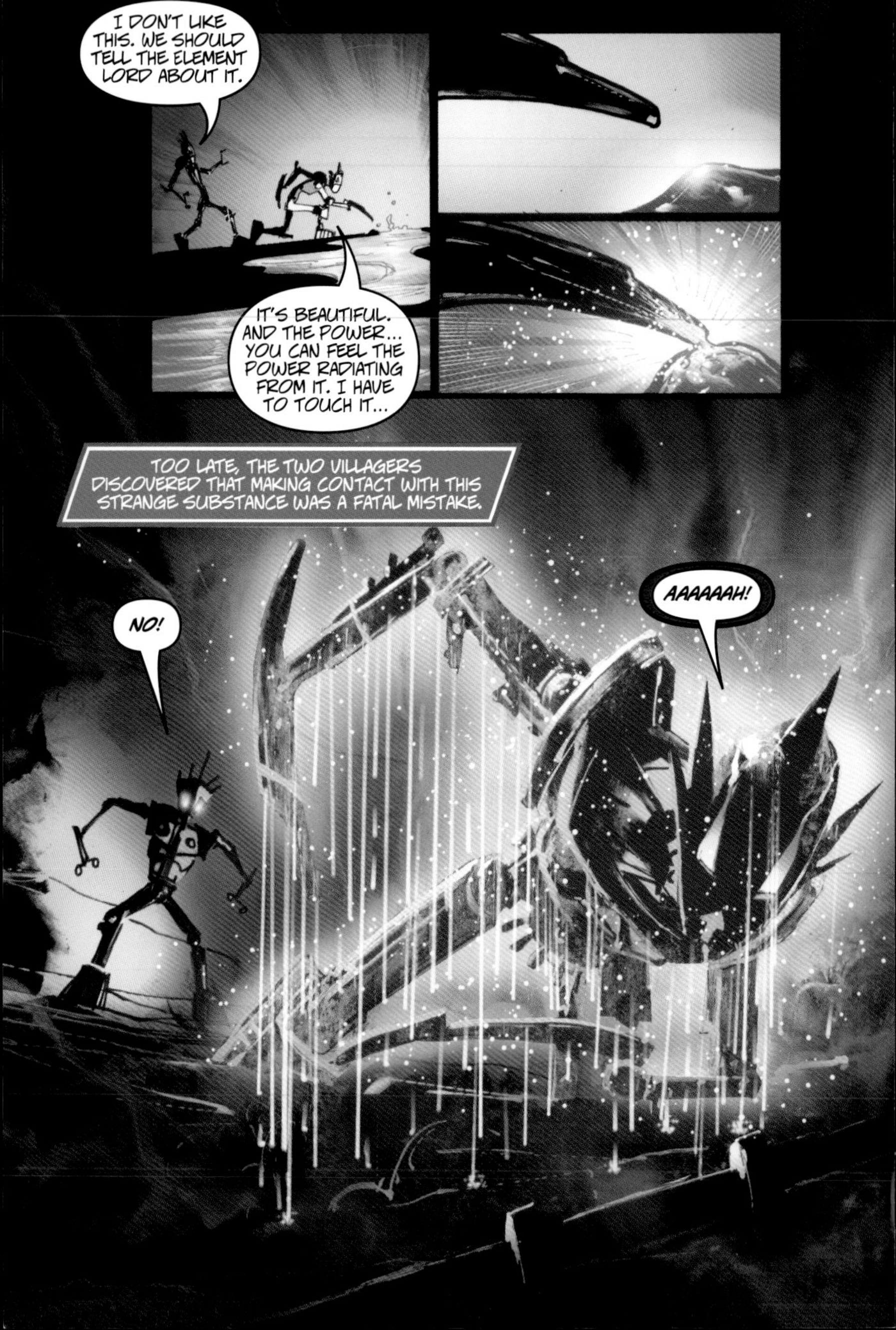
I DON'T LIKE THIS. WE SHOULD TELL THE ELEMENT LORD ABOUT IT.
IT'S BEAUTIFUL. AND THE POWER... YOU CAN FEEL THE POWER RADIATING FROM IT. I HAVE TO TOUCH IT...
TOO LATE, THE TWO VILLAGERS DISCOVERED THAT MAKING CONTACT WITH THIS STRANGE SUBSTANCE WAS A FATAL MISTAKE.
NO!
AAAAAAH!

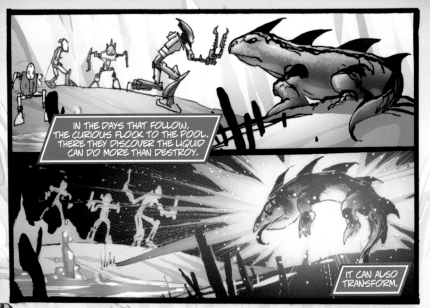

IN THE DAYS THAT FOLLOW, THE CURIOUS FLOCK TO THE POOL. THERE THEY DISCOVER THE LIQUID CAN DO MORE THAN DESTROY.

IT CAN ALSO TRANSFORM.

...SOMETIMES WITH SHOCKING RESULTS.

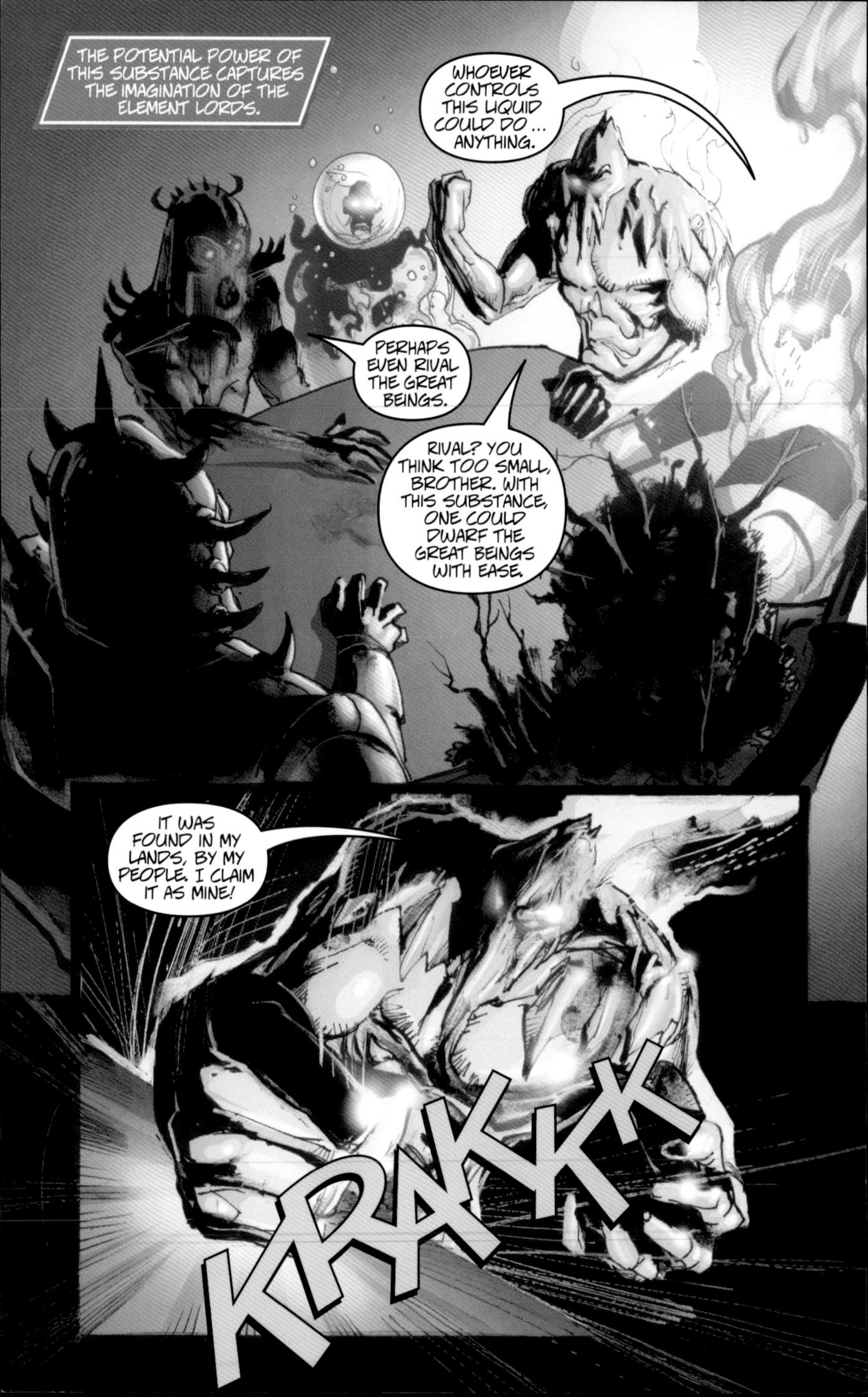
THE POTENTIAL POWER OF THIS SUBSTANCE CAPTURES THE IMAGINATION OF THE ELEMENT LORDS.
WHOEVER CONTROLS THIS LIQUID COULD DO... ANYTHING.
PERHAPS EVEN RIVAL THE GREAT BEINGS.
RIVAL? YOU THINK TOO SMALL, BROTHER. WITH THIS SUBSTANCE, ONE COULD DWARF THE GREAT BEINGS WITH EASE.
IT WAS FOUND IN MY LANDS, BY MY PEOPLE. I CLAIM IT AS MINE!
KRAKK

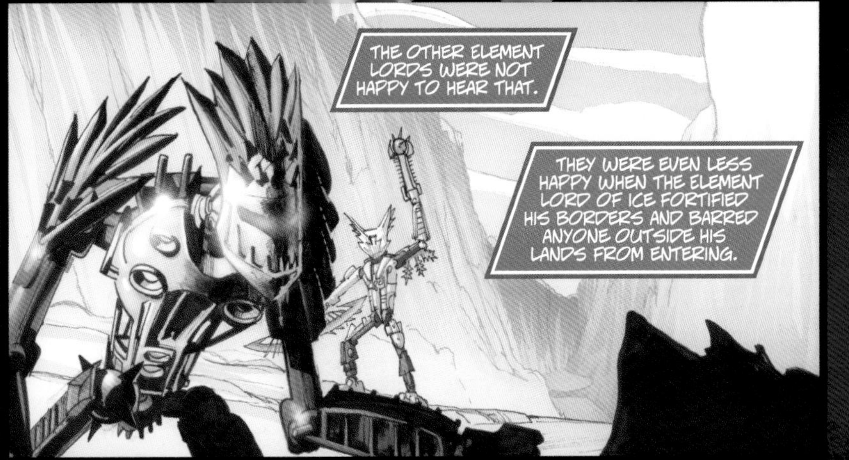
THE OTHER ELEMENT LORDS WERE NOT HAPPY TO HEAR THAT.
THEY WERE EVEN LESS HAPPY WHEN THE ELEMENT LORD OF ICE FORTIFIED HIS BORDERS AND BARRED ANYONE OUTSIDE HIS LANDS FROM ENTERING.
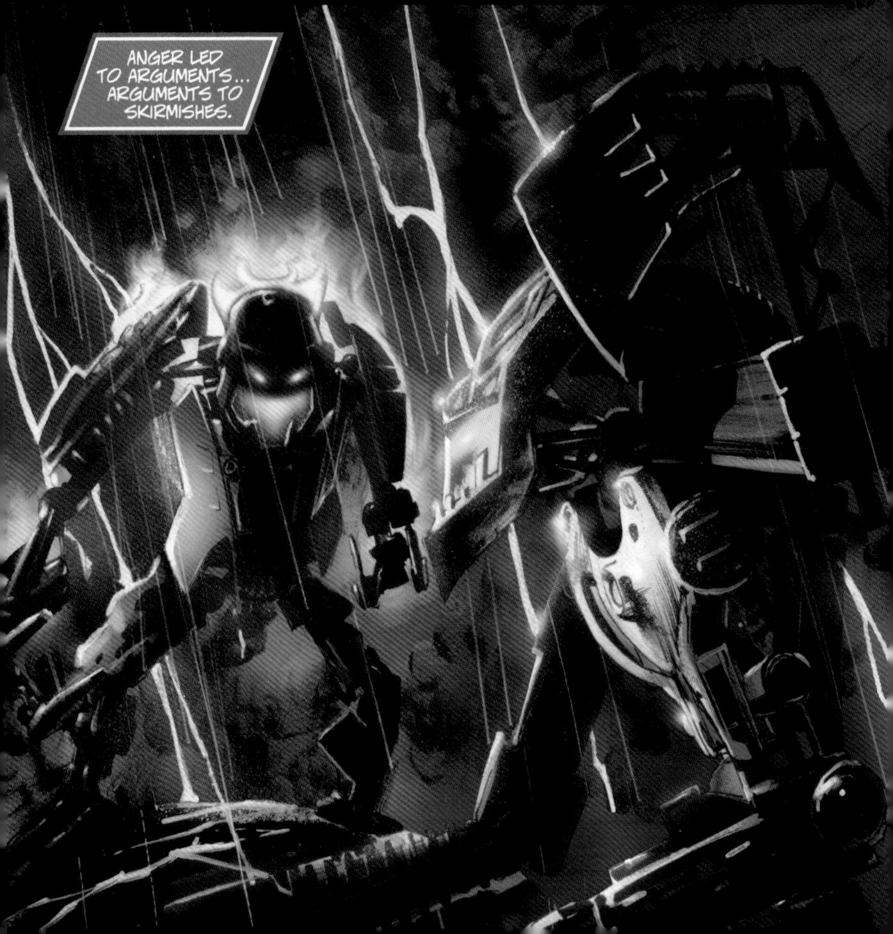
ANGER LED TO ARGUMENTS... ARGUMENTS TO SKIRMISHES.

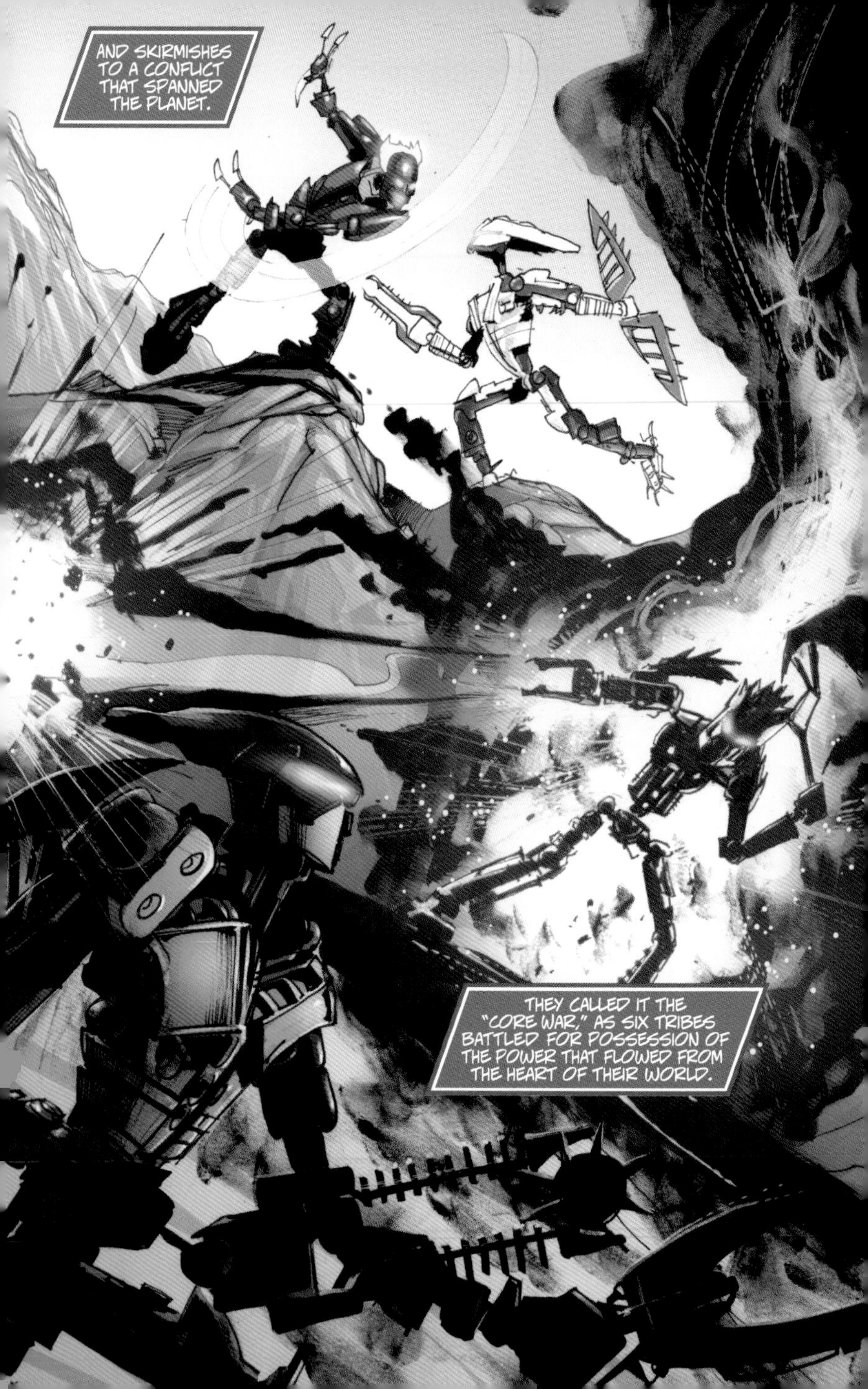
AND SKIRMISHES TO A CONFLICT THAT SPANNED THE PLANET.
THEY CALLED IT THE "CORE WAR," AS SIX TRIBES BATTLED FOR POSSESSION OF THE POWER THAT FLOWED FROM THE HEART OF THEIR WORLD.

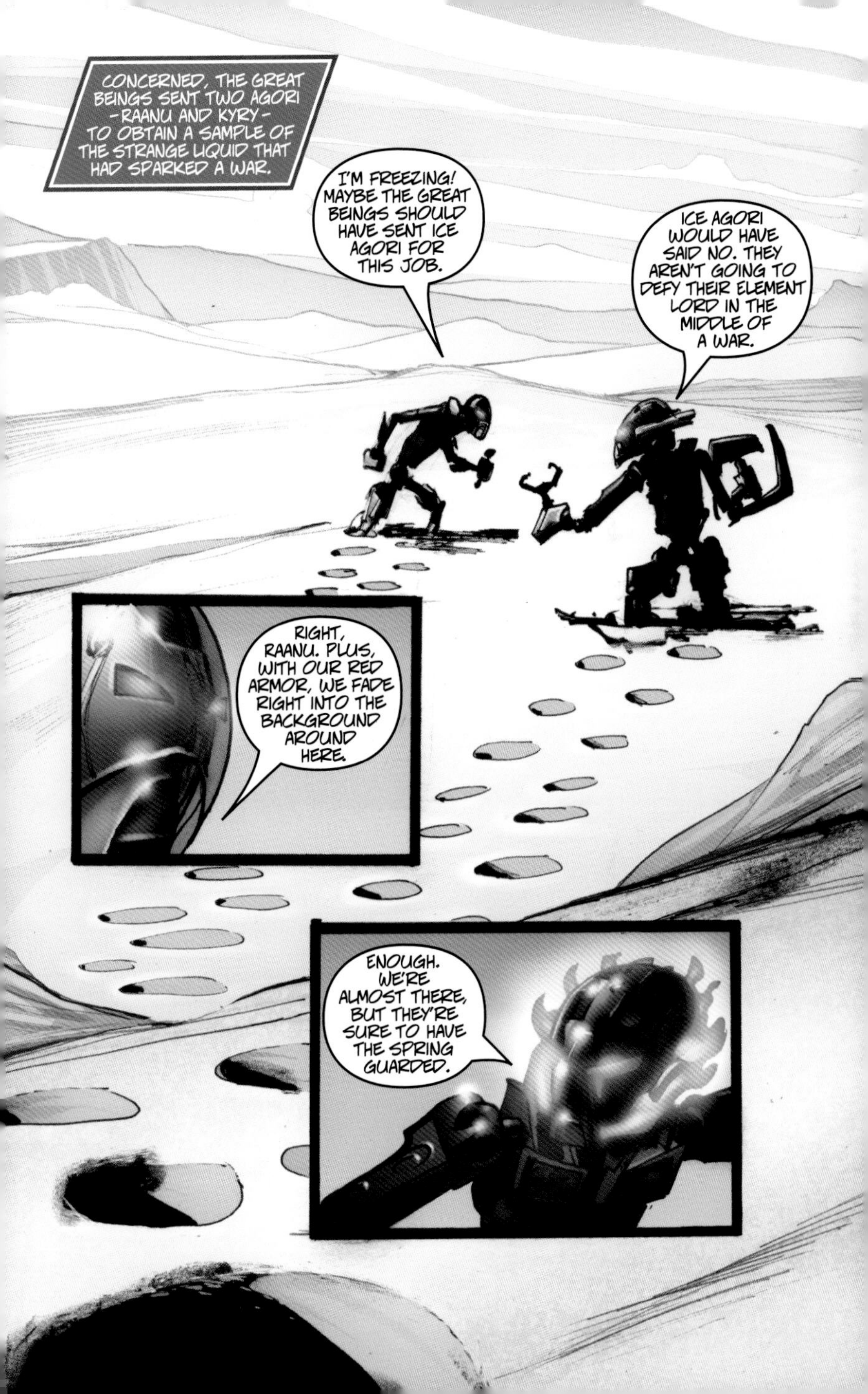
CONCERNED, THE GREAT BEINGS SENT TWO AGORI -RAANU AND KYRY- TO OBTAIN A SAMPLE OF THE STRANGE LIQUID THAT HAD SPARKED A WAR.
I'M FREEZING! MAYBE THE GREAT BEINGS SHOULD HAVE SENT ICE AGORI FOR THIS JOB.
ICE AGORI WOULD HAVE SAID NO. THEY AREN'T GOING TO DEFY THEIR ELEMENT LORD IN THE MIDDLE OF A WAR.
RIGHT, RAANU. PLUS, WITH OUR RED ARMOR, WE FADE RIGHT INTO THE BACKGROUND AROUND HERE.
ENOUGH. WE'RE ALMOST THERE, BUT THEY'RE SURE TO HAVE THE SPRING GUARDED.

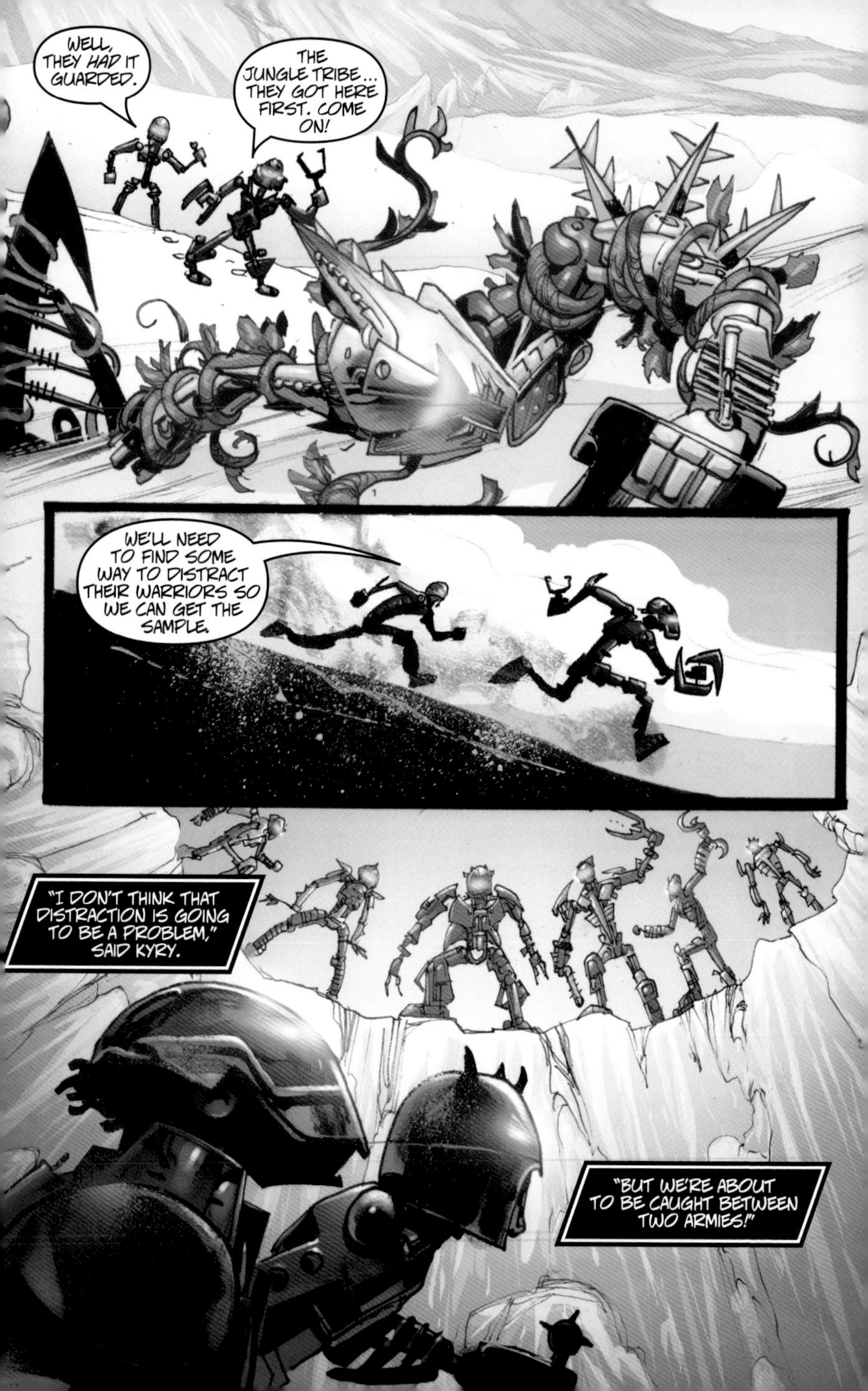
WELL, THEY *HAD* IT GUARDED.
THE JUNGLE TRIBE... THEY GOT HERE FIRST. COME ON!
WE'LL NEED TO FIND SOME WAY TO DISTRACT THEIR WARRIORS SO WE CAN GET THE SAMPLE.
"I DON'T THINK THAT DISTRACTION IS GOING TO BE A PROBLEM," SAID KYRY.
"BUT WE'RE ABOUT TO BE CAUGHT BETWEEN TWO ARMIES!"

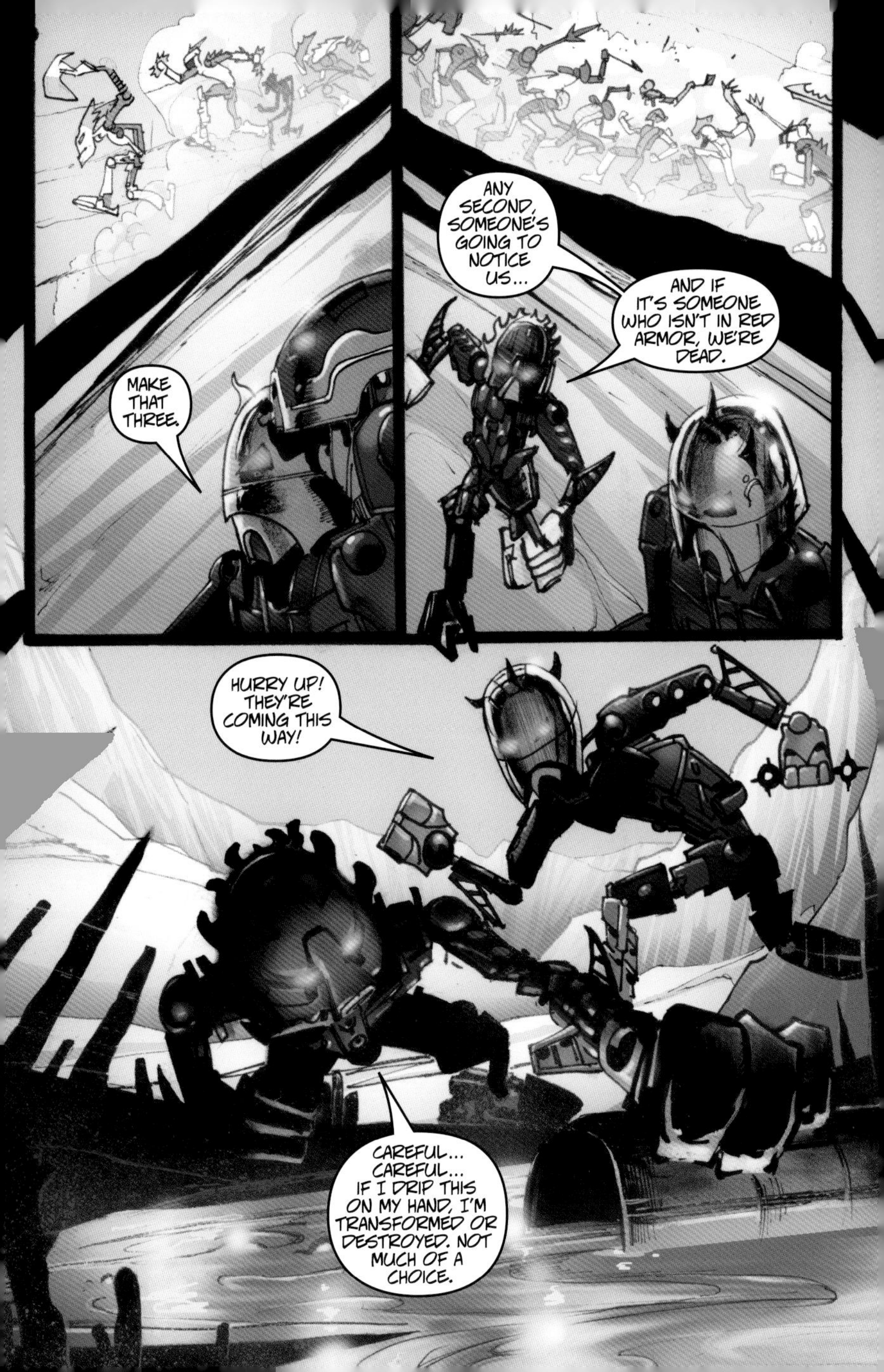
MAKE THAT THREE.
ANY SECOND, SOMEONE'S GOING TO NOTICE US...
AND IF IT'S SOMEONE WHO ISN'T IN RED ARMOR, WE'RE DEAD.
HURRY UP! THEY'RE COMING THIS WAY!
CAREFUL... CAREFUL... IF I DRIP THIS ON MY HAND, I'M TRANSFORMED OR DESTROYED. NOT MUCH OF A CHOICE.

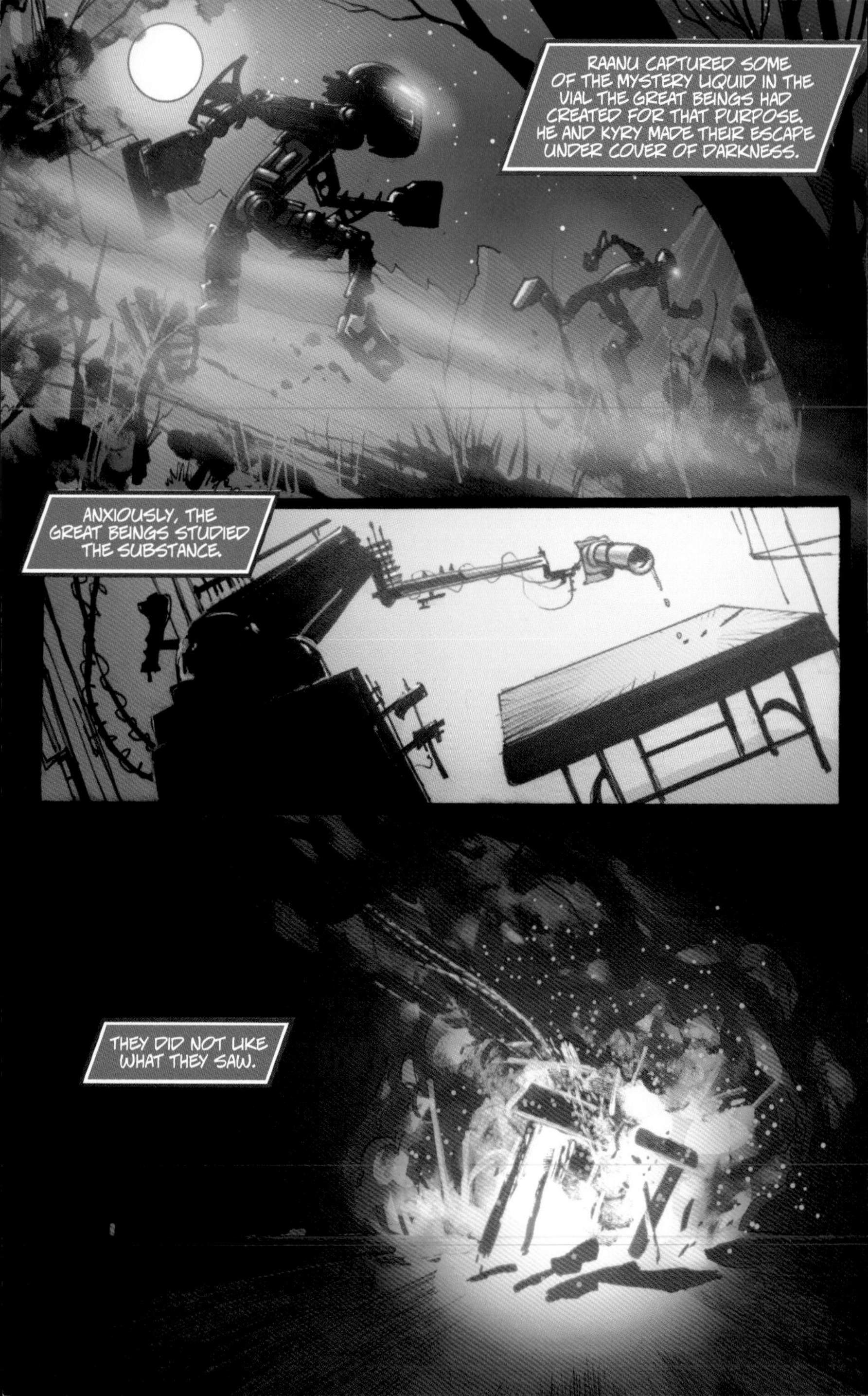
RAANU CAPTURED SOME OF THE MYSTERY LIQUID IN THE VIAL THE GREAT BEINGS HAD CREATED FOR THAT PURPOSE. HE AND KYRY MADE THEIR ESCAPE UNDER COVER OF DARKNESS.
ANXIOUSLY, THE GREAT BEINGS STUDIED THE SUBSTANCE.
THEY DID NOT LIKE WHAT THEY SAW.

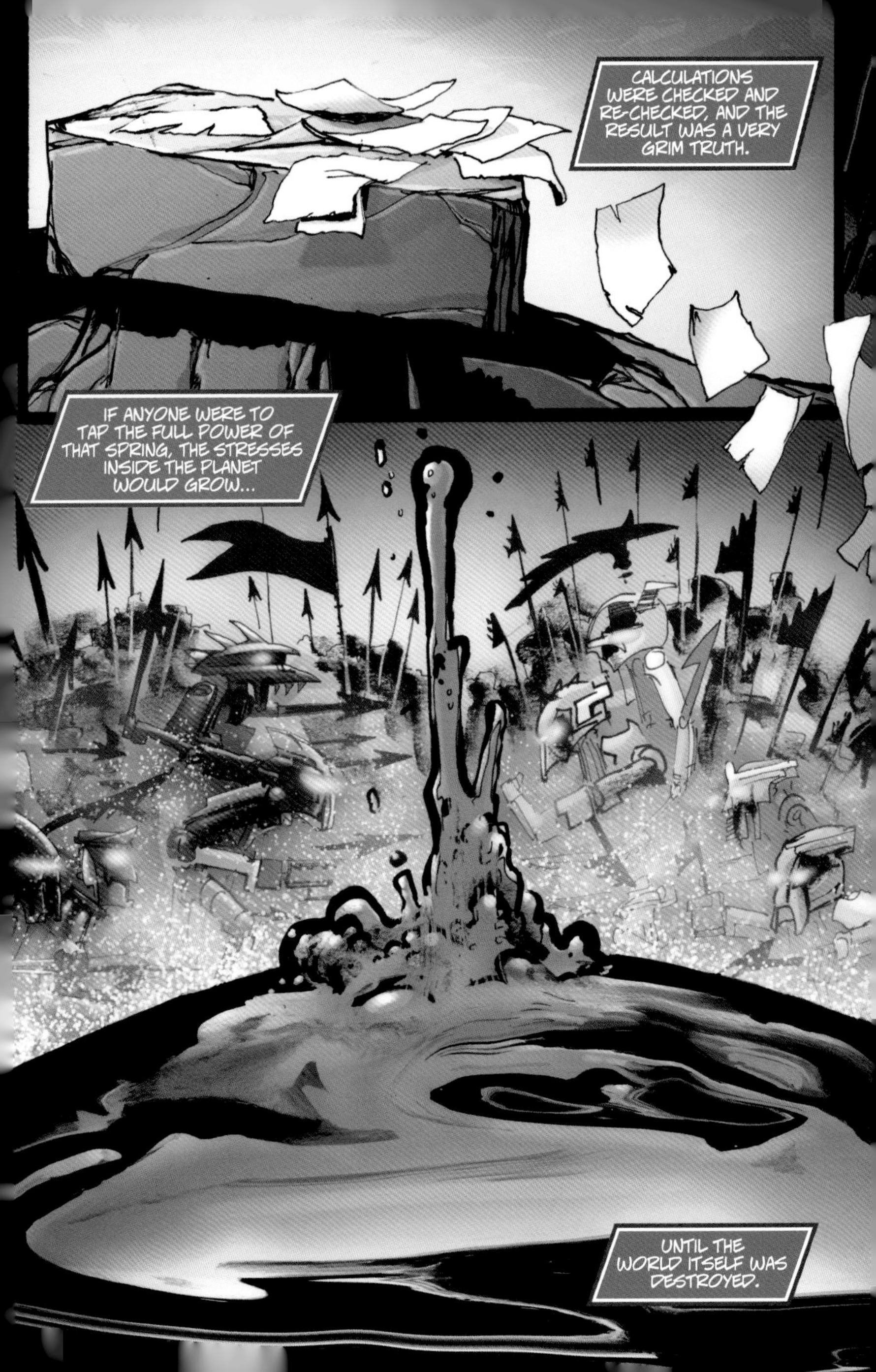
CALCULATIONS WERE CHECKED AND RE-CHECKED, AND THE RESULT WAS A VERY GRIM TRUTH.
IF ANYONE WERE TO TAP THE FULL POWER OF THAT SPRING, THE STRESSES INSIDE THE PLANET WOULD GROW...
UNTIL THE WORLD ITSELF WAS DESTROYED.

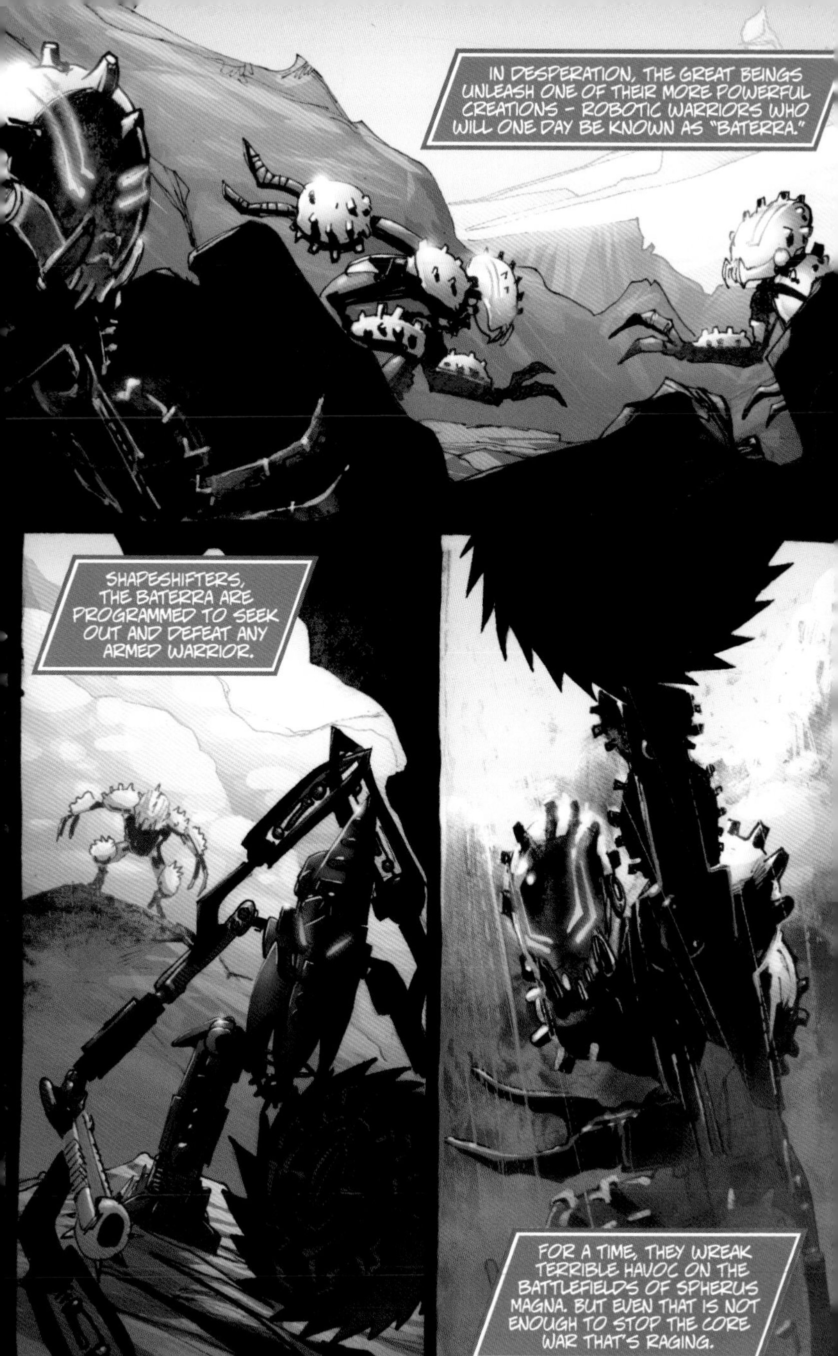
IN DESPERATION, THE GREAT BEINGS UNLEASH ONE OF THEIR MORE POWERFUL CREATIONS - ROBOTIC WARRIORS WHO WILL ONE DAY BE KNOWN AS "BATERRA."
SHAPESHIFTERS, THE BATERRA ARE PROGRAMMED TO SEEK OUT AND DEFEAT ANY ARMED WARRIOR.
FOR A TIME, THEY WREAK TERRIBLE HAVOC ON THE BATTLEFIELDS OF SPHERUS MAGNA. BUT EVEN THAT IS NOT ENOUGH TO STOP THE CORE WAR THAT'S RAGING.

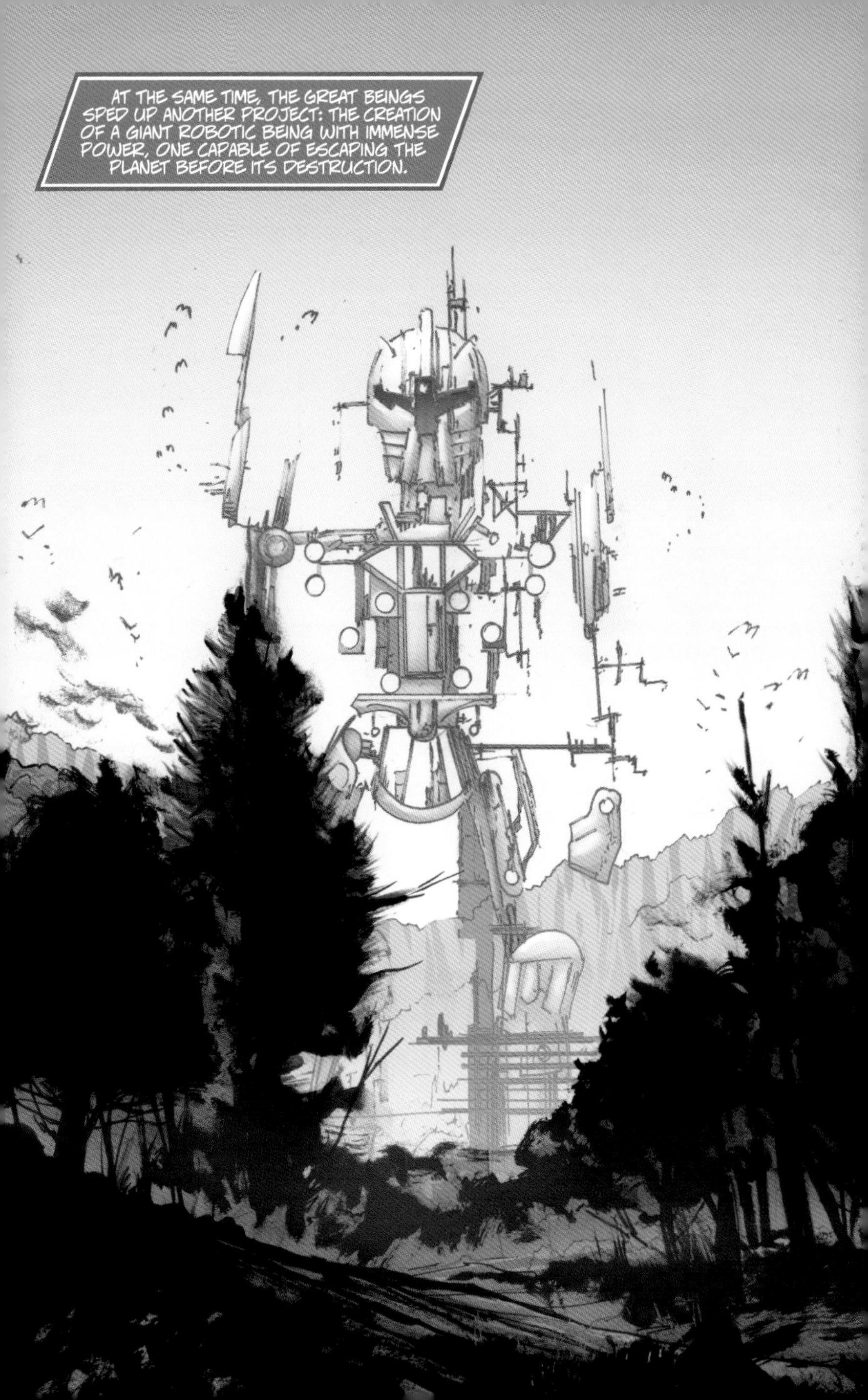
AT THE SAME TIME, THE GREAT BEINGS SPED UP ANOTHER PROJECT: THE CREATION OF A GIANT ROBOTIC BEING WITH IMMENSE POWER, ONE CAPABLE OF ESCAPING THE PLANET BEFORE ITS DESTRUCTION.

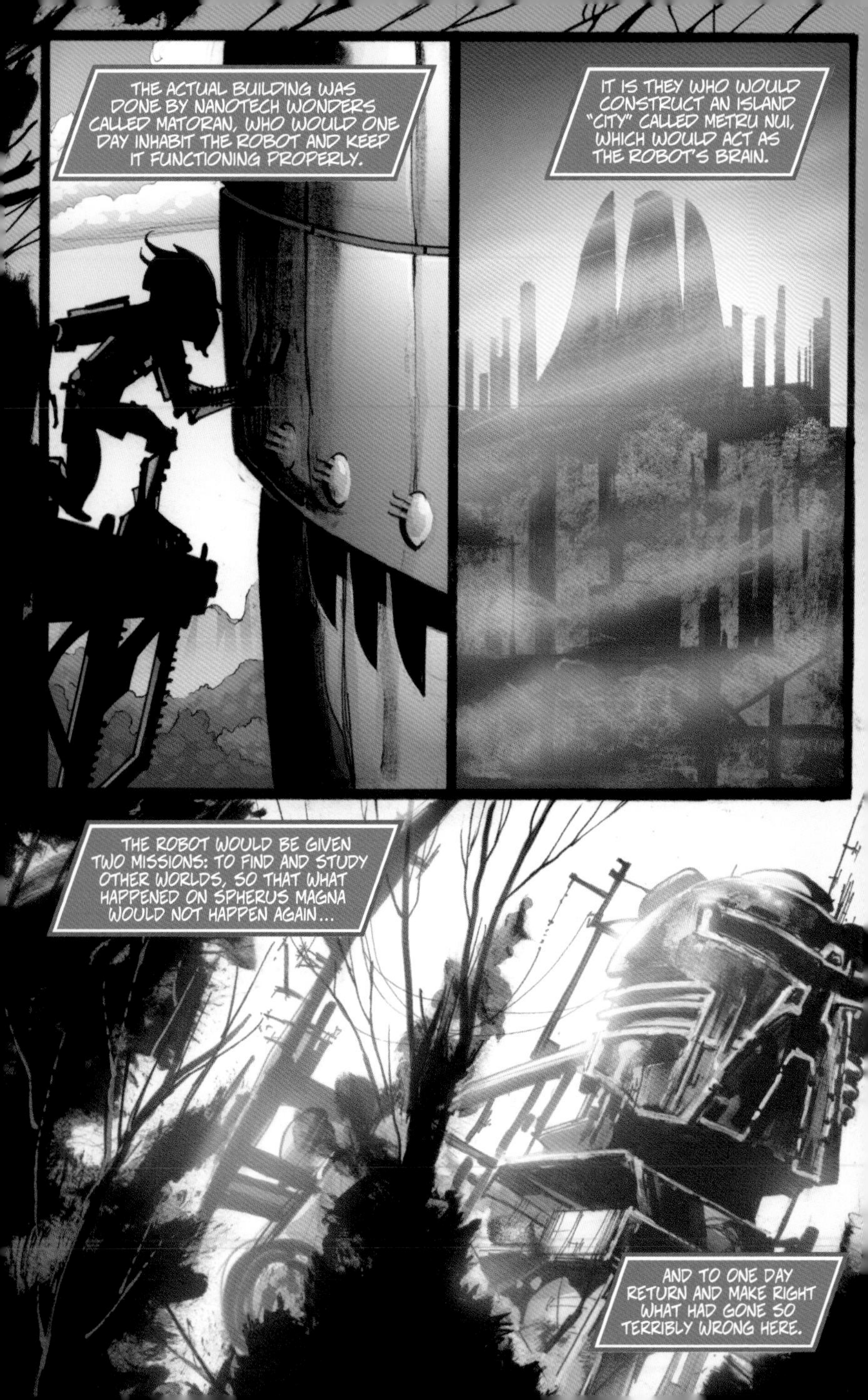
THE ACTUAL BUILDING WAS DONE BY NANOTECH WONDERS CALLED MATORAN, WHO WOULD ONE DAY INHABIT THE ROBOT AND KEEP IT FUNCTIONING PROPERLY.
IT IS THEY WHO WOULD CONSTRUCT AN ISLAND "CITY" CALLED METRU NUI, WHICH WOULD ACT AS THE ROBOT'S BRAIN.
THE ROBOT WOULD BE GIVEN TWO MISSIONS: TO FIND AND STUDY OTHER WORLDS, SO THAT WHAT HAPPENED ON SPHERUS MAGNA WOULD NOT HAPPEN AGAIN...
AND TO ONE DAY RETURN AND MAKE RIGHT WHAT HAD GONE SO TERRIBLY WRONG HERE.

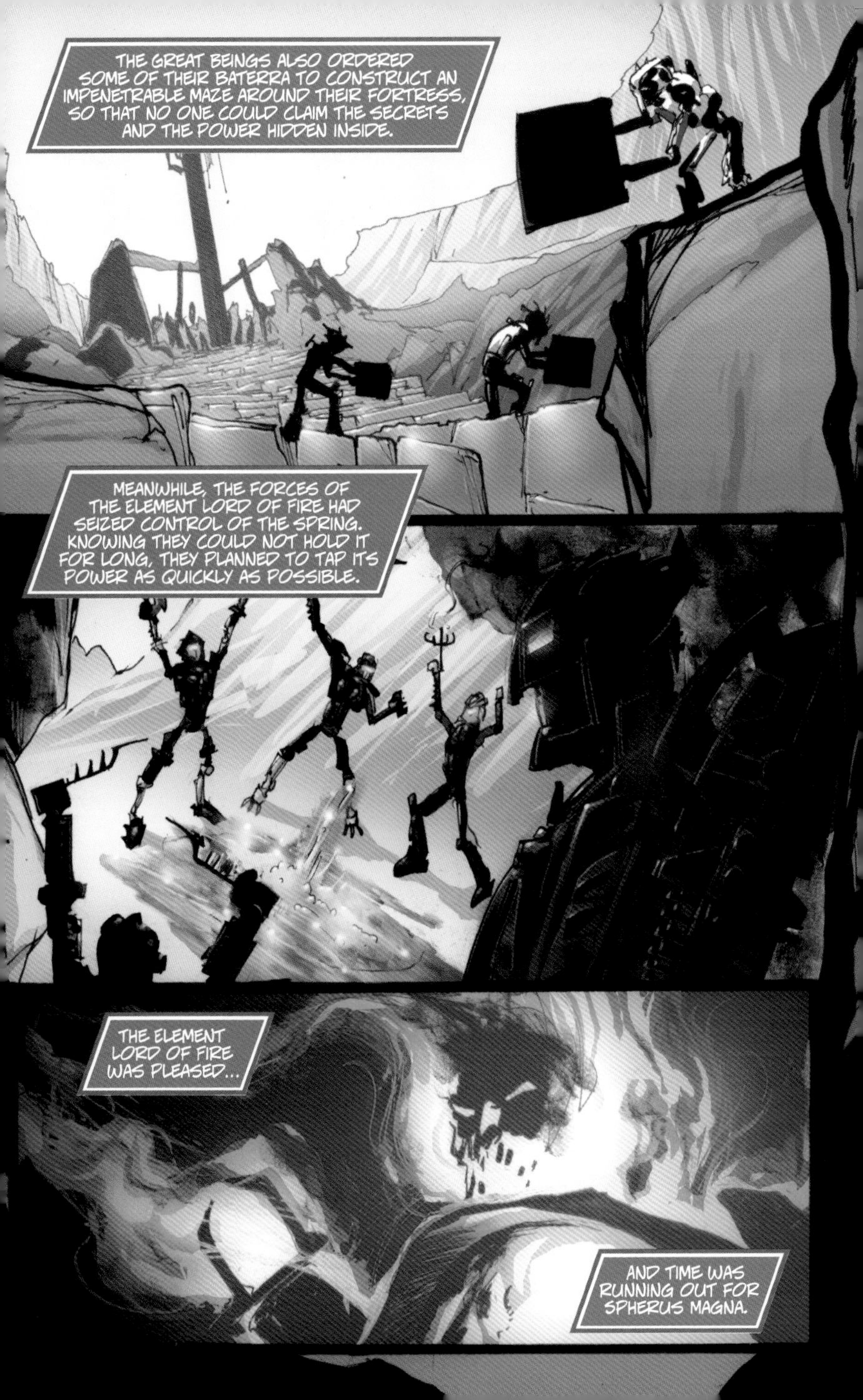
THE GREAT BEINGS ALSO ORDERED SOME OF THEIR BATERRA TO CONSTRUCT AN IMPENETRABLE MAZE AROUND THEIR FORTRESS, SO THAT NO ONE COULD CLAIM THE SECRETS AND THE POWER HIDDEN INSIDE.
MEANWHILE, THE FORCES OF THE ELEMENT LORD OF FIRE HAD SEIZED CONTROL OF THE SPRING. KNOWING THEY COULD NOT HOLD IT FOR LONG, THEY PLANNED TO TAP ITS POWER AS QUICKLY AS POSSIBLE.
THE ELEMENT LORD OF FIRE WAS PLEASED...
AND TIME WAS RUNNING OUT FOR SPHERUS MAGNA.

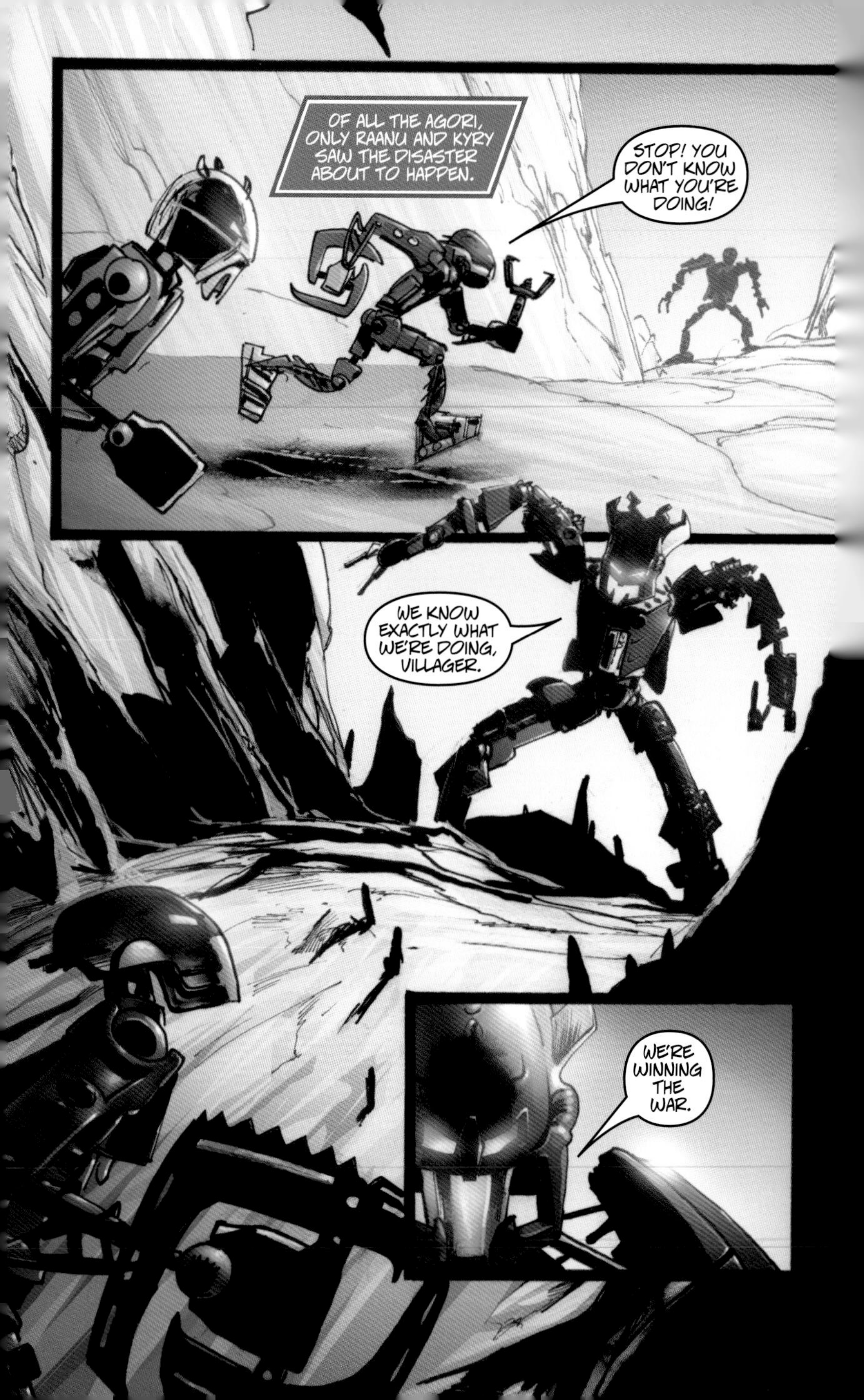
OF ALL THE AGORI, ONLY RAANU AND KYRY SAW THE DISASTER ABOUT TO HAPPEN.
STOP! YOU DON'T KNOW WHAT YOU'RE DOING!
WE KNOW EXACTLY WHAT WE'RE DOING, VILLAGER.
WE'RE WINNING THE WAR.

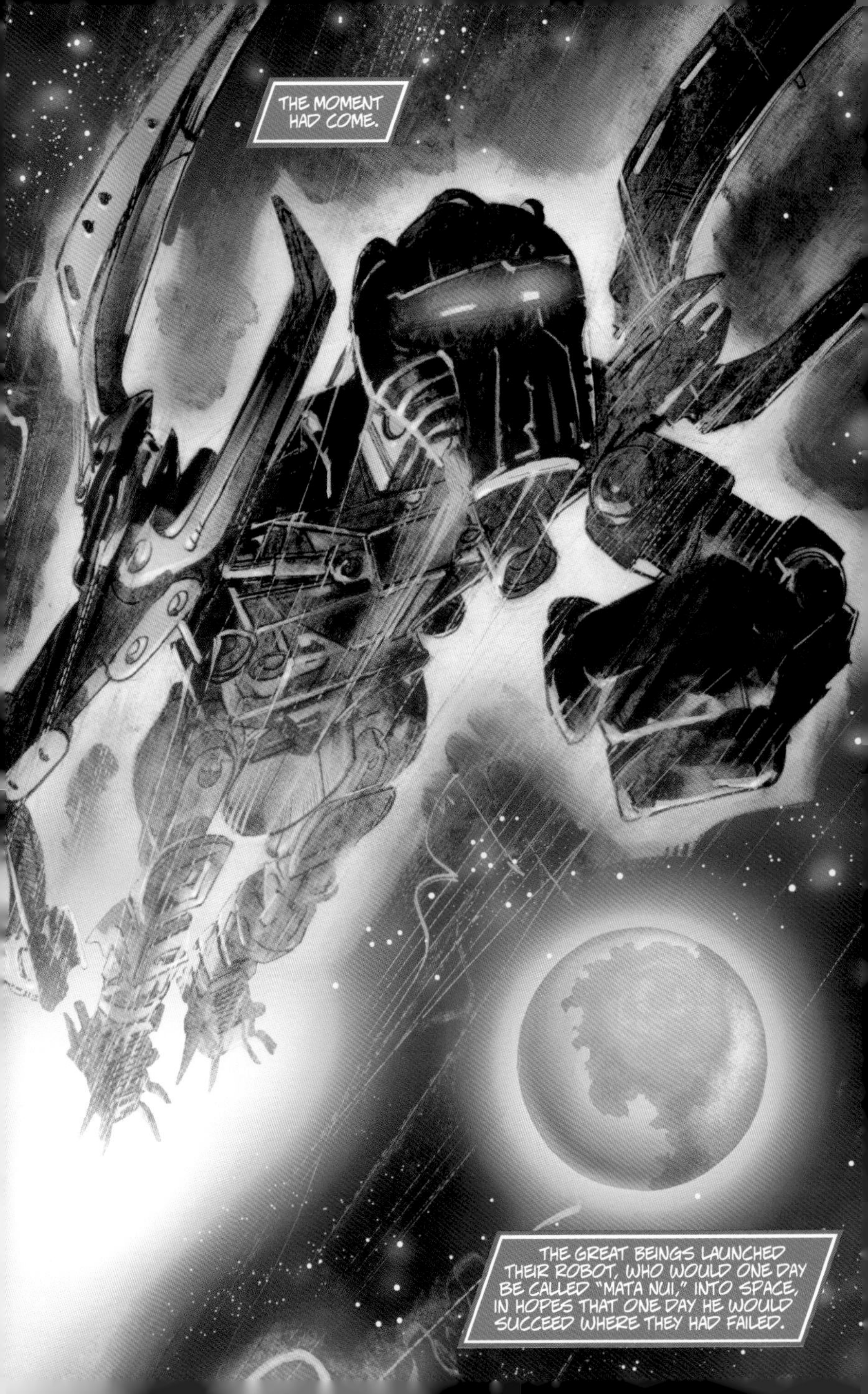
THE MOMENT HAD COME.
THE GREAT BEINGS LAUNCHED THEIR ROBOT, WHO WOULD ONE DAY BE CALLED "MATA NUI," INTO SPACE, IN HOPES THAT ONE DAY HE WOULD SUCCEED WHERE THEY HAD FAILED.

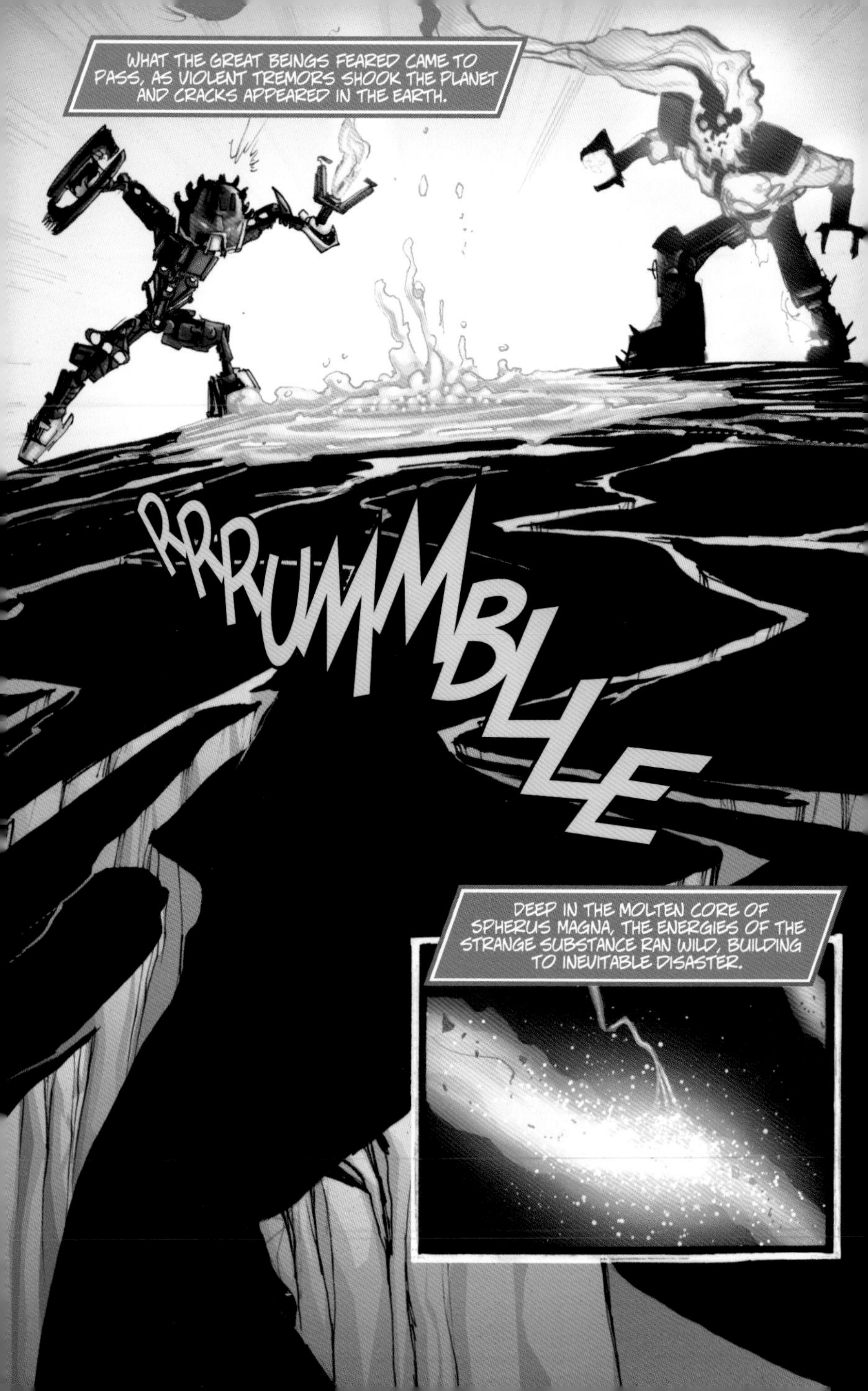
WHAT THE GREAT BEINGS FEARED CAME TO PASS, AS VIOLENT TREMORS SHOOK THE PLANET AND CRACKS APPEARED IN THE EARTH.
RRRUMMBLLE
DEEP IN THE MOLTEN CORE OF SPHERUS MAGNA, THE ENERGIES OF THE STRANGE SUBSTANCE RAN WILD, BUILDING TO INEVITABLE DISASTER.

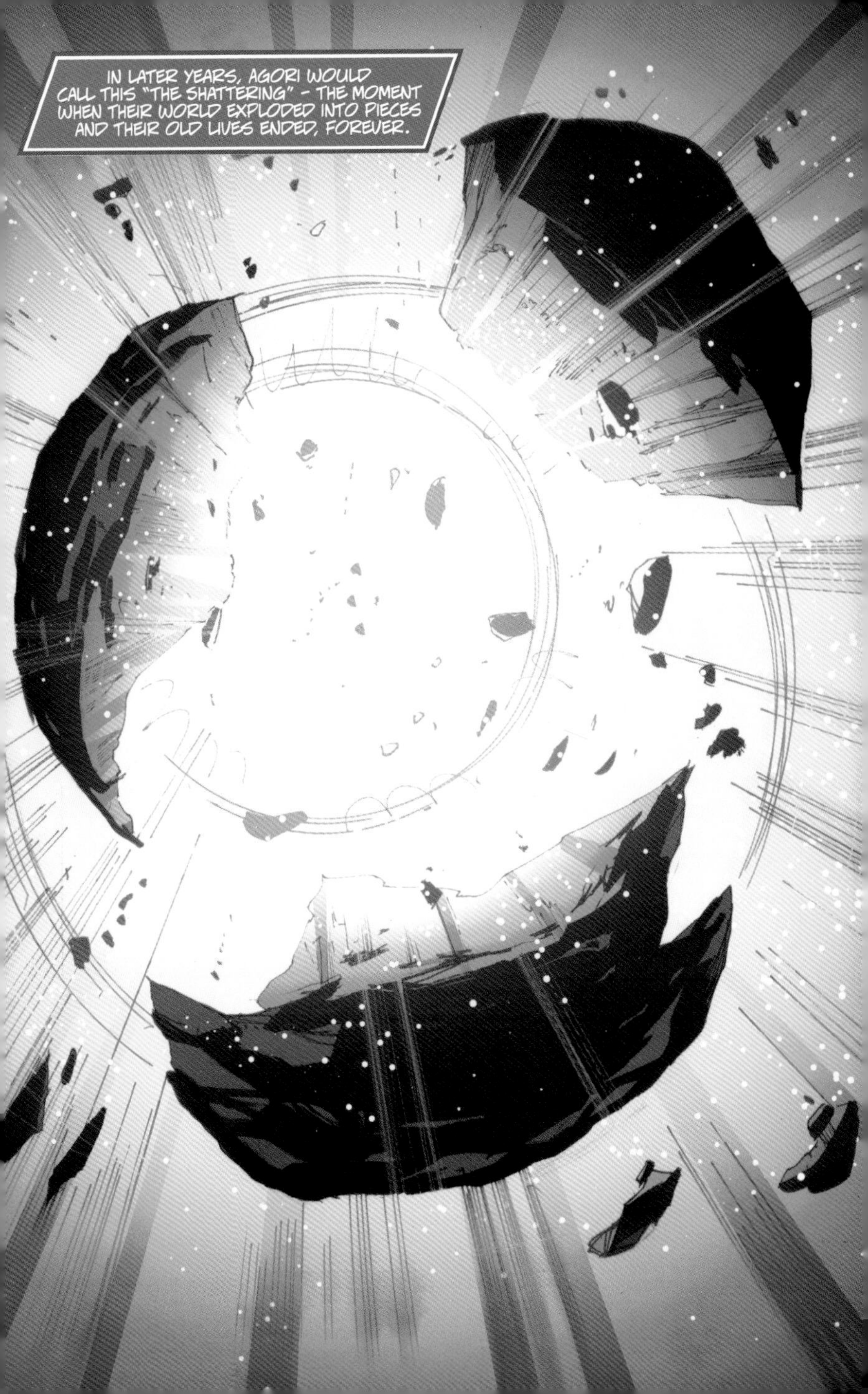
IN LATER YEARS, AGORI WOULD CALL THIS "THE SHATTERING" - THE MOMENT WHEN THEIR WORLD EXPLODED INTO PIECES AND THEIR OLD LIVES ENDED, FOREVER.

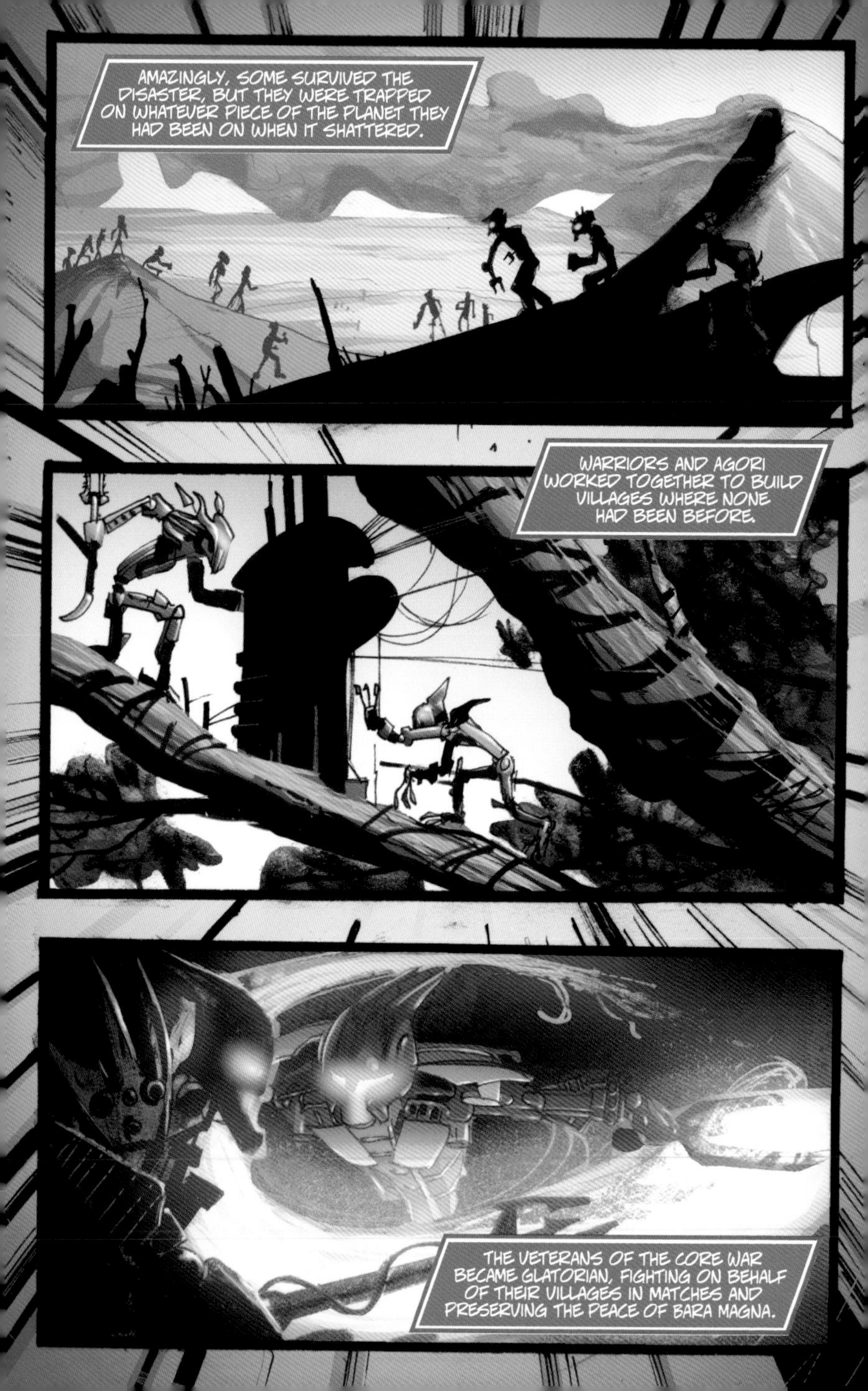
AMAZINGLY, SOME SURVIVED THE DISASTER, BUT THEY WERE TRAPPED ON WHATEVER PIECE OF THE PLANET THEY HAD BEEN ON WHEN IT SHATTERED.
WARRIORS AND AGORI WORKED TOGETHER TO BUILD VILLAGES WHERE NONE HAD BEEN BEFORE.
THE VETERANS OF THE CORE WAR BECAME GLATORIAN, FIGHTING ON BEHALF OF THEIR VILLAGES IN MATCHES AND PRESERVING THE PEACE OF BARA MAGNA.

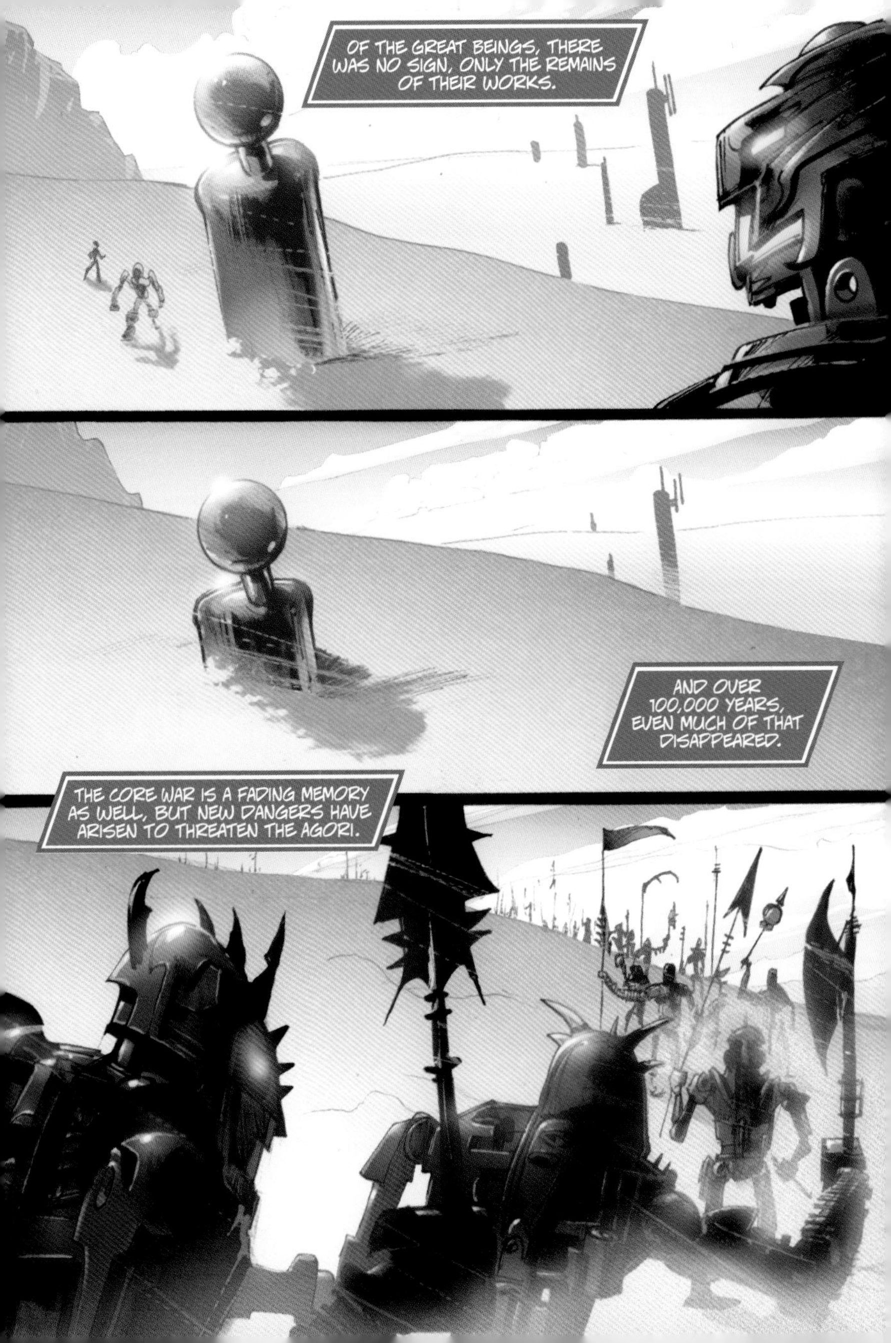
OF THE GREAT BEINGS, THERE WAS NO SIGN, ONLY THE REMAINS OF THEIR WORKS.
AND OVER 100,000 YEARS, EVEN MUCH OF THAT DISAPPEARED.
THE CORE WAR IS A FADING MEMORY AS WELL, BUT NEW DANGERS HAVE ARISEN TO THREATEN THE AGORI.

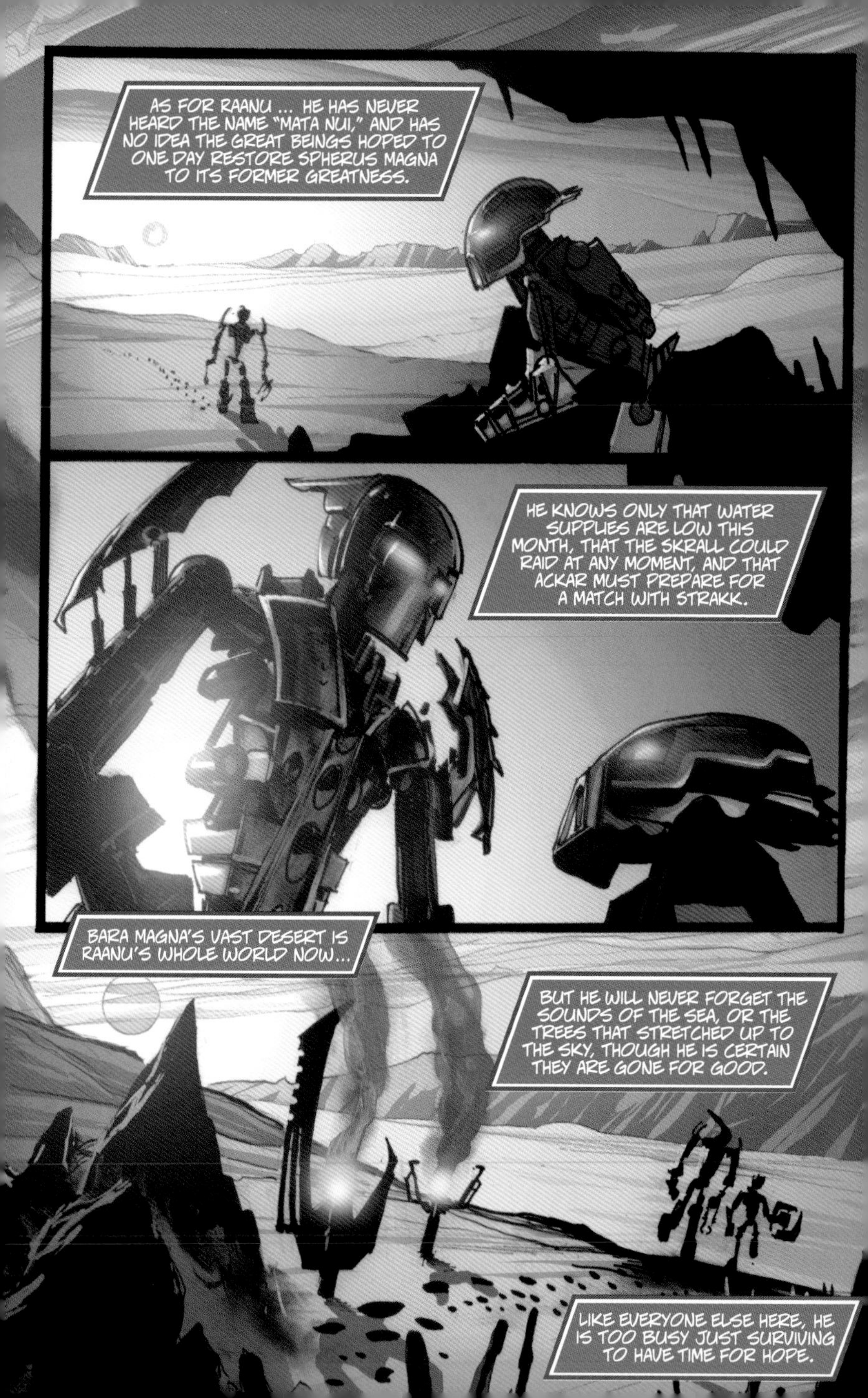
AS FOR RAANU ... HE HAS NEVER HEARD THE NAME "MATA NUI," AND HAS NO IDEA THE GREAT BEINGS HOPED TO ONE DAY RESTORE SPHERUS MAGNA TO ITS FORMER GREATNESS.
HE KNOWS ONLY THAT WATER SUPPLIES ARE LOW THIS MONTH, THAT THE SKRALL COULD RAID AT ANY MOMENT, AND THAT ACKAR MUST PREPARE FOR A MATCH WITH STRAKK.
BARA MAGNA'S VAST DESERT IS RAANU'S WHOLE WORLD NOW...
BUT HE WILL NEVER FORGET THE SOUNDS OF THE SEA, OR THE TREES THAT STRETCHED UP TO THE SKY, THOUGH HE IS CERTAIN THEY ARE GONE FOR GOOD.
LIKE EVERYONE ELSE HERE, HE IS TOO BUSY JUST SURVIVING TO HAVE TIME FOR HOPE.

Special Preview of BIONICLE #9
"The Fall of Atero"

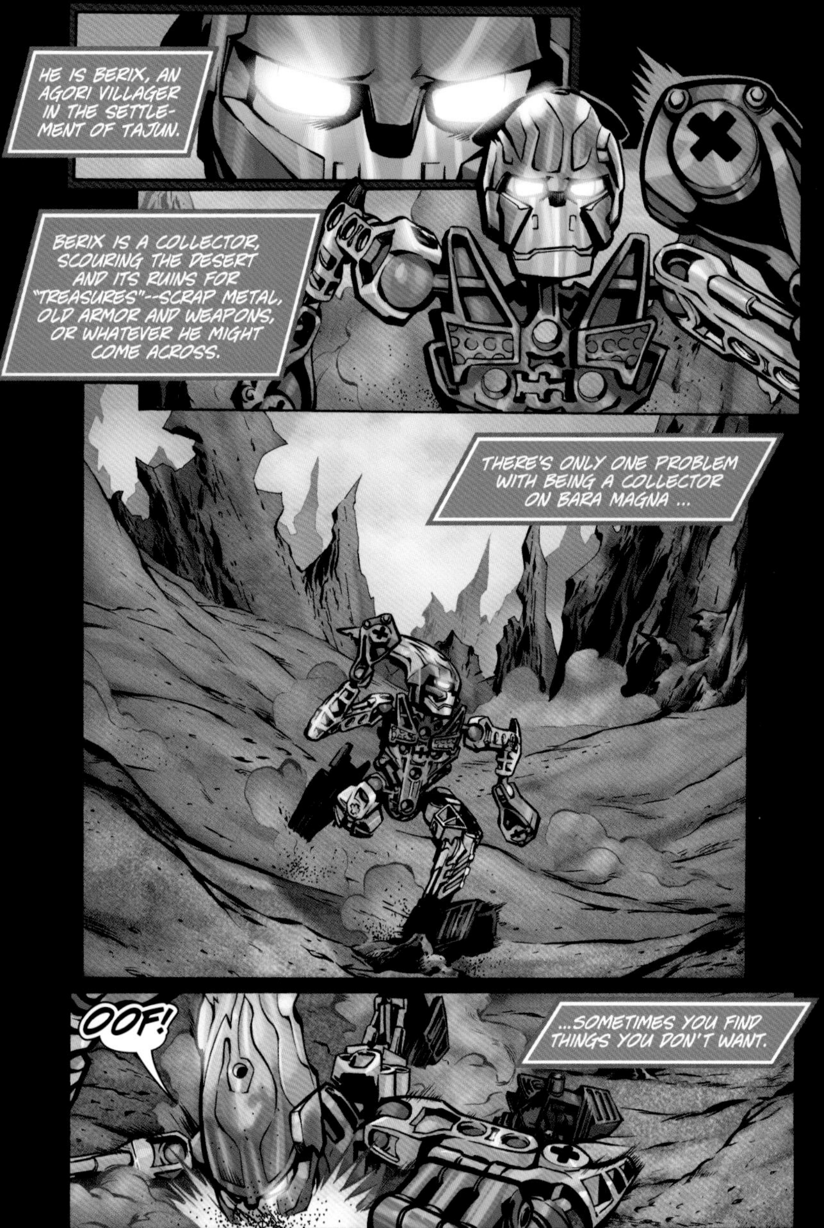
HE IS BERIX, AN AGORI VILLAGER IN THE SETTLE-MENT OF TAJUN.
BERIX IS A COLLECTOR, SCOURING THE DESERT AND ITS RUINS FOR "TREASURES"--SCRAP METAL, OLD ARMOR AND WEAPONS, OR WHATEVER HE MIGHT COME ACROSS.
THERE'S ONLY ONE PROBLEM WITH BEING A COLLECTOR ON BARA MAGNA ...
OOF!
...SOMETIMES YOU FIND THINGS YOU DON'T WANT.

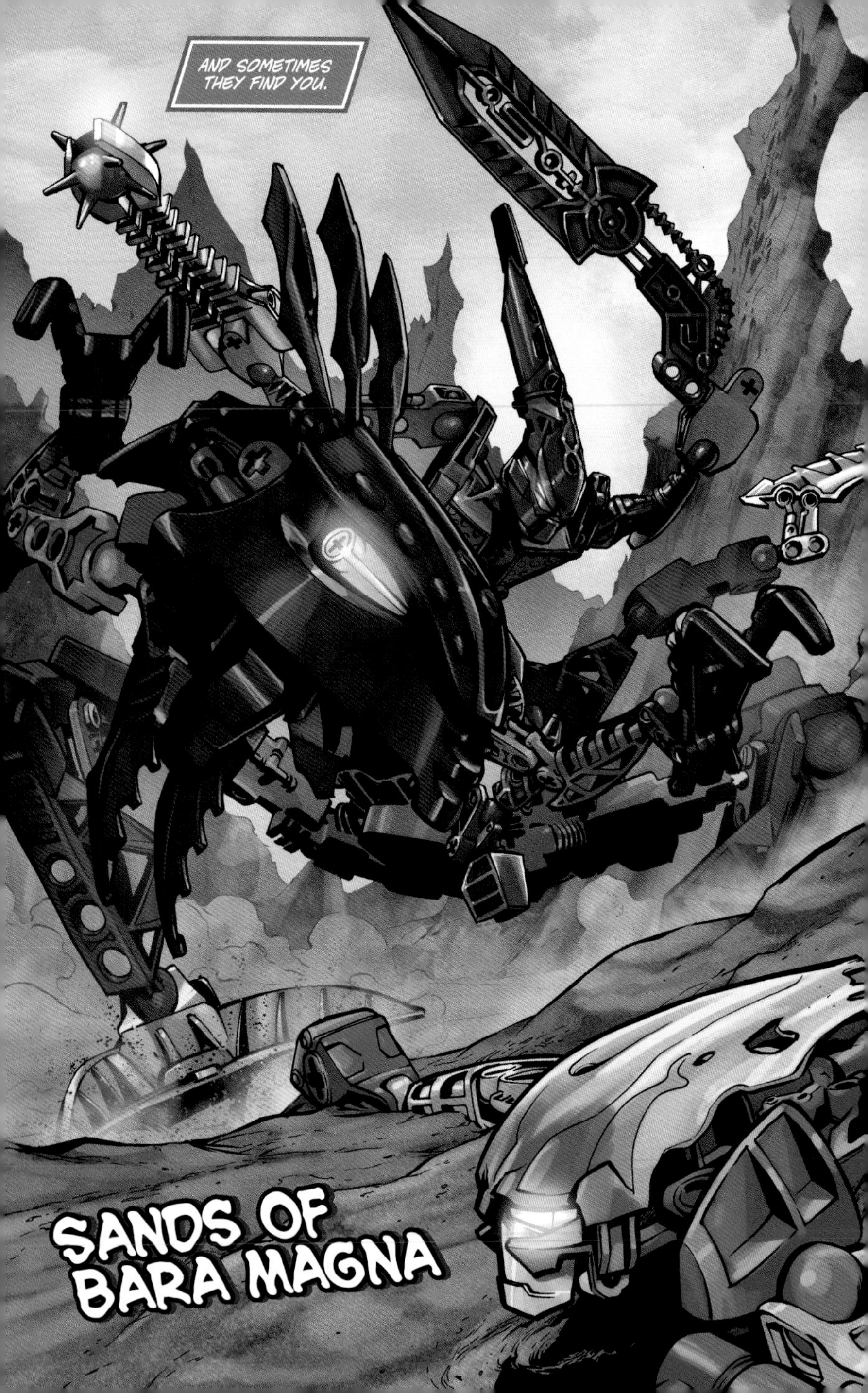
AND SOMETIMES THEY FIND YOU.
SANDS OF BARA MAGNA

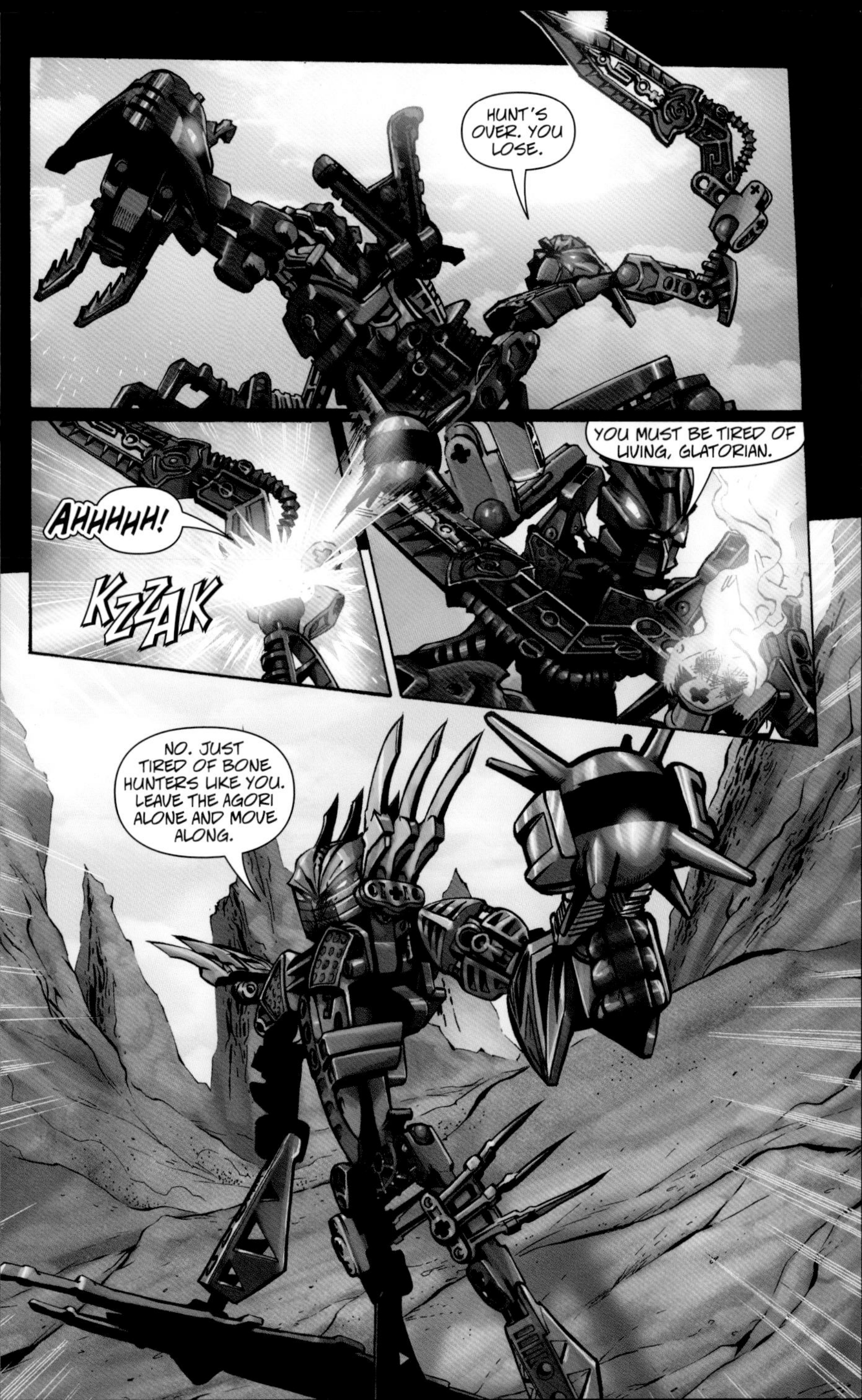
HUNT'S OVER. YOU LOSE.
YOU MUST BE TIRED OF LIVING, GLATORIAN.
AHHHHH!
KZZAK
NO. JUST TIRED OF BONE HUNTERS LIKE YOU. LEAVE THE AGORI ALONE AND MOVE ALONG.

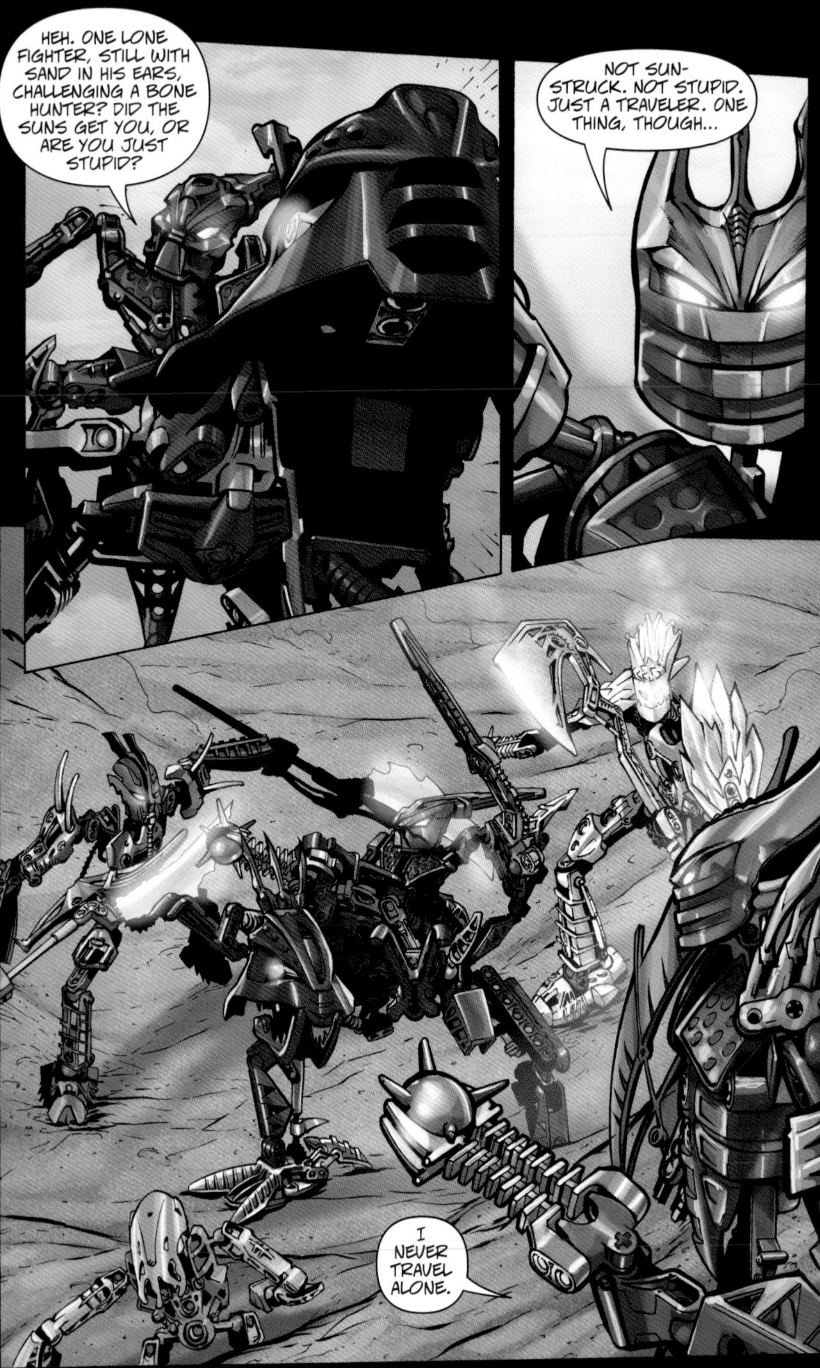

HEH. ONE LONE FIGHTER, STILL WITH SAND IN HIS EARS, CHALLENGING A BONE HUNTER? DID THE SUNS GET YOU, OR ARE YOU JUST STUPID?
NOT SUN-STRUCK. NOT STUPID. JUST A TRAVELER. ONE THING, THOUGH...
I NEVER TRAVEL ALONE.

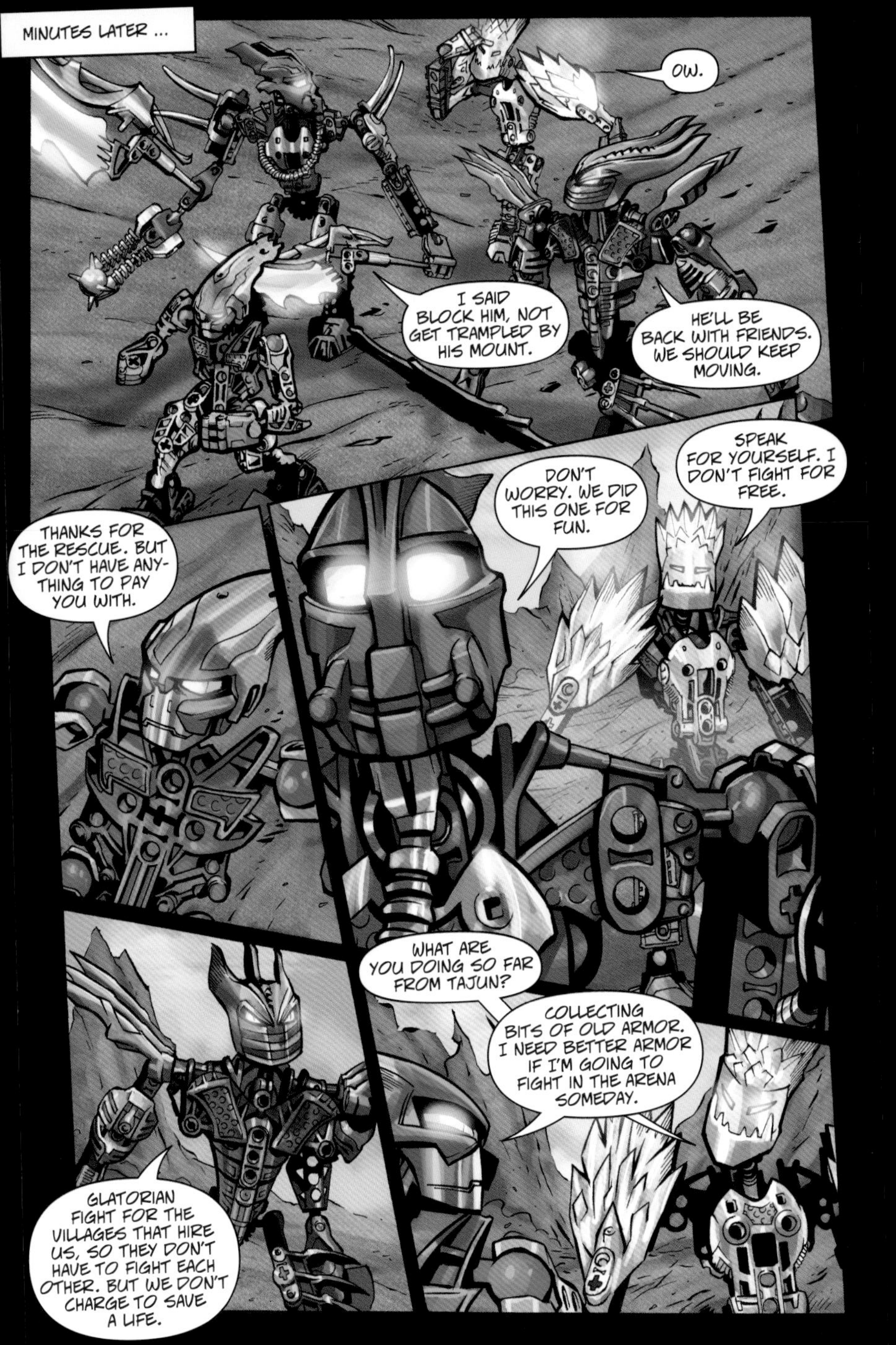
MINUTES LATER ...
OW.
I SAID BLOCK HIM, NOT GET TRAMPLED BY HIS MOUNT.
HE'LL BE BACK WITH FRIENDS. WE SHOULD KEEP MOVING.
THANKS FOR THE RESCUE. BUT I DON'T HAVE ANY-THING TO PAY YOU WITH.
DON'T WORRY. WE DID THIS ONE FOR FUN.
SPEAK FOR YOURSELF. I DON'T FIGHT FOR FREE.
GLATORIAN FIGHT FOR THE VILLAGES THAT HIRE US, SO THEY DON'T HAVE TO FIGHT EACH OTHER. BUT WE DON'T CHARGE TO SAVE A LIFE.
WHAT ARE YOU DOING SO FAR FROM TAJUN?
COLLECTING BITS OF OLD ARMOR. I NEED BETTER ARMOR IF I'M GOING TO FIGHT IN THE ARENA SOMEDAY.

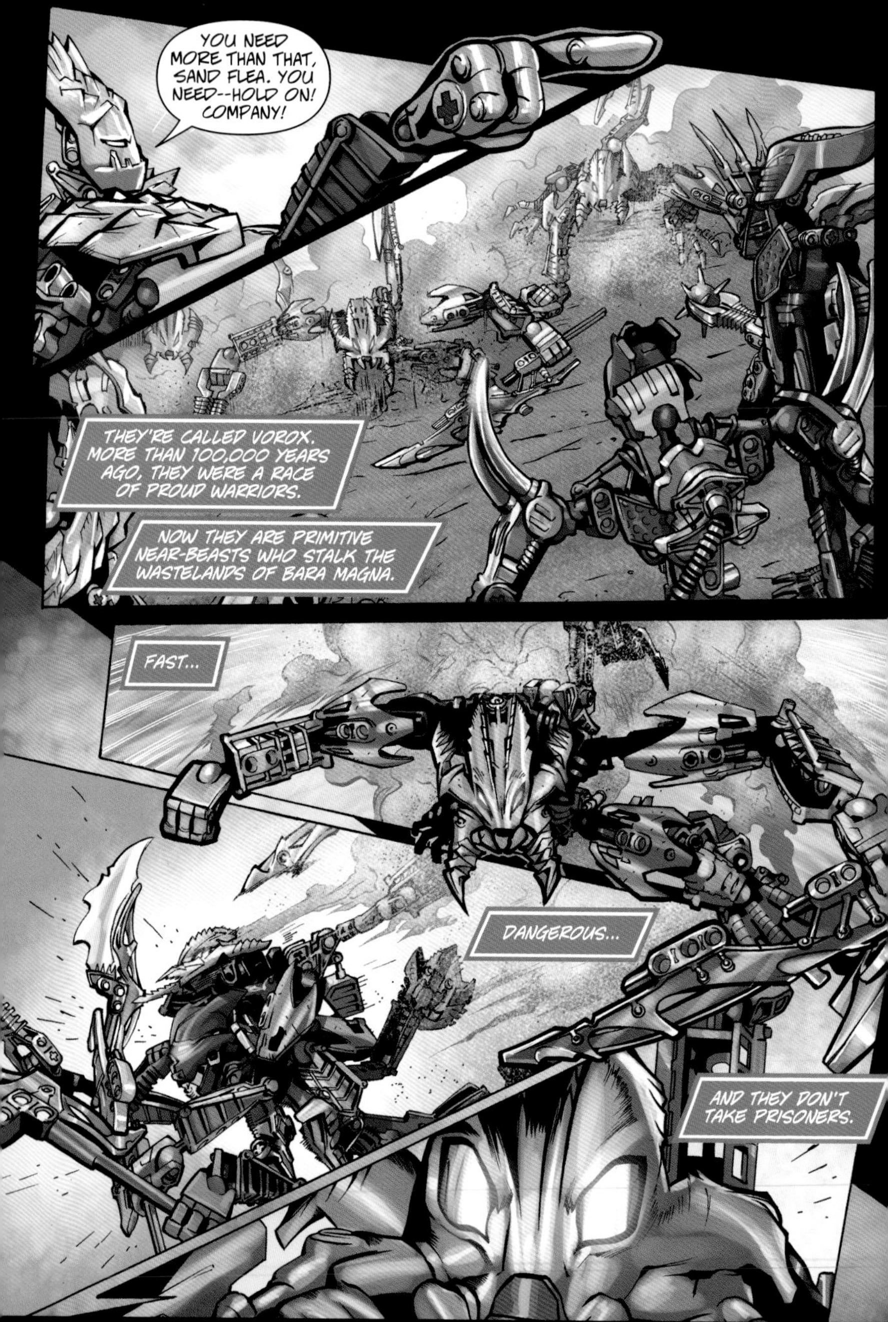
YOU NEED MORE THAN THAT, SAND FLEA. YOU NEED--HOLD ON! COMPANY!
THEY'RE CALLED VOROX. MORE THAN 100,000 YEARS AGO, THEY WERE A RACE OF PROUD WARRIORS.
NOW THEY ARE PRIMITIVE NEAR-BEASTS WHO STALK THE WASTELANDS OF BARA MAGNA.
FAST...
DANGEROUS...
AND THEY DON'T TAKE PRISONERS.

DON'T MISS BIONICLE GRAPHIC NOVEL #9
"THE FALL OF ATERO"

WATCH OUT FOR PAPERCUTZ™

Welcome to BIONICLE® #8, I'm your proud-as-can be Papercutz Editor-in-Chief Jim Salicrup. Well, we finally did it—an entire all-new BIONICLE graphic novel produced just for you! Now, we didn't just get anybody to write these new mini-epics. Oh, no—we went to the man who knows these characters and mind-blowing concepts better than anyone, the amazing Greg Farshtey!

Greg's been involved behind-the-scenes at LEGO® group since the very beginning of the BIONICLE line concept, and not long ago he posted this insightful and informative piece on the early history of the BIONICLE® line on the Papercutz.blog:

"BIONICLE got its start in 1999-2000, when an international team of people employed by the LEGO Group were tasked with coming up with a storyline-based LEGO® line. The early working title was, believe it or not, 'Bone-Heads of Voodoo Island.' The first story bible (a summary of the year's story) for 2001 actually ended with Mata Nui awakening! No one could be sure if the BIONICLE stories would be big enough to last for more than one year …

"The BIONICLE line was introduced with a comicbook, truck tours, a 'build your own website' contest, and, of course, the first six Toa canister sets. The six villager sets (who would later come to be called 'Matoran') were available only through a McDonald's promotion.

"As the Toa were originally planned, they were all different ages and they would all sound sort of 'godlike' when they spoke. I had a long conversation with story team head Bob Thompson as I worked on the first comic, and suggested that the characters might be easier to relate to if they had different personalities, and spoke differently from each other, rather than all sounding like Thor or Superman. He agreed, and that was how the initial characters were born in print."

There's a little more revealed, and you can see it on the March 12th 2009 Papercutz blog entry at www.papercutz.com.

We're out of room, but before we go we want to send out a big THANK YOU to Stuart Sayger, who did such a great job on "All Our Sins Remembered," and of course, Christian Zanier, who did his usual super-detailed impressive work on both "Fall and Rise of the Skralls" and "The Exile's Tale," and remind you to not miss BIONICLE #9: The Fall of Atero—it's the start of the BIONICLE Glatorian series, and features the return of Mata Nui!

Thanks,

Jim

Bone-Head of Manhattan Island

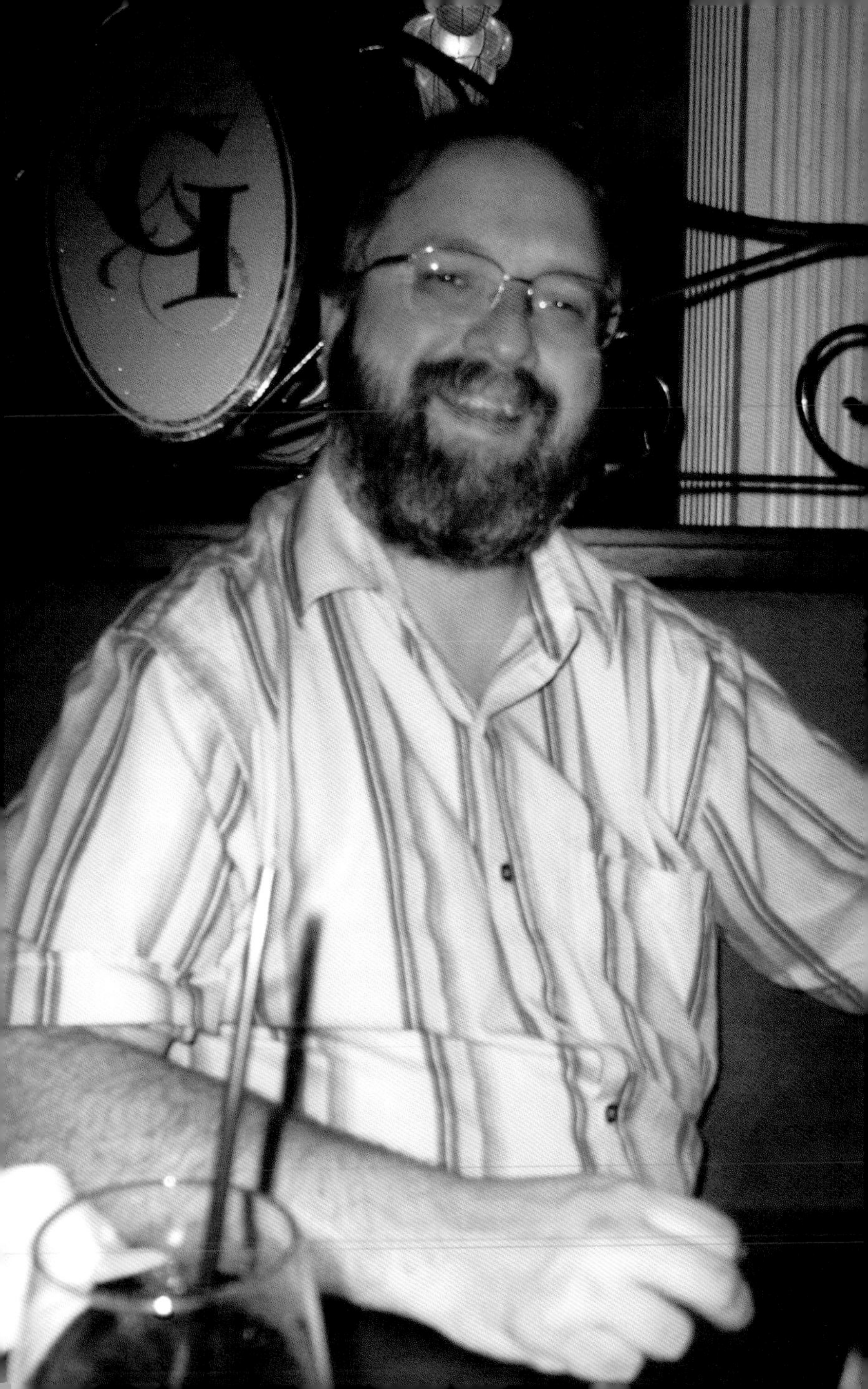

MEET BIONICLE® GRAPHIC NOVELS WRITER

GREG FARSHTEY!

A PAPERCUTZ Profile

We emailed a bunch of questions to the brilliant brain behind the BIONICLE® graphic novels, to better get to know this talented writer. Here are the fun-filled, insightful results…

PAPERCUTZ: When and where were you born?

GREG FARSHTEY: I was born in 1965 in Mount Kisco, NY.

P: What were your favorite toys?

GREG: Mego action figures, and when I was older, LEGO bricks (LEGO bricks didn't come to the US until I was 9). I had a ton of action figures and used to make up stories with them that lasted for months.

P: At what age did you start to read?

GREG: I was reading pretty young. I was reading

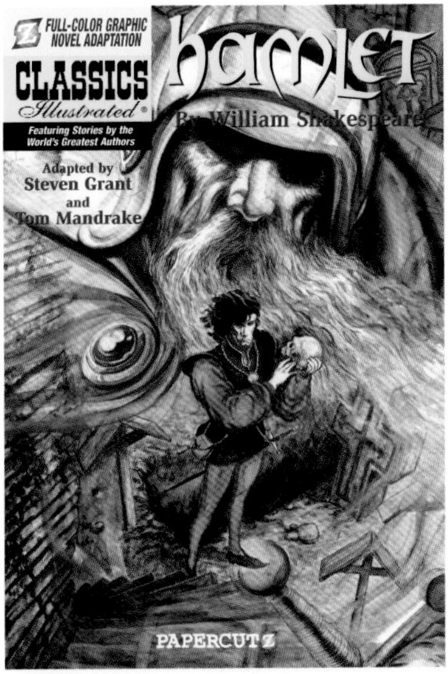

FULL-COLOR GRAPHIC NOVEL ADAPTATION
CLASSICS Illustrated®
Featuring Stories by the World's Greatest Authors
Hamlet
By William Shakespeare
Adapted by Steven Grant and Tom Mandrake
PAPERCUTZ

Shakespeare for fun when I was in first grade, I remember. Plus I learned a lot of vocabulary from comicbooks.

P: What did you read when you were a young boy?

GREG: Comics, especially Batman, Encyclopedia Brown books. The Great Brain books, Sherlock Holmes, and history books.

P: When did you start to write?

GREG: I think the first writing I did was in fourth grade, but I didn't really get serious about it until high school.

P: Who were your favorite writers and artists?

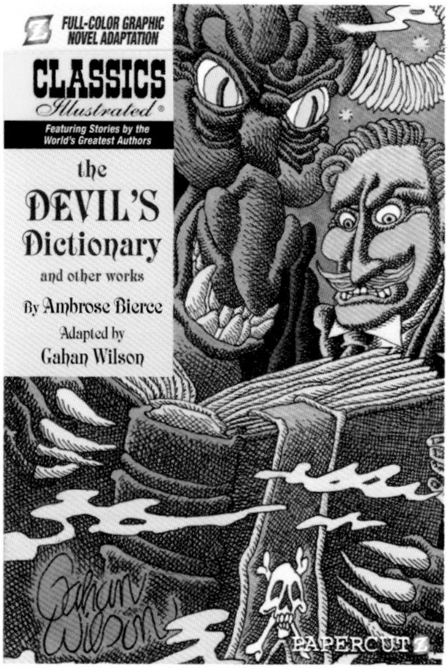
FULL-COLOR GRAPHIC NOVEL ADAPTATION
CLASSICS
Illustrated
Featuring Stories by the World's Greatest Authors
the DEVIL'S Dictionary
and other works
By Ambrose Bierce
Adapted by
Gahan Wilson
PAPERCUTZ

GREG: My favorite writers are Ambrose Bierce (see above), Jeffery Deaver, Raymond Chandler, and most recently, Christopher Fowler. I don't really have favorite artists, though I loved Gene Colan's comicbook work.

P: Did you take any special courses in school to become a writer?

GREG: No. I don't really believe you can teach someone to write. I think you can teach them to read, and to read things that will, in the long run, improve their writing. But I think a lot of writing is instinctive, you can do it or you can't.

P: What was your first published writing?

GREG: I self-published an underground paper in high school, and in college I had a short story published in a literary magazine. The first creative writing I was paid for was a humor column called Town Crier in the first paper I worked at.

P: How did you wind up working on BIONICLE comics?

GREG: I was hired at the LEGO® Group in 2000 as the Club writer, to work on the LEGO Magazine. They were just getting ready to launch BIONICLE line then. I knew they were going to do a comic, but figured I was too new to get to do it. I wrote a couple pages just for fun and showed them to my boss. Turned out they needed the first script right away, so I got the chance to do it.

P: Why was the BIONICLE concept ever called "The Bone-Heads of Voodoo Island"?

GREG: Well, I wasn't working on the BIONICLE line at that time, but I suspect that was a combination of placeholder name and code name. Toy and game companies often use code names for projects, just in case the competition gets wind of what you're doing before you release. I once worked on a very, very serious science fiction game whose code name was "Dogs in Space."

P: Did you know when you started writing the BIONICLE stories how sprawling an epic it would become?

GREG: Not really. When I first started working on BIONICLE comics, the story was largely being dictated to me and I was just adapting it to comics. It really wasn't until the novels started that the universe started to expand.

P: How do you write a BIONICLE story-- what are your working methods?

GREG: Basically, I write it like I do any other fiction -- I let the characters do the heavy lifting. If you create a character the right way, he/she/it becomes like a real person in some ways -- you know what they do and don't like, what they would and wouldn't do, the same way you know that about a friend. Then it becomes easy to know how they would react in a given situation, how they would get along with others or not get along, what would anger them or frighten them. The trick is to not force your character to do something he wouldn't normally do, because at that moment, it becomes impossible to predict his actions and your story grinds to a halt.

P: Which story, in any of the books, comics, or DVDs is your favorite?

GREG: BIONICLE Adventures 10: Time Trap. It's the "smallest" story I have written, in that it really only focuses on two characters, Makuta and

Vakama. It was also the story in which I rebooted Makuta and turned him from a super-villain who always lost to a really complex character who sometimes ALLOWED himself to lose to throw off his opponents.

P: Do you have a favorite BIONICLE character?

GREG: Makuta Teridax and Kopaka (see illustration above). I also like a Dark Hunter named Lariska a lot and the Glatorian named Kiina.

P: Which is your favorite BIONICLE toy? And why?

GREG: I'm not sure I have a favorite set. I tend to like the bigger, more elaborate ones, like the Skopio, because I like longer builds.

P: Do you have a favorite experience meeting BIONICLE fans?

GREG: Yes. I met a young boy named Evan back in 2003, who was a huge BIONICLE fan and had Asperger syndrome. I became close friends with him and his family and we exchanged birthday gifts for years. I am still friends with his Mom and have gotten to see him grow up in photos.

P: What's the best way for BIONICLE fans to contact you?

GREG: Most BIONICLE fans send me questions through a website called BZPower.com, where I am on under the screen name GregF. So that is probably the easiest way to get in touch.

P: Thanks so much, Greg! And keep up the great work!

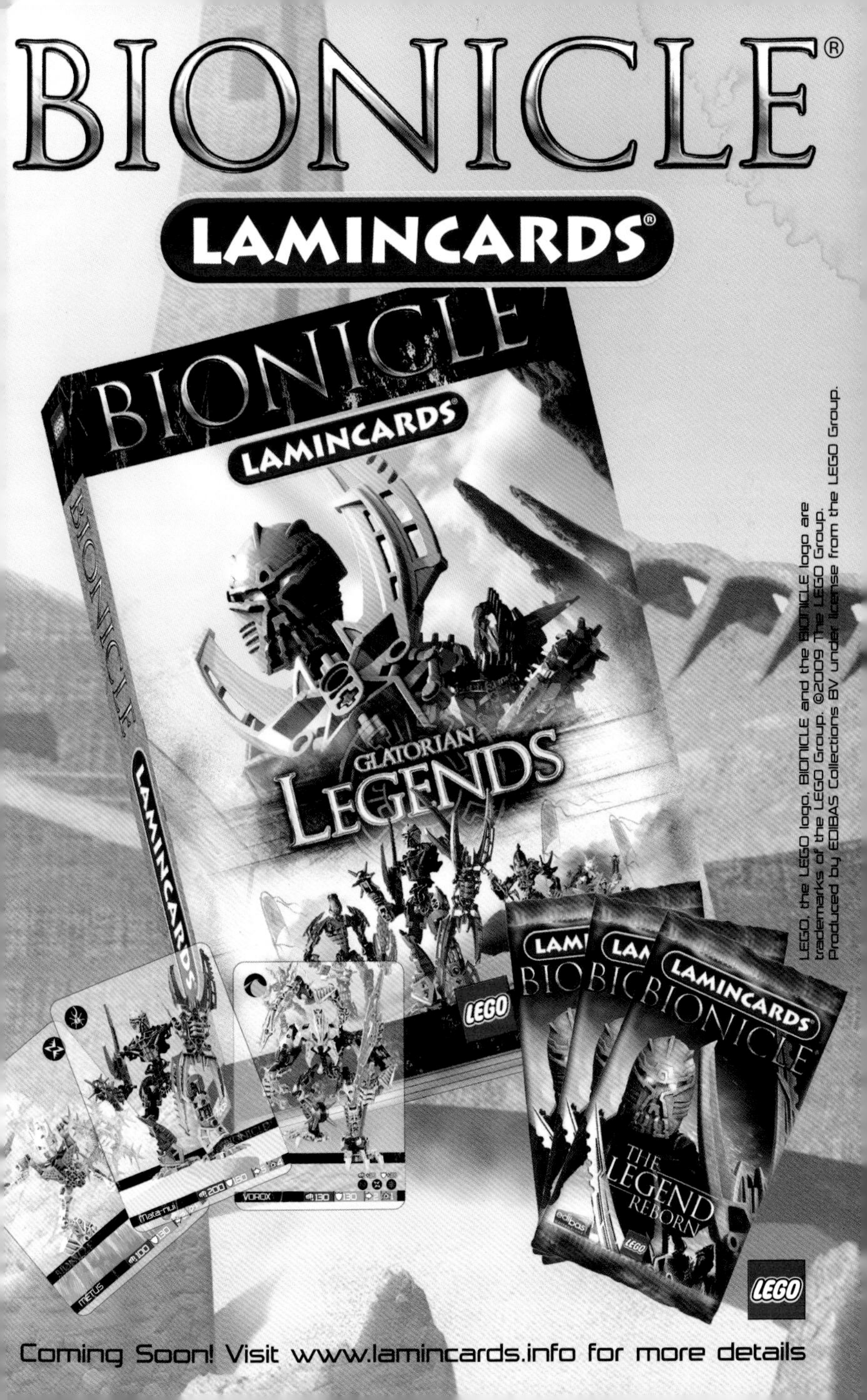
BIONICLE®
LAMINCARDS®
BIONICLE
LAMINCARDS®
GLATORIAN
LEGENDS
LAMINCARDS
LEGO
VOROX
Mata-nui
METUS
LAMINCARDS®
BIONICLE
THE LEGEND REBORN
LEGO
LEGO, the LEGO logo, BIONICLE and the BIONICLE logo are trademarks of the LEGO Group. ©2009 The LEGO Group.
Produced by EDIBAS Collections BV under license from the LEGO Group.
Coming Soon! Visit www.lamincards.info for more details

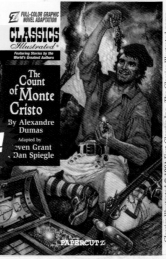